Praise for the Davis

MW00329639

"Seriously funny, wickedly ente

– Janet Evanovich

"As impressive as the amount of sheer fun and humor involved are the details concerning casino security, counterfeiting, and cons. The author never fails to entertain with the amount of laughs, action, and intrigue she loads into this immensely fun series."

– *Kings River Life Magazine*

"Fasten your seat belts: Davis Way, the superspy of Southern casino gambling, is back (after *Double Dip*) for her third wild caper."

– *Publishers Weekly*

"It reads fast, gives you lots of sunny moments and if you are a part of the current social media movement, this will appeal to you even more. I know #ItDoesForMe."

– *Mystery Sequels*

"Fast-paced, snarky action set in a compelling, southern glitz-and-glamour locale...Utterly un-put-down-able."

– Molly Harper,
Author of the Award-Winning Nice Girls Series

"A smart, snappy writer who hits your funny bone!"

– Janet Evanovich

"Archer's bright and silly humor makes this a pleasure to read. Fans of Janet Evanovich's Stephanie Plum will absolutely adore Davis Way and her many mishaps."

– *RT Book Reviews*

"Snappy, wise-cracking, and fast-paced."

– *New York Journal of Books*

"Hilarious, action-packed, with a touch of home-sweet-home and a ton of glitz and glam. I'm booking my next vacation at the Bellissimo!"

– Susan M. Boyer,
USA Today Bestselling Author of *Lowcountry Bonfire*

"Funny & wonderful & human. It gets the Stephanie Plum seal of approval."

– Janet Evanovich

"Filled with humor and fresh, endearing characters. It's that rarest of books: a beautifully written page-turner. It's a winner!"

– Michael Lee West,
Author of *Gone with a Handsomer Man*

"Davis's smarts, her mad computer skills, and a plucky crew of fellow hostages drive a story full of humor and action, interspersed with moments of surprising emotional depth."

– *Publishers Weekly*

"Archer navigates a satisfyingly complex plot and injects plenty of humor as she goes....a winning hand for fans of Janet Evanovich."

– *Library Journal*

"Archer's writing had me laughing out loud...Not sure if Gretchen Archer researched this by hanging out in a casino or she did a lot of research online. No matter which way, she hit the nail on the head."

– *Fresh Fiction*

"In the quirky and eccentric world of Davis Way, I found laughter throughout this delightfully humorous tale. The exploits, the antics, the trial and tribulation of doing the right thing keeps this story fresh as scene after scene we are guaranteed a fun time with Davis and her friends. #LoveIt #BestOneYet."

– *Dru's Book Musings*

DOUBLE
DOG DARE

DOUBLE DOG DARE

A DAVIS WAY CRIME CAPER

Gretchen Archer

HENERY PRESS

DOUBLE DOG DARE
A Davis Way Crime Caper
Part of the Henery Press Mystery Collection

First Edition | March 2018

Henery Press
www.henerypress.com

Trade Paperback ISBN-13: 978-1-63511-316-7
Digital epub ISBN-13: 978-1-63511-317-4
Kindle ISBN-13: 978-1-63511-318-1
Hardcover ISBN-13: 978-1-63511-319-8

Printed in the United States of America

This one's for my Beckys

ACKNOWLEDGMENTS

Thank you Deke Castleman, Stephany Evans, and Henery Press.

ONE

Security called Saturday morning at seven forty-five to say I had a visitor.

My name is Davis Way Cole. I live on the twenty-ninth floor of the Bellissimo Resort and Casino in Biloxi, Mississippi, with my husband and our twenty-month-old twin daughters. At any given time, there were three thousand employees and ten thousand guests below us, so security screening to our private residence was necessary. The security screening that Saturday morning was a necessary formality, because the visitor was my only sibling and younger sister, Meredith.

Except it wasn't.

"Vree."

It was Vreeland Howard, my sister's best friend.

Meredith was supposed to arrive at eight, Vree at ten. I was expecting Meredith, but it was Vree at the door. I didn't get the memo. I was still in my pajamas. I'd had one sip of coffee.

Vree, between two tall stacks of hot pink luggage, opened her mouth to speak. I braced myself for what I knew was coming. In ten seconds flat, Vree managed to get all this out without taking a breath: "Hi, Davis! It's me! I couldn't sleep knowing tomorrow would be today. And then it was today. I was awake and packed and I couldn't wait one more minute, so here I am! I left before the sun came up and only stopped once for Starbucks in Mobile. Am I too early? Meredith isn't answering her phone. She's here, right? Meredith! Bubbles? Bubbly Girl? Bubblegum? It's Mommy!"

And that was why I had Meredith arriving first. It wasn't that I didn't like Vree. I'd known her my whole life; I liked her just fine. It was that I didn't want to be in charge of Vree. I wanted Meredith here first so she could handle her. I opened my mouth to speak, but not fast enough.

"Davis?" She dragged my name out. "Are Meredith and Bubblegum not here yet?"

Bubblegum was Vree's Westie. Her West Highland White Terrier. Cute little dog. The most spoiled rotten cute little dog to ever prance on four paws, and reigning Grand Champion of the Southern Canine Association, who would be staying in our home, defending her title at this year's Bellissimo-hosted SCA dog show. So, for a week, an entire week, I had my sister, Vree, and Vree's dog.

My husband, Bradley, would be out of town.

And who could blame him.

"They're not here yet, Vree." I opened the door wider. "Come on in."

She came on in, rolling her hot pink luggage towers. She moved faster than she talked.

"I can't believe I beat them. Traffic, you think? No. There was no traffic. It's Saturday morning. Saturday morning is the best time to be on the road for that very reason, because there's no traffic. Everyone's still in bed. You can't sleep and drive at the same time, right?"

Four little hands were tugging my robe.

Bexley and Quinn, my baby girls, didn't know Vree. They'd met her a few times when we'd been home to see my parents in Pine Apple, Alabama, where Vree and Meredith lived and where I was from too, but at their ages, my daughters were out-of-sight-out-of-mind unless the person in front of them was family or a regular. Vree was neither. The girls were busy assessing her for playmate potential and eyeing her hot pink luggage for climbing possibilities, and all from behind my legs. Bex peeked around one of my knees and Quinn the other. Bradley, who'd been out of bed all of ten minutes on his only day off called out from the terrace, where he was waking up with the *Sun Herald* and a hot cup of coffee. "Hello, Meredith!"

"It's not Meredith!" I yelled down the hall. "It's Vree!"

Nothing back from Bradley, because he, like me, was probably trying to figure out who crossed which wires.

I reached for the extended handle on one of the hot pink suitcase stacks and pointed Vree in the direction of the guest wing. Bex and Quinn ran ahead. "Settle in, Vree. Make yourself at home. Let me grab a quick shower, then we'll have breakfast on the terrace with Bradley. Meredith will be here by then."

Except she wasn't.

Bradley ordered breakfast and dressed the girls, or better put, Bradley was with the girls when they dressed. I passed the coffee pot for the adults and sippy cups of chocolate milk for the princess-cowgirl and the ballerina-fireman. I think. I wasn't sure what the girls were going for, because Quinn topped off her blue ball gown with a pirate hat, and Bex, her red fireman jacket over pink tutu with a plush purple wizard's hat. Between them, there were four purses, three different shoes, two unmatched socks, and a dusty cowgirl boot. Saturday was one of their favorite days of the week, in direct competition with the other six. Saturdays were extra special, though, because Daddy was in charge, and that meant wardrobe freedom. They'd stay in their Saturday get-ups until they were ready for pajamas again, unless Bradley let them play in mud, run through sprinklers, or like last Saturday, decorate their own cupcakes at Frostings, the bakery on the mezzanine level of the hotel. My phone was stuffed with Saturday pictures of my husband and daughters. And my phone was right in front of me. Vree's was too. Both of us waiting to hear from Meredith, who was officially an hour late, hadn't called, and wasn't picking up. Something stopped me from calling my parents to ask if they'd heard from her. That something was Vree.

"Let me get this straight." She zoomed in on my husband. "You're the president of the casino? This whole place? Every square inch? You're large and in charge? Like the buck stops here? I can't imagine how much money you make. I mean, look around. You're making the big bucks. And you've never been married before you married Davis? And you're from Texas? And you don't have any brothers or sisters? Neither do I. I love being an only child. Do you? You know who you remind me of? Young Paul Newman. Remember that movie where Paul Newman was in jail and ate all those eggs? I swear, I can't even eat eggs because of that movie. My husband Gooch loves eggs. He has three brothers, and if I wasn't glad I was an only child before I married Gooch, I tell you what, I was glad after. When his brothers show up, which is every single Friday night of my life, Double Bubble and I hit the road. Those Howard boys are horrible one at a time, you can't even image what it's like when they're together. They were raised by their aunt because their parents got in a race with a train and lost. Splat. So their aunt, the creepiest woman on God's green earth, raised them. She smells like eye of newt. Or bat wings. And she smells that way because she's a rip-roaring witch. Certified. Papers. I swear, she casts spells on me. Her name is Bootsy. Her name should be Broomhilda."

Vree could talk the stars out of the sky.

I believed she talked so she wouldn't have to listen; there was always something Vree didn't want to hear. When we were little girls, she didn't want to hear my mother say it was time for her to go home and tried to talk Mother into letting her stay. When we were in elementary school, she didn't want to hear her parents were divorcing and tried to talk them back together. When we were in high school, she didn't want to hear she was failing, again, and talked herself all the way into a cap and gown. Vree talked over, under, and all the way through her life. I always thought she'd grow out of it, yet here we were, and she was still talking her head off. I wasn't sure what it was adult Vree didn't want to hear.

Bex and Quinn said, "Shiny, shiny, shiny."

Something she did want to hear.

She looked at them curiously.

"They're saying you're pretty, Vree. That's their word for pretty."

She thanked them for the next five minutes.

They didn't catch a bit of it.

They were right, though, Vree was pretty. She'd always been pretty, in a Marilyn Monroe sort of way. Think Marilyn Monroe on Red Bull. She was thirty-four years old with waist-length flyaway blonde hair, cocoa brown eyes, perfect skin, and wore her clothes two sizes too small. Her husband, Gooch the egg eater, looked like a tall Yosemite Sam—the ten-gallon hat, the handlebar moustache, the six-shooters. And Vree might be right about Gooch's Aunt Bootsy. That woman was spooky. Unlike Vree, who truly believed, I gave up the notion Bootsy was a bona fide witch around the time I learned the truth about the Easter Bunny. Was Bootsy terrifying? Yes. A witch? No. Probably not. Surely to goodness, not. There was no such thing.

(Was there?)

"Who cooked all this food?"

Plethora, Vree didn't give me time to answer, the buffet just inside the casino. One of the many perks of living above a resort. That, plus no lawn to mow and no neighborhood-association fees.

"I barely cook anymore," she said. "We have nachos every single night of our lives. I tell Gooch all the time we need to eat better. Like stir-fry. Or whole-grain organics. Or at least Lean Cuisine. But no, every night, I'm dragging out the Velveeta for nachos. Unless we order pizza."

I wondered what she'd ordered from Starbucks. Triple espresso? I could see Bradley mentally counting down the hours between now and tomorrow morning when he would leave for a conference. Bex and Quinn stared. They'd never seen, or heard, anything like Vree in their little lives.

"This is the most beautiful place in the world." She took a breath to admire the view past our terrace, the city of Biloxi waking up behind Bradley and the morning sun cutting a shimmering line through the Gulf waters behind me. "I don't know when I've seen anything as beautiful as this. I'm so happy to be here I can't see straight and Bubblegum is going to go crazy loving it. She's going to run in circles for hours when she gets here. Where *are* they? Did you ever think in a million years you'd live in a place this nice, Davis? I mean, you know, growing up like you did in your parents' little house? It's like I tell Mer all the time, you were born under a lucky star. You're the luckiest person alive. It's like you rolled in a field of four-leaf clovers or you were hit over the head with a horseshoe when you were little. Another thing I tell Mer all the time is if I'd had any idea you'd wind up here and we'd end up stuck in Pine Apple, I'd have hitched my wagon to yours and left her in the dust. Not that I don't love Meredith, you know I do, thick and thin, but you've got it going on, Davis. You really do."

A cardinal sang an April song from a high branch of the terrace cherry tree. Bex and Quinn's hats whipped around. They said, "Bird, bird, bird."

"Are they in school yet?" Vree asked. "Do they play musical instruments or speak Japanese? Kids are so super smart these days.

How old are they now? Two? Four? I don't even remember when they were born. A year ago? Three? They're not afraid of dogs, are they? It's so funny how the baby bug bit such a big chunk out of you, Davis, and didn't even light on me. Everyone keeps telling me I should have a dozen by now, because everyone else does, which they actually don't. I mean, there's Brenda Gray, who has seven kids, maybe eight by now, but she's the exception, not the rule. I tell everyone Bubblicious is all the baby I need, and it's the truth. She's every bit my baby, just like yours are yours, and the only difference is mine has fur. And she's the cutest furbaby ever born. Not that your kids aren't cute too. They're really cute. Adorable. They don't look a thing like you, Davis, but, I mean, you know they're yours because you had them, right? I guess it's a good thing I don't have any of my own because they'd be six feet tall and look just like Gooch. Can you imagine? I can't. I'm too busy with Bubble Pop to think about kids anyway."

Bradley, who hadn't blinked once since Vree sat down and opened her mouth, pushed his chair back and stood. "Who's ready to go help Dad in the office?"

I raised my hand.

(No, I didn't.)

"Ladies." Bradley kissed the top of my head.

He was barely out the front door with the girls when a notification flashed across my phone. It wasn't Security, telling me Meredith had finally arrived, but it was the next best thing, a notification I had an email from her.

"What is it?" Vree placed a heavy hand on my arm.

"It's an email from Meredith." I clicked it open.

"Email? Why? Is something wrong with her phone? Do you think she dropped her phone and busted it? No, because she probably sent the email from her phone. If her phone's not busted, why wouldn't she just call? I bet because her hands are full of

Bubble Trouble. But wait. Texting is easier than emailing. And calling is easier than texting. She sent an email? That doesn't make sense. What does it say?"

Davis, it's Pastor Gully. Meredith is with me, and for the time being, she's safe. We're on our way to Guadalajara, Mexico.

What? Meredith was safe? Why in the world wouldn't she be? She was with a preacher. Gilford Gully was the pastor at Pine Apple Baptist Church, had been all my life. He'd baptized me when I was ten. He dressed up as Noah every year for Vacation Bible School. Why did Gully have Meredith's phone? And what did he say about Guadalajara? All I knew of Guadalajara was organized crime, drug trafficking, and don't drink the water. Meredith was with the preacher and his wife, yes. She left Pine Apple with the Gullys the day before in their new-used motorhome for a stop at Orange Beach, two hours away in Alabama, on her way here. Not Mexico. Meredith didn't even have a passport.

We didn't go to the beach and I'm not dropping Meredith off in Biloxi. We're on our way to Guadalajara and we're staying in Guadalajara until you wire me $1,000,000. That's a million dollars, Davis.

I didn't put the phone down so much as I threw it down.

"What?" Vree asked. "What? I mean, what? Is something wrong with Bubblegum? What's wrong?"

I leaned over the phone lying on the table, one hand clasped over my mouth, the other over my heart, and read the rest.

I'm giving you five days. You have until Friday morning

to figure out how to get a million dollars out of that den of iniquity you live in or I will leave Meredith and Vreeland Howard's dog on the street corner in downtown Guadalajara. I've prayed without ceasing over this, Davis, and I am confident this is the Lord's will. Heed his message: I was put on this earth to show men the way, the truth, and the light. If word of this were to get out, my work for the Almighty would be finished. To ensure you and Sister Loose Lips don't destroy my holy mission, I am sending a disciple to be my eyes, ears, and courier. If you or Vreeland Howard speak one word to one person, I will know, and I will leave your sister in the middle of Mexico with nothing but the clothes on her back. The dog too. You're a child of God, Davis. Do his will. Do it swiftly, stealthily, and in secret, so that you may soon be reunited with your loved one. God be with you.

I pushed the phone to Vree.

She read the email, then the phone dropped out of her hands.

She didn't say a word.

I hadn't begun to process what I'd just read and Vree was in a mute paralytic trance when my phone rang. It was Security. Calling to say I had another visitor on the way up. I don't remember running to the front door. I do remember almost tearing it off the hinges, praying it would be my sister, but there stood Aunt Bootsy.

The witch.

TWO

"I don't have a million dollars, Bootsy. I can't believe Gully is stupid enough to think I do. Who has a million dollars lying around? What does Gully need with a million dollars anyway? An even better question, Bootsy, is what does his needing a million dollars have to do with my sister? What's she done to him? What have I done to him?"

"My *dog*!" Vree wailed. "What has my dog ever done to him?"

Bootsy Howard had marched in my front door, dropped an ancient tapestry bag on the travertine floor of my foyer, and said, "Where's Vreeland? I'm only saying this once." A sorrowful howl floated in from the terrace. Bootsy's head jerked. "There she is." She followed the cries to the terrace, me on her heels, where she kicked the chair Vree was slumped over in, told her to stop blubbering, then helped herself to a heaping plate of cold breakfast before she sat down in the chair my husband had occupied not ten minutes earlier. Mouth full, she said, "Have a seat, Davis."

I didn't want to have a seat so much as I wanted to have a fit. But sit down I did, because my legs wouldn't hold me up another second.

"Bootsy. Where is my sister?"

"Pass the potatoes."

Vree was still bent over double, sobbing into her knees.

"Vreeland!" Vree's head jerked up. Her face was a mascara mess. "Pass the potatoes."

I hijacked the hash browns, guarding them with my life, and said, "Bootsy! Where is my sister?"

"Where's my *dog*?"

Bootsy Howard, mid-fifties, never married, mean as a rattlesnake, had a long face atop a long scraggy neck atop a long lanky body. She'd been buttoned up in dark clothes from her chin to her ankles since birth, mine, anyway, even in the dead of summer, so the only exposed skin on her body was her face and hands, and they were ravaged, either by the sun, meanness, or standing over a boiling cauldron. She dropped the croissant she'd been buttering, pushed her plate away, and clasped her hands on the terrace table. Her fingernails were long, Cabernet red, and filed to points. She cleared her throat, and the two cardinals who nested in the cherry tree bolted.

"You know where Meredith is, Davis." She turned to Vree. "And you know where your silly dog is. You've read the message from Pastor Gully, I know you have, so you know where they are, and that being said, you know why I'm here."

A gust of wind blew a white linen napkin off the table.

"They're in Mexico," she said. "And they'll be in Mexico until you come up with the money."

That was when I told her I didn't have a million dollars.

"This is federal, Bootsy," I said. "Aggravated kidnapping and extortion. You're aiding and abetting. You're going to prison for the rest of your life. Get yourself out of this mess while there's still time. Call Gully." I pushed my phone past the potatoes. "Tell him to turn the camper around and bring Meredith back this minute."

"And my *dog*!"

Bootsy looked me in the eye. She had black dot lasers for pupils. "Go to the casino and get the money, Davis. Bring it to me.

The minute you do, I'll make the call and your sister will be on her way."

"*Why?*" Vree sobbed. "*Why?*"

"Why isn't your concern, Vreeland. The only thing you need to concern yourself with is keeping your mouth shut and helping Davis get the money." Bootsy forked her fingers and toggled them at us. "You tell no one. Either of you. And that includes your husband, Davis." She tapped her hollowed temple. "I'll know. You say a word about this and I'll know." Bootsy pushed back from the table and stood. She stepped behind me and used the back of one of her veiny hands to smack Vree. "Get up, Vreeland. Show me to my room."

I shot out of my chair and wedged between them. "You're not staying in my home, Bootsy. You weren't invited, you're not welcome, and you're not staying."

Bootsy rolled her eyes. "You don't understand, do you, Davis?"

She was right; I didn't understand. Twenty minutes earlier, my daughters had been at the same table eating strawberry pancakes. An hour earlier, I'd woken up and remembered my sister was coming—my funny, sweet, smart, loyal, beautiful sister. A day earlier, I'd been fluffing pillows on the guest beds, getting ready for my guests, and Bootsy Howard's name hadn't been on the list. So, no. I didn't understand.

"I'm here for the money." Bootsy paused to use a long pointy pinkie fingernail for a toothpick. "And to keep an eye on you two until I get it. Make no mistake, this isn't a test. Gully's dead serious and so am I. Get the money, give it to me, or good luck getting your sister back in one piece."

Vree wailed, "My *dog*!"

I fell back into my chair.

"No money?" Bootsy popped Vree's arm again. "No dog."

Vree gasped for air.

Bootsy said, "I'll find my own room." And left.

In her wake, my phone rang. Maybe it would be a dose of reality on the other end. Someone calling to tell me it was a hoax, April Fool's. Maybe it would be Meredith, and by tonight we'd be on the road to putting this nightmare behind us. The caller ID said it was Bradley, which hit me like another, the tenth, bucket of ice water dumped over my head in as many minutes. For the first time in forever, maybe since I met my husband more than five years ago, I didn't want to talk to him, because I didn't know what to say. Nothing? Everything? Something in the middle? I hadn't begun to process the onslaught of the incoming, so I wasn't in any position to manage anything outgoing, like conversation. I rescued my arm from Vree, who was trying to pull it off, and the babble coming out of her was incoherent. I caught every thirtieth word. Those were "Bubbles," "Clint Eastwood," and "Mexico."

"Bradley?"

"Hey, you."

He sounded fine. I could hear one of the girls, Quinn, I think, giggling. Nothing wrong. Everything right on his end. When it most certainly wasn't on mine.

"I didn't know Vree's mother-in-law was coming."

"What?" I was up and circling the terrace table. "Vree's what? Who?"

"Vree's aunt, mother-in-law, husband's aunt. I'm not sure. Tall? Older lady? Looks like my middle-school assistant principal? She was waiting on the lobby level when the girls and I stepped out of the elevator. She had two of those carnival suckers, the huge rainbow lollipops, for the girls."

"You didn't let them have them, did you?"

"I didn't unwrap them."

Good.

"I had Security send her up. Did she make it?"

"She made it."

"Is she staying with us too?" he asked.

I scratched my head.

"It doesn't matter," he said. "If any more of Pine Apple shows up, we'll put them in hotel rooms. Bex! Davis, hold on."

I stopped lapping the table to stare out at the Gulf, in the direction of Mexico, looking for my sister.

"She jumped on a luggage cart and was on her way to the tenth floor with a bellman."

I'd forgotten I was holding the phone with my husband on the other end. "Who?"

"Your daughter," he said. "Bexley."

I rubbed the back of my neck. "Did you need me, Bradley?"

He didn't answer right away, probably because he wasn't used to me rushing him off the phone. "Is she driving you crazy?" he asked. Then, "Quinn! Get back here!"

"Who?"

"Meredith's friend. The talker. Is she driving you crazy?"

Speaking of, where was Vree? Her chair was empty. She could have slipped into the house and have her hands throttled around Bootsy's throat by now, which wouldn't help my sister a bit. I scanned the terrace and found her on the other side of the cherry tree, sobbing over the balustrade.

"Are you there, Davis?"

"Here."

"Are you okay?"

"I'm fine. Sorry. Just busy."

"The girls and I are on our way to the convention center, where the show dogs are checking in. I have a feeling we may be there a while."

No doubt. Bex and Quinn loved dogs.

And ladybugs.

And witches with carnival suckers.

"You're sure you don't mind if I skip the...girl talk?"

"No. Not a bit."

"About that," he said.

"About what?"

"The girl talk."

I was having so much trouble keeping up.

"I have good news," he said. "One of the judges cancelled."

"What? Who?"

I could hear my scattered self, and if I didn't calm down, just a little, I might as well blurt it out. Which I fully intended to do, the minute I figured it out.

"A dog-show judge, Davis. A woman from Atlanta, a judge in the dog show, isn't going to make it. A dental emergency. Something."

"And?"

"It's good news," he said.

I could use some good news, but couldn't figure out how that was.

"They want Bianca to fill in."

I dropped into Vree's vacated chair. Bianca Sanders, the Bellissimo owner's wife, who lived above us in the penthouse, wouldn't be caught dead judging a dog show. We looked alarmingly alike, Bianca and me, and as such, I was her celebrity double. I had been for years. The news my husband was delivering was that I would be filling in for the missing dog judge. If they asked for Bianca, they would get me. "How is that good news, Bradley?"

"You won't have to entertain Motormouth and the aunt-in-law. You'll be at the dog show."

How was I supposed to get my hands on a million dollars, get my sister back, take care of my daughters with him out of town, manage Vreeland and Bootsy Howard, and judge a dog show at the same time?

I looked up to see Vree with one leg on this side of the terrace wall and one leg on the other. "Bradley, I have to go." I hung up. Then pulled Vree off the ledge.

We sat on the cool marble ground, our backs against the stone balustrade, and panted.

"There's nowhere to go, Vree."

"I figured that out."

Parents of toddlers who live twenty-nine stories in the air don't take chances. Thanks to three levels of Plexiglass balcony shields, there was no jumping, falling, tripping, or otherwise exiting our home except by elevator, emergency stairwell, or helicopter from the roof.

Vree was slumped beside me, her face buried in her hands. "What are we going to do, Davis?"

"First, we're going to find out if it's true."

"How?"

I found my phone. "My father will know."

"But we can't tell!"

"Vree, Daddy will tell me what he knows without me telling him what I know."

Doe-eyed, she said, "That's so smart."

But when my father, the chief of police and mayor of Pine Apple, did learn two of his residents, under his jurisdiction, were holding his youngest daughter hostage and demanding a ridiculous amount of ransom from his oldest, if he didn't shoot them on sight, he'd throw them under the Pine Apple jail until they could be carted off to Federal Prison Camp in Montgomery. What in the world were Gully and Bootsy thinking? Had they lost their minds?

I speed dialed; he answered on the first ring. "Daddy."

"Sweet Pea."

I was almost-mid-thirties, married with children, and my

father still called me Sweet Pea. He'd probably call me Sweet Pea when I was sixty. Or a hundred and sixty, like Bootsy, who must have been spying on me, because she suddenly appeared. The terrace doors blew open and Bootsy blew through them. She towered over us, her long shadow blocking the sun, with her feet planted wide and her hands balled into fists on her hips. Vree scooted closer to me, out of defiance, solidarity, or terror.

"Hold on a second, Daddy." I tucked the speaker end of the phone under my leg.

Bootsy growled a low-pitched warning. "Don't you say a word to him, Davis."

"Bootsy." I lowered my volume to a loud whisper. "Let's get one thing straight. Whatever it is Gully has dragged you into, and whatever you think your role is here, you don't own me, and I don't follow your rules. This is my home, my father, and my phone." I glared at her, picked up my phone, and said, "Daddy."

"Can you believe your sister?"

"Daddy, is Riley with you?"

"Yes." He said it in an of-course-she-is way. "She's been here for two days. She'll be here all week. You knew that."

I didn't know a thing at that moment, except Riley, my ten-year-old niece and Meredith's only child, was where she was supposed to be. Safe in Pine Apple with my parents, and that Daddy sounded fine. "What did you say about Meredith?" I asked. "Can I believe what about my sister?"

There was a pause, just a beat, before he answered. "You don't sound good, Davis."

Bootsy's witchy eyes bore down on me.

"Bex and Quinn," I lied. To my own father. "No sleep last night."

He said sweet somethings about his granddaughters, then asked what I thought about Meredith's sudden change of plans.

I tried to keep my voice steady. "I don't know what to think, Daddy. What do you think?"

"Well, for one," he said, "I can't imagine that Vreeland Howard isn't upset with her. For another, your mother and I think it's odd that Meredith would want to spend the week with Gilford and Gina."

My heart sank. "Did she say why?"

"Something about Americana, the open road, landscapes, sunrises and sunsets."

Which was preposterous. Meredith didn't have an ounce of wanderlust. If she did, she wouldn't still live in Pine Apple. And she was the worst person in the world to be stuck in a vehicle with because she didn't sit well. Vree didn't have a quiet button; Meredith didn't have an idle button. "When did you talk to her, Daddy?"

"Last night. She called from Gilford's phone, because she'd misplaced hers. She said she'd changed her mind about spending the week in Biloxi, and wanted to stay on the road with the Gullys. Have she and Vreeland had a falling out?"

On the other end of the phone, Daddy waited for my response in comfortable silence. It was anything but comfortable on my end with Bootsy lurking over me, tapping a witch boot, ready to snatch the phone out of my hand.

"Not that I know of."

"Don't be mad at your sister, Davis."

"I'm not, Daddy."

"Let her have her fun. She's done little in her life on a whim."

"She deserves a whim."

"And get some earplugs."

Head bent, so Bootsy wouldn't have the satisfaction, I blinked back tears. It was all so very real, this confirmation from my father: If Daddy said Meredith wasn't coming, Meredith really wasn't coming. And that meant Gully really did have her, and Bootsy really did expect me to come up with a million dollars to get her back. "Earplugs?" My voice cracked.

"Vreeland."

Right.

"Davis," Daddy said, "your sister said to tell you everything would be okay and she'd see you soon."

I turned as far away from Bootsy Howard as I could. "I love you, Daddy."

"We'll talk soon, Sweet Pea."

Bootsy pushed back a dark sleeve and checked the time on her witch watch. She kicked my foot to get my attention, as if she didn't already have it. "This can be finished faster than it started. Go downstairs and get the money. I'll be resting in my room." She turned on her witch heels. "And Davis..." She paused at the French doors. "I'm no happier about this than you are. Make it easy on us both. Get the million dollars, give it to me, and this will all be over." Then she was gone.

Beside me, as quiet as she'd been in her life, and probably for the longest stretch since she'd spoken her first baby word, Vree broke her silence. "Did your dad say anything about Bubblegum?"

He hadn't. I patted her leg.

She tipped her head onto my shoulder. "What are we going to do?"

"I don't know yet."

The cardinals returned. They circled. Coast clear, they settled in their tree.

"I'll tell you one thing we're not going to do, Vree."

"What's that?"

"Go downstairs, get a million dollars, then give it to Bootsy Howard."

"Isn't there so much money in the casino, Davis? Like millions and millions and millions? Would anyone really miss one of them? Can't you just sneak it out?"

"Yes, Vree, I could. But it's not my money. And I'm not going to rob the casino."

THREE

I was the perfect person to rob the casino, because it was my job to keep the casino from being robbed. I knew every trick in the casino heist book. It had either been tried here, or I'd learned from attempts at other casinos, plus I'd seen all the Ocean's movies. I knew how it wasn't done. I could figure out how it was.

Not that I had any intention of robbing the casino.

What I wanted to do was march out my front door, find my husband, and tell him everything. For several reasons, Bootsy's and Gully's demands for secrecy not one of them, I didn't. Before Bradley was president and CEO of the Bellissimo, he was an attorney. He saw things in black and white, including kidnapping and extortion. He'd have the FBI and their international counterparts here in five minutes.

I was a spy. Spies don't call the feds until they have their man.

Or preacher.

Or witch.

Five years ago, I joined an elite internal security team at the Bellissimo. After a nice long maternity leave when Bex and Quinn were born, I'd recently returned to work, in a part-time job-share capacity with my best friend, Fantasy Erb. We reported to the head of security, Jeremy Covey, and we had a fourth on our team, Baylor. Just Baylor. He was mononomous. Like Beyoncé. And Snoopy.

Before I took the Bellissimo position, I was a police officer for seven years in Pine Apple. Given my background, very different from my husband's, I saw every shade of gray. Bradley went straight from A to Z. I meandered, often getting stuck around G, shot at near M, without a hope by T, but somehow pulled it together by Z.

I wasn't sure what I was dealing with, and I wasn't going to drag Bradley into it until I was. Too much was at stake—my own sister—for me to rush, trip, and possibly fall. I had too many questions. First, was Gully really on his way to Mexico with Meredith? I believed he had her, but for all I knew he had her across the street. I needed to find him. If I found Gully, I'd find my sister. Second, why did he need so much money? Because Gully had a million-dollar problem. If I knew what it was, maybe I could help find a solution other than grand larceny, with me being the grand larcenist. Third, I needed to level the playing field. As it stood, Gully held all the cards.

Typically, my first move would be to gather my team. Four heads, you know.

I couldn't, because I couldn't tell them.

I couldn't tell them before I told Bradley.

(Marriage, you know? I had a good one and wanted to keep it that way.)

I couldn't go to the police. What would I say? A preacher kidnapped my sister and a witch wants me to steal a million dollars?

I couldn't, and wouldn't if I could, tell my parents. My father survived one heart attack. I wasn't about to give him another.

And that left...Vree?

"Are we going to sit outside all day?" she asked. "Shouldn't we be doing something? Should we at least go inside? Make missing flyers and staple them to telephone poles? Call the milk box people? You know how they used to put pictures of missing people on milk boxes? We could call the police and have an Amber Alert issued for Bubblegum. Think, Davis, think. I can't even think. You're going to have to do the thinking. I'm way too confused to think. I can't think past us going to Mexico and saving them. But if we go to Mexico, what about your babies? Can you take babies to Mexico? Could you leave them with a babysitter? Is there an app for babysitters? Like Lyft? Where you just ask for a babysitter, then one shows up? And once we get there, how will we find Meredith and Bubbles? Or should we do what Gully wants? Davis, please, let's go to the casino and get the money. Just...go get it. You know where the money is. I mean, surely you know. Get the money, give it to Bootsy, then get Meredith and Bubbs back."

"Vree." I patted her leg again. "Of all that, we should probably go inside."

"And then what? Get the money from the casino?"

"I can tell you right now, Vree, we're not going to the casino and stealing a million dollars. That's not happening."

Tears sprang to her eyes. "If we don't give Bootsy the money, how do we get Meredith and Bubbs back?"

We launch Operation Sister Rescue was how we'd get them back. I picked up my phone, lying still on the terrace tile. I whispered, "Gully has Meredith and Bubbles. We're taking Bootsy."

The blood drained from Vree's face.

"Go stand at the door. Watch for her."

Vree pulled herself up, skirted the table, then positioned herself between the double French doors. She cupped her eyes with her hands and pressed her face against the glass. "I don't see her."

I speed-dialed. "Hey. It's me. I need you to help me relocate someone."

"From where to where?" Fantasy asked.

"From here to anywhere else."

"Are you home?" she asked.

"Yes."

"And there's someone there you want gone?"

"Yes."

"Who?"

"Does it matter?"

"I guess not," she said. "When?"

"Immediately."

"I have a nail appointment."

"Cancel it."

"How big is he?"

"It's a she. And why does it matter how big she is?"

"I need to know if this is a bag-over-the-head job, a chloroform job, or a gun job."

That's the thing about a best friend.

"Do you still have the pink gun you got for Christmas?"

"As a matter of fact, I do."

"Bring the pink gun."

"Good idea."

Vree's head whipped around. "We can't get money from the casino, but we can shoot Bootsy with a pink gun? Not that that's not a good idea. But isn't killing worse than stealing?"

"Who's that?" Fantasy asked.

"Meredith's friend, Vree."

"Oh, right. The chatterbox. Is that who I'm relocating?"

"No," I said. "Her fake mother-in-law."

"Why's her fake mother-in-law there? And what's a fake mother-in-law?"

"Long story, Fantasy. Just get over here and help get this woman out of my house."

"And what is it you want me to do with her once I get her out of your house?"

"I need to park her somewhere. Can you put her in your bonus room?"

"If all you need is to park her somewhere, why can't we park her in a guest room at the hotel? Does she have to come here?"

"Housekeeping would find her."

"Right."

"How much trouble is she?"

"Not much," I lied.

"For how long?"

"A few days. One or two."

"How am I supposed to explain this to Reggie and the boys?"

Reggie was Fantasy's husband. The boys were Fantasy's three sons. The boys, all middle-school aged, played every sport under the sun, some I'd heard of, some I hadn't. Lately, it'd been basketball. "I thought they were out of town at a basketball tournament."

"They are."

"Then why do you have to explain anything?"

"Good point," she said.

"And go through your bonus room, Fantasy. Load it up with a few days of groceries and get anything out she could use for a weapon or to escape."

"This is getting more interesting by the minute," she said. "What else? Should I bring donuts?"

"No," I said. "We just finished breakfast. But I need a West Highland White Terrier."

"A what?"

"A dog. Cute little white dog with pointy ears."

"A Westie," Fantasy said. "I love Westies. Where am I supposed to get one?"

"I have no idea."

"How about we take this one step at a time. The fake mother-in-law first, then we'll worry about the dog."

I closed my eyes in relief. And gratitude. And hope.

"What's this about?" Fantasy asked.

I didn't answer.

"Davis, is Meredith there? Today's the day Meredith and her friend are coming, right? The friend is there. Is Meredith?"

I didn't answer.

"What, Davis? What's happened?"

Again, I didn't answer.

She said, "I'll be there as soon as possible."

Vree flipped around, then let the French doors hold her up. In the smallest voice, she asked why we needed a Westie.

"Because we don't want to tell anyone yet, Vree. Which means we need to act normal. And that means you need a dog for the dog show."

My phone rang in my hand. I looked at the caller ID and with its news, decided I'd had all I could take for one morning. "Bianca." I said it on a sigh, an exhausted sigh.

"DAVID!"

*　*　*

Richard Sanders owned the Bellissimo. He bought it from his father-in-law, Salvatore Casimiro. Mr. Sanders was at times happily, and at other times, unhappily, married to Casimiro's only daughter, Bianca. My doppelganger. Our coloring was off: I have red hair, more caramel than red, and eyes about the same color, while she's honey blonde, with pistachio green eyes. But we were the same height, build, and weight, with alarmingly similar features, and with one can of B Blonde, which I bought by the case at Walgreens, plus tinted contact lenses, only our husbands could tell us apart. I'd been Bianca's celebrity double since I walked through the Bellissimo doors, and I was good at it. Bianca was addicted to it. So addicted, she rarely went out. Which meant very little interaction with humans past her staff, who she didn't even acknowledge as human, and that left me: I was her human. And she thought I was her staff. Not only did I represent her to the outside world, I was her only link to it. To beat it all, she fully believed my name was David. I hadn't managed, in five long years, to convince her otherwise.

"David," she said, "a person from *Georgia*—" she said it like, "A person from *The Ninth Circle of Hell*" "—came to my home with textbooks. Large, filthy, and unattractive textbooks about *dogs*. As in *bow-wow*. Several dilapidated boxes containing dozens of oversized, soiled, and musty canine reference manuals. He's under the impression I'm going to study them, then take part in an activity downstairs involving dogs. Is the casino now filled with dogs? Am I living above a kennel and no one's bothered to tell me? You, of all people, know I would risk Gianna and Ghita's health, at their tender ages, by consorting with common street dogs exactly never, and I'd like you to stop whatever you're doing and take care of this."

By "tender ages," she meant "senior citizens." Bianca's Yorkshire Terriers had to be twelve or thirteen years old. Maybe twenty. And the older they got, the less they liked me.

"The casino is still below us, Bianca," I said. "The dogs are in the convention center, not the casino. They're here for a show. A dog show."

"As in Westminster?"

"Like that," I said.

"These are European dogs?"

"Not exactly."

"These dogs are from *Georgia*?"

She did it again.

"All over the South, Bianca."

She huffed. "Why have these Southern dog people invaded my home with their filthy library?"

"They want you to be a judge."

"Never."

"I'll do it," I said.

"You most certainly will, David."

(It's Davis.)

*   *   *

I called Plethora and asked for a terrace makeover. I wasn't going back in my house until Bootsy Howard was on her way out of it, and I couldn't look at breakfast one more minute. "And bring a fresh pot of coffee," I said.

"For how many, Mrs. Cole?"

"Two."

Bootsy was on her own. She wasn't getting anything from me—coffee, hospitality, or a million dollars.

Vree and I sat facing each other at the table, positioned to see Bootsy coming.

"Start at the beginning." I kept my voice down. "And be efficient with your words. Try to answer my questions as accurately and concisely as you can."

"Okay, but—"

I held up a stop-sign hand. "Just okay."

"What? I mean—"

I stop-signed her again. "'Okay' was the answer. That was all you needed to say. When I do this—" stop sign "—it means stop talking."

"How am I supposed to—"

I gave her the stop sign. She slumped.

I scanned again for Bootsy. No Bootsy. She was probably busy casting spells all over my house.

"Vree, what's the connection between Gully and Bootsy?"

"What do you mean? Like does Bootsy go to church? Or do you mean is she friends with Gina Gully? That's a no, because no one is friends with Gina. You know that dead stare of Gina's? How it makes everyone so nervous? People can't take it. She's just about goofy, and I think it's from listening to Gully's sermons too long. You say, 'Good morning, Gina,' and after she stares straight through you for ten minutes, she throws her head back and her arms up in the air, then screams, 'Praise be to the Almighty! Jesus, take the wheel! Lazarus and Mary Magdalene!' She's, like, on another planet—"

Stop sign. "Vree, there has to be a connection between Gully and Bootsy. Think. Think hard. Gully didn't knock on Bootsy's door and say, 'I'm going to kidnap Meredith Way, haul her to Mexico, and get a million dollars out of her sister. I'd like you to help.' That didn't happen, Vree. Tell me something, anything, that connects the two of them."

Vree squirmed. "I can't think of anything. I mean, I can't hardly think. My brain is frozen. Like, shocked."

"Try," I said. "Try hard, Vree."

Ten minutes later, I gave up trying to dig a connection between Pastor Gully and Bootsy out of her endless babble because it wasn't coming any time soon, and time was something we didn't have much of. "Next question," I said. "Why was your dog with Meredith?" I might have known, Meredith may very well have told me during one of the ten conversations it had taken to set up the week's adventures, but I'd either forgotten or missed it altogether.

Vree took a deep breath—a bad sign. "You know The Front Porch."

I let out the deep breath she'd taken. Of course, I knew The Front Porch. My sister and niece lived on Main Street in the antebellum my father was born and raised in. They lived on the second and third floors, above Meredith's shop, The Front Porch. She sold antiques, collectibles, rare first-edition books, and vintage clothing. She served banana splits and milkshakes in the former kitchen she'd remodeled into an old-fashioned soda fountain. "Vree?" It was a warning.

"Right. Don't stick your hand in my face. I'll hurry and answer. How am I supposed to answer in, like, one word? Or two words? I mean, I have to start at—"

Double stop signs.

Vree crossed her arms. "Photoshoot."

"See?" I asked. "How hard was that?" I could fill in the blanks. My sister was part stylist, part decorator, part retail genius, and all gold, as in everything she touched turned to. (Gold.) Meredith could take an eighty-year-old piece of unidentifiable furniture, a few milk crates, a bolt of ugly fabric, and a roll of duct tape, then turn it into elegant dinner seating for eight. A year ago, maybe, I'd been busy with newborn twins, she bought an antique camera collection at an estate sale. She'd tinkered with the cameras until they were in working order, but instead of selling them at the Porch, she started snapping photographs.

Gold photographs.

Meredith was good at everything.

And without a doubt, our mother's favorite.

"Let me get this straight," I said. "You let Bubblegum go with Meredith for a photoshoot."

"Sunset on the beach. In her bikini."

(The dog had a bikini?)

"Whose idea was it?"

"What idea? You mean for Meredith to take Bubblegum's picture? Mine. For us to ride down here in Gully's new Winnebago? His."

Premeditated.

"When did Gully get the Winnebago, Vree?"

"Like, maybe, last week?"

Recently. Gully had planned his hostage-taking road trip recently.

"Did he offer you a ride too, Vree? Why didn't you ride with them?" I asked.

"I was going to. But then, Gooch? He—"

Stop sign.

"Package."

Maybe I needed more than one or two-word answers. Less than a thousand, but more than one. I rolled a hand.

"My FedEx didn't get there in time. And Gooch—"

Stop sign.

"I've known Gooch my whole life, Vree. You've been married to him since high school. This story isn't about Gooch and we can talk about him another time."

She pouted, then let it go. Then she squeezed her eyes closed, searching, I think, for an answer that wouldn't get her a stop sign. "Bubblegum has a cocktail dress for the evening-wear competition on Thursday. Maybe Wednesday. I'd have to look at the schedule of events. Pink taffeta, with a little line of pearls—"

Guess what I did.

Vree rolled her eyes. "The matching booties didn't fit. They were open-toe, to show her glitter polish—"

I did it again.

Vree drooped in frustration. "I was waiting for the booties. They made her outfit—" Vree actually stop-signed herself. "At the last minute, I didn't ride with the Gullys and Meredith and Bubbles because I had to stay home and wait on the booties."

Saved from abduction by open-toe dog booties.

FOUR

Room service restored order to the terrace. I followed the busboy to the front door, hoping to get a visual on Bootsy Howard without having to actually hunt her down in the guest wing, where she was and Meredith wasn't. Where she was supposed to be, anyway. For all I knew, she could be witching her way through my walls.

I glanced down the hall—everything was quiet—then returned my attention to the front door, where the busboy's silver bus cart couldn't get out because Fantasy's canvas laundry cart was coming in. It was a traffic jam of carts.

"What is that?" I asked around the busboy.

She answered over him. "Transportation."

Right. We had to get Bootsy out, and dragging her by her witch hair might draw unwanted attention.

They went in opposite directions, both backing away from the door.

"Come on," Fantasy said.

"After you, ma'am," the busboy said.

This dance went on until I nudged the busboy aside, pushed his cart out, then pulled the laundry cart in. I dusted my hands. I said thank you to the busboy, then closed the door behind Fantasy.

"Let's go," I whispered. "She's this way." I took off for the guest wing.

"Hold on." Fantasy caught my sleeve. "We need to talk first."

Well, we couldn't.

I turned around to tell her as much, but she was bent over, halfway in the laundry cart. She reappeared with an insulated lunchbox. Then Vree, probably tired of no one to talk to on the terrace, showed up.

"Oh, hey." She craned for Bootsy. No Bootsy. "I didn't know if I was supposed to wait, or help kill Bootsy, or what I was supposed to do. I mean—"

Double stop signs.

Vree clapped a hand over her mouth.

"Fantasy, Vree. Vree, Fantasy. You can exchange pleasantries later."

Fantasy, holding her lunchbox, said to Vree, "We're not killing anyone." Then to me, "Where can we talk?"

Back to the terrace. We dragged chairs to the shade under the cherry tree and arranged them facing the French doors. Fantasy sat in the middle, her lunchbox on her lap. She leaned up, reached behind, and pulled a pink gun from the waistband of her jeans. Vree let out a little scream. "You said we weren't killing anyone!"

"We're not, Vree," I said.

"Who is this woman?" Fantasy unlatched the lunchbox. Inside were three darts and two vials. Of something.

"Me?" Vree poked her chest.

"No," Fantasy said. "I know who you are. Who is the woman we're not killing?"

"The woman who raised Vree's husband," I said.

Fantasy picked up a dart. "How much does she weigh?" She unscrewed the gold tip.

"I don't know," Vree said. "I've never asked. I mean, I don't like it when people ask how much I weigh, so I never ask anyone how much—"

Stop sign.

Vree clamped her mouth closed.

"I need to know," Fantasy said. "Too much of this stuff and we will kill her."

"It's hard to tell what she weighs," I said. "She wears thick canvas dresses with mandarin collars, no waist, and they button all the way down to her ankles. It's hard to say what's under there."

"Just guess."

I shrugged. "One-fifty? Two-fifty?"

"Canvas?" Fantasy asked. "Who wears canvas?"

"Sometimes burlap," Vree said.

"Burlap?" Fantasy said. "Burlap clothes? Well, canvas or burlap, we're going to have to get her naked first."

"Oh, hell, no," Vree said. "We just ate."

"Why naked?" I asked.

"Because the tip is sharp." Fantasy showed us. "But not canvas or burlap sharp."

"How in the world are we supposed to get her naked?" Vree asked.

"That's for you two to figure out. I have to figure out how much to zap her with." Fantasy bit her lower lip and closed her eyes, which meant leave her alone, she was doing math.

"What is she doing?" Vree whispered.

"She's dividing. Or subtracting," I said. "Be quiet."

"I'm trying to calculate the right dosage," Fantasy said. "Because the effective dose is very close to the lethal dose, and again, we don't want to kill anyone today."

"What kind of gun is that?" Vree was staring. "I've never seen a pink gun. It's cute. One time—"

"It's a tranquilizer gun," I interrupted before Vree could start telling gun stories. "She got it in her stocking for Christmas."

"Cool," Vree said. "I love Christmas stockings. Last year—"

"Open this," Fantasy interrupted, passing us drugs. Small glass vials. "Here, Free."

"It's Vree," she said. "My name is Vreeland. Everyone calls me Vree. I'm named after Diana Vreeland, who was the editor of *Harper's Bazaar*. My mother was going to name me Harper Vreeland, but at the last minute, went with Vreeland Harper—"

"Got it," Fantasy stopped her. "You're Meredith's best friend, you're staying with Davis this week, and your dog is in the show."

Like a light switch, Vree sobbed.

Fantasy turned to me. "Davis?"

I studied my lap.

We sat in almost perfect silence, a few sniffs from Vree, while Fantasy weighed her options. She knew something was wrong, very wrong, I wasn't talking, and she was being blindly dragged into it. Now was the time for her to get up and go or stay and help. After what felt like an hour of her trying to decide, she broke the spell, asking, "Is this burlap woman allergic to anything?"

I let out the breath I'd been holding.

"Free." Fantasy snapped her fingers.

"It's *Vree*. And no. Not that I know of."

One of the cardinals chirped.

Vree's neck looked like it was about to snap as she tipped her head all the way back to find the cardinal. "How can birds live this high? I mean, I know they fly, and flying means up in the air, but what about their babies? I mean, kicking them out of a high-rise nest seems like, I don't know, harsh parenting. And how can they have enough oxygen up here? Well, wait." Her head came down. "We have enough oxygen, so I guess they do too. And do they think they're in a tree on a mountain? Do they know they're in a tree at the top of a building? And for that matter, how did the tree know to grow up here?"

I leaned past Fantasy and said, "Vree. A landscaper brought

the tree. The birds came with it."

To not answer a Vree question was to invite her to ask four hundred more.

It was easier to answer.

"What? Like the landscaper planted the tree, then passed you a cage and said, 'Here are your birds, lady.' Was it like buy one tree, get two birds?"

Sometimes answering Vree's questions was just as bad.

"The birds showed up a few days after the tree. And they come back every spring to nest."

Fantasy said, "Would you two mind talking about the birds and the trees later? Like after I leave? Bust into those bottles. I don't have all day."

"It's expired." Vree had the vial up to her nose. "Azaperone. What's Azaperone? Whatever it is, it expired last month."

"It'll be okay," Fantasy said. "It's been in the refrigerator."

I took a closer look at my vial. Fentanyl. "Mine's expired too. Fantasy, you said yourself we're not going to kill her. These drugs are old."

The dart she'd been holding landed in the lunchbox with a crack. "Who called who here? Who said, 'Bring your pink gun'?" She picked up the pink gun and used it as a pointer. She waved it around, mostly back and forth at us. Vree and I plastered ourselves against the chair backs. "There's a reason everyone with a badge isn't issued one of these. And that's because they're not anesthesiologists. Hello? Neither am I. I'm doing my best here. You think this is easy?" Still waving the gun. Vree and I were about to hit the deck. "I'm trying to override this woman's central nervous system long enough to get her in my car and you two are sitting here talking to me about expiration dates. We're not injecting her with cottage cheese," she said. "This is Big Pharma trying to make me buy Schedule One drugs every three months, and I'm not playing their game. Now, last time," she said. "Is this woman fat?"

I said, "We don't know."

"Does she have a fat face?" Fantasy asked.

"No," Vree said. "But she has a fat mouth."

"Then we're going with skinny." Fantasy held her hand out for my vial, then carefully measured several drops into the tubular body of the dart. She did the same with Vree's vial. Then she screwed the tip on and loaded the dart into her pink gun.

Vree and I shot out of our chairs, ready to get it over with.

Fantasy said, "Wait a minute, you two."

We sat back down.

"I'm going to shoot her in the thigh," Fantasy said. "So, you two have to hike up the burlap high enough for me to get to her thigh."

"Ewww," Vree said.

I was rethinking everything. My whole life. "Why her thigh? Just shoot her in the neck."

"If I shoot her in the neck, it could kill her."

"Then shoot her in the arm."

"We're trying to get the drug into her bloodstream," Fantasy said. "Her neck would be too fast and her arm not fast enough. Arms aren't very vascular."

Vree held her arms out. She examined them.

"Thigh it is," I said.

"And it's not going to work right away," Fantasy said. "It's going to take a minute to get into her bloodstream. Like, five minutes, at least. So be ready to subdue her until she conks out."

"We'll sit on her," I said.

Vree's face dropped into her hands. "Gooch is going to kill me."

Fantasy raised her eyebrows at me.

I said, "Gooch is Vree's husband."

Fantasy checked her pink gun again. "Are you girls ready?"
(No.)

* * *

Easy enough, Bootsy was asleep. Laid out on her back like a cadaver, arms crossed over her middle, hands cupping opposite elbows, mouth wide open, on top of the duvet in Meredith's room. Which went a long way in restoring my shaky faith in what we were doing. Bootsy had no business being in Meredith's room.

We gathered at the foot of the bed.

Bootsy snored. A repetitive sucking noise on the intake, a whistle coming out.

"Lord, help," Fantasy whispered. "Who is this woman?"

Vree geared up to tell Bootsy's life story when I stop-signed her.

"You know who she looks like?" Fantasy whispered. "The Wicked Witch of the West."

Vree and I shared a quick glance.

Fantasy whispered, "Put a black hat on her, paint her face green, and she'd be a dead ringer."

"She needs an ambush makeover, that's for sure," Vree whispered.

"She's looked like this since the day I was born," I whispered.

"So, do we undress her now?" Vree asked.

"She's really asleep," Fantasy whispered. "Like in-a-coma asleep. We may not need to."

Fantasy's words had no sooner left her lips when Bootsy's arms and legs shot out, her head raised up, she stared straight at us, let out a yelp, then as quickly as she'd startled, she collapsed back into the prone position she'd been in not two seconds earlier.

I think we had three mini heart attacks.

Vree's head bobbed in time with the pants escaping her.

We were life-boat huddled at the foot of the bed.

"Hypnic jerk." I barely got the words out. "She jumped in her sleep. Everyone settle down."

Fantasy's eyes were closed, and she had the heel of a palm pressed to her forehead. "Davis," she whispered. "I swear—"

I said, "Let's just get it over with."

"Are those bloomers?" Vree whispered. "What the hell is she wearing? Does she have panties on under them? Is it old lady Spanx? What the hell?"

Luckily, or unluckily, considering three sets of eyeballs needed Clorox, Bootsy's black dress had settled above her knees after her in-sleep fit, which exposed her boney legs, and she was wearing dingy cotton...something under her dress that hit her mid-calf.

"You two stand back." Fantasy pushed up her sleeves.

Gladly.

She tiptoed to Bootsy's left, used her fingertips to lift the edge of the black dress, and with her pink gun pressed against the dingy cotton, popped Bootsy one with the tranquilizer gun.

I had another mini heart attack.

Vree went down. I didn't see it, but I heard it.

Bootsy kicked once, but otherwise slept right through it.

After the longest five minutes of my entire life, Fantasy carefully lifted one of Bootsy's arms, then let it fall.

Bootsy was out of it.

She shook her. "Hey, you, Bloomers. Wake up."

Bootsy sucked in a snore.

Glancing over her shoulder at Vree, Fantasy leaned over passed-out Bootsy and whispered to me, "What's this woman done to you?"

I didn't answer.

"You realize we're kidnapping her, right?"

I realized that.

"Davis?"

I studied the stitching on the duvet comatose Bootsy Howard was stretched out on.

"Go get the laundry cart." Fantasy looked at her watch. "I have to be at work at noon."

"Why are you working today? The dog show doesn't start until tomorrow."

Vree was still on the floor, head between her knees.

"I'm not working the show," she said. "I'm working the slot tournament that goes with the show. Today, tomorrow, and all next week. You took the week off because Meredith was coming. I'm on dog-show slot-tournament duty."

It had been a long, confusing, taxing morning, to say the very least. I'd been hit with so much, so fast, and all I wanted was my sister. The dog show had temporarily slipped my overloaded mind, including the slot tournament that went with it. I'd clicked through the stack of dog-show emails not paying a bit of attention to the details, because at the time, I hadn't needed them. I needed them now. "Who's in the slot tournament?"

Vree, still on the floor, raised her hand.

"The dog owners, trainers, and groomers. Part of the dog-show package."

"What's the payout?"

"What?" Fantasy asked.

"What are the stakes? How much can the dog people win?"

"The jackpot is five-hundred thousand a night."

"For how long?" I asked.

"Every night they're here," she said. "Sunday through Thursday. It's a cute game. Double Dog Dare. It barks."

We wouldn't have to steal the money to get Meredith back.

Vree could win it.

If we found her a dog.
No dog, no slot tournament.
Vree needed a dog.

FIVE

"Is Meredith here yet? Send her down with her camera. And the girls might need flea baths. There's no way we'll get through next week without a dog, Davis. Put puppy chow on our grocery list."

"Are they having fun?" I knew the answer.

"They're having so far past fun."

Pitter-patter, my heart.

After Project Evict Bootsy, of the twenty things I needed to do immediately, I returned my husband's calls first. I'd missed two while Fantasy, Vree, and I rode the freight elevator down with the laundry cart full of snoring Bootsy, strapped her upright in the backseat of Fantasy's Volvo, then threw her tapestry bag in the back. I'd gone through her bag, purse, and pockets, keeping her phone, a twine-bound crossed-twigs contraption, and three equally suspicious amber bottles with black rubber drop-stoppers. I sent her with her prison warden clothes, her blood-pressure pills, and a dog-eared witch book by Anne Rice.

I slapped the back of the car. "Clear."

Fantasy peeled off.

Vree looked around. "Where are we?"

"The loading dock behind the hotel. Come on, Vree. Let's go."

"Where's your friend taking Bootsy?"

Over my shoulder, I said, "To her house. About four miles

from here. Fantasy lives in a subdivision that backs up to the dog beach."

"A beach just for dogs?"

"The stretch of beach where dogs are allowed. With their owners."

The freight elevator doors clanked closed.

"I'd love to live close to a dog beach," Vree said. "Can you imagine? How fun would that be? How many dogs does Fantasy have?"

"None. She has three tall skinny sons, an unemployed husband, and a new bonus room over her garage. Her husband turned the garage attic into a bonus room. Bootsy will be in the bonus room."

"I love bonus rooms. Like for arts and crafts? Or a home gym? Or a media room? Storage? What?"

Vree wanted to know everything. Every single thing. Which would come in handy with what we had ahead of us—I would need to pull from her stockpiles of Pine Apple trivia—but being on the receiving end of her useless information gathering was draining. "More like a playroom. He built it for the boys."

"Why? I mean—"

"Because they hogged the television in the family room."

"Gooch and his brothers hog mine. NASCAR."

"I think it's Xbox at Fantasy's house."

"Right. Gooch and his brothers play Xbox too. Some days I think—"

"The boys don't like the bonus room," I said.

"Why not? What's not—"

"It has low ceilings, no windows, and Fantasy's housekeeper was locked in it for three days."

"What? Locked in? Like trapped? Stuck? Stranded? That's horrible. Why couldn't she get out? They didn't hear her? Was her car in the driveway? Couldn't they see it?"

"Reggie bought the door at a Home Depot clearance, and found out the hard way it was a security door that automatically deadbolted from the outside. They were at a hockey tournament in Hattiesburg with the boys, so no one was home to hear the housekeeper. Or see her car. Her phone was dead, so she couldn't call anyone." I kept going, answering her endless questions before she had the chance to ask them. "The police found her after her daughter reported her missing. They retraced her steps to Fantasy's."

"That's awful! Do you remember—"

"When they found her, she was wearing a Saints jersey and playing *Red Dead Redemption.*"

Vree said, "Harsh. One time—"

"She was okay. The bonus room has a little kitchen, bunk beds, and a shower."

"Still, though. I'd have clawed my way out. I have mild, sometimes medium, sometimes raging claustrophobia. Do you? I mean, like this elevator—"

Finally, *ding ding*, twenty-ninth floor.

"What happened to the housekeeper?"

"She quit."

"I guess so." Vree stepped off the elevator. "I'd have quit too. Did you see that movie—"

I closed my ears.

I couldn't take one more word.

I'd missed two calls and ten pictures from Bradley. I clicked through the photographs of my girlie girls with dog after dog after dog. Not because I had the time, but because I needed the respite. I dialed Bradley. "Sorry I missed your calls."

"I thought maybe you were wearing noise-cancelling headphones and didn't hear the phone ring."

"What?"

"Motormouth," Bradley said. "Speaking of, she needs to register her dog."

She didn't have a dog to register.

Vree needed a dog.

I needed a sister.

I needed off the phone too, but didn't want to raise red flags.

"Davis? Is everything okay?"

Too late.

I told a partial truth. "Bradley, I'm...jumpy. Just...jumpy."

"Understandable," he said, quickly followed by, "Quinn! Don't pull his ear! Davis? I need to go."

I took a minute to gather my strength, then set about finding my sister.

*　*　*

I found Vree on my sofa in the living room. She was clicking through pictures of Bubblegum on her phone, baby-talking to them and bawling.

I sat down beside her. I held my hand out. She passed me her phone and I shut it down. She used a sleeve to mop her eyes. Clearly, I couldn't leave Vree alone, even to talk to my husband for five minutes. Left to her own devices, she came unglued. So to add to my load, I would need to keep her by my side.

"Vree, listen to me."

She nodded.

"Has Gully ever hurt a flea that you know of?"

Vree sniffed. "No."

"He won't start now," I said. "Gully needs money, Vree, this is about money, not Meredith and Bubblegum. Meredith is his path to money. You have to believe he's not going to hurt them. *I* have to believe he's not going to hurt them. If you don't believe, I can't believe. If I don't believe, we won't be able to do this."

"Do what? I mean—"

"Find them," I said. "Then get them back. I can't do it without you, Vree. I need your help."

"I'll help, Davis. You bet I will. All day long. All week long. As long as it takes, every single minute. But what I don't understand is, if this is about money, and Meredith is his path to money, why did he take Bubblegum too? How did she get mixed up in this? She doesn't have any money. I mean—"

"Bubblegum was an innocent bystander, Vree. She doesn't have a thing to do with it. And Gully's not going to hurt either one of them. He just needs money."

If I said it enough, I'd believe it.

"Why would Gully need money, Davis? He's making a fortune off Jesus Water."

Jesus Water, pffft. Gilford Gully had a brother who worked for a beverage-filling plant, Dixie Cola, maybe, in Greenville, twenty miles from Pine Apple. Years earlier, or decades earlier, Dixie relocated their operations to Mexico. Pastor Gully teamed up with Brother Gully, they leased the abandoned filling plant, and Jesus Water was born. Pastor Gully blessed the water, Brother Gully filled the bottles, and they couldn't possibly still be in business, much less making money. Blessings in a Bottle. Drink the water, and be blessed. "Vree, Gully isn't making a dime off Jesus Water. He never has and he never will."

"He is, Davis." Vree was bright eyed, either with enthusiasm or lingering tears. "He must be making money. His brother hired Bootsy. If they weren't making money—"

"What?" This time I grabbed Vree's arm. "What about Bootsy?"

"Bootsy works for Jesus Water."

She could have told me this earlier.

"How long has she worked for Jesus Water, Vree?"

"A year? Maybe longer. Gooch's youngest brother grew up and moved out, which was more like Bootsy got tired of him drinking all night and sleeping all day, and she kicked him out. Then all the boys were gone and Bootsy didn't have anything to do. You know how that is when you don't have anything to do? She got a job. Bootsy went to work for Gully's brother at Jesus Water. I mean—"

Stop sign.

Gully, Bootsy, Gully's brother, Jesus Water.

I'd asked her point blank for a connection between Gully and Bootsy, and there it was. Jesus Water. I stood. "Let's go, Vree. Up and at 'em."

"Where are we going?"

"To my office. We're going to find Meredith and Bubblegum."

*   *   *

"How are we going to find them in your office?" She was on my heels. "I didn't know you had an office. Is it where your husband's office is? Same place? Do you share an office? One of these days I'm—"

"We're here." My office was through my kitchen. I pointed to the chair across from my desk. She sat. She opened her mouth; I beat her to the punch. "Vree." I pulled Bootsy's phone from the pocket of my jeans. "I need to think and work. So I need you to sit there and keep quiet. Just like before. Only speak to answer my questions, and give me the shortest answers you can."

She zipped her lips and nodded. Then, through her locked jaw, she eked out, "What are you going to do?"

I looked up from Bootsy's phone.

"Right." She zipped her lips again. "But I still want to know what you're going to do."

"Vree, whispering is still talking, and I'm going to find them."

"How?"

So far, the be-quiet-and-let-me-think program wasn't going so well. I laid Bootsy's phone down, drew a deep breath, and said, "If Gully has a lick of sense, he'll be on a burner phone."

Vree nodded. "Like a prepaid—"

"Exactly. If he's not on a burner phone, I can pinpoint his location. There's a good chance he's not and I'll be able to. Because Gully doesn't have a lick of sense." The good news was my sister did. Pit the two of them against each other on any field, level or otherwise, and Meredith would be the victor. In fact, I expected her call any minute. She'd say, "I left that nut Gully on the street in downtown Guadalajara. I have Vree's dog and I'm on my way."

My phone wasn't ringing, and neither was Bootsy's.

I picked Bootsy's up and waved it at Vree. "Quiet time."

She said, "You go ahead, Davis. I'm going to sit here and shut up."

I didn't know Gully's number, Vree didn't either, and I wasn't about to call anyone in Pine Apple to ask for it, then have to explain why I wanted it. His Jesus Water employee and kidnapping accomplice had his number. According to the recent call list on Bootsy's phone, they'd talked four times the day before and twice during the night, at two, then again at four that morning. No wonder Bootsy had been sleeping so hard. She'd been up all night.

So premeditated.

There was one text-message exchange, when Gully let Bootsy know he'd received a notification that the email had been read. (By me.) Bootsy responded, *10-4 Pastor*. I checked the times, and they matched. Bootsy, who must have been lying in wait for hours, in the lobby, the casino, or the parking garage, had shown up at my door minutes after I read the email and Gully texted her. Their last phone call, less than two minutes in duration, was half an hour later, which was when I was sending out an SOS to Fantasy.

I powered up my system to look for Gully's phone. I worked on a Mydlar SPRO personal super computer. I had two college degree notches on my belt—one in criminal justice and the other in computer information science. In my professional career, I'd used them both. Extensively. After the girls were born, I took myself out of the line of fire as far as live criminals were concerned, and earned my Bellissimo paycheck tracking criminals down from the computer-processing side. Several months ago, I built a big one. (Processor.) I had a knack for computing, and a system large enough to accommodate my knack. In what was intended to be a laundry room behind my kitchen, I had 600GB of DDR4 EEC memory, five hard drives, four Quadro and Tesla acceleration cards, and three monitors the size of movie screens.

The tower whirred to life and the monitors woke up.

Vree said, "Whoa."

I hacked into Gully's cellphone service provider's mainframe and plugged in his phone number. Then I asked for a location. A dot pulsed red on the screen. It wasn't pulsing in Mexico. Gully's phone was in Houston. And Houston was in Texas.

Relief flooded through me.

He had Meredith, against her will, and while he wasn't far from the Mexican border, he hadn't crossed it. His phone's tracker gave me a ten-mile radius where Gully could be. Ten miles in midtown Houston was a needle-haystack proposition, but that didn't dampen my spirits. Meredith was on American soil and the dot wasn't moving.

My phone rang, scaring Vree to death. It was Fantasy.

"Hey."

"Don't hey me, Davis. I called to tell you I'm on my way to work and I'm bringing this crazy Pine Apple woman with me. You can have her back."

"No! You can't!"

"Oh, yes, I can."

"Fantasy, I have to have more time."

"For what, Davis? What do you need more time for?"

Instead of answering her question, I asked one of my own. "What's wrong?"

"She started a fire is what's wrong. I had to stomp it out with my brand new Givenchy loafers."

"The ones with the chain trim?"

"Those."

"What happened?"

"She started a fire. Flames and smoke?"

"How?"

"That's a very good question. Because the fire was in the stairwell outside the bonus room."

"Where was she?"

"Inside."

Oh, no.

"Explain to me, Davis, how she started a fire outside the bonus room from inside. I'd like to know."

So would I.

"You can't bring her back yet. Seriously, Fantasy, you can't."

"Dammit, Davis."

SIX

Gully's phone plan included a feature called Sharing is Caring. It looked a lot like AT&T's Family Plan, times ten. It was maxed out with all ten share spots filled, giving Gully access to those ten phone numbers' data—activities and locations. Bootsy's name was fourth on Gully's share list, after his wife Gina, and between his brother, Greene Gully, and Pine Apple's latest ridiculous excuse for a doctor, Leverette Urleen, MD. No surprise to find Bootsy on the list, considering what I'd learned in the space of one morning. But my name was on the list too—what?—and so was my father's. Big unauthorized surprises.

Preachers got away with murder.

I clicked the S&C icon on Bootsy's phone and nosed around. Circles to the left of member names filled white when other sharers were on their phones, and lit green when sharers were talking to each other. Which was how Bootsy had known I was on the phone with Daddy—we were sharers and carers. And how she hadn't known I was on the phone with Fantasy or Bianca. Bianca didn't share and she sure didn't care.

Bianca.

I'd forgotten all about her. And the dog show I had to judge.

This was supposed to have been a fun week with my sister.

Now look.

I didn't remove myself from Gully's share and care list, which he would have noticed. Instead, I cloned my phone, then blocked him from the clone. Next, I placed a tracker on his—goose, gander, all that—and programmed my phone to notify me if his moved an inch. Next, from Bootsy's phone, I texted him: *Davis wants proof of life.* He texted back: *Come again?* I shot back: *Send a picture.* He texted back: *Of what?* This went on until I almost lost my marbles, then ten of the longest minutes of my life later, Bootsy's phone dinged with a photograph of Meredith. Since nine o'clock that morning I'd been telling myself Meredith was in no real or immediate danger, because both Gully and Bootsy were incapable of truly harming anyone. We were inconvenienced, starting with Meredith, and in a compromising position, starting with me, but Meredith wasn't in any real danger. That's what I'd been telling myself, anyway, until the proof-of-life photograph appeared on Bootsy's phone screen. It hit me hard.

It wasn't an image of Gully with a knife to her throat, but something about it was terrifying all the same. Meredith, against a backdrop of the dark interior of the twenty-year-old Winnebago, was sitting at the small kitchenette table, Bubblegum beside her, both staring blankly out the motorhome window. The view past the window, the sliver I could see, was concrete. As in parking lot. I could see boredom in Meredith's posture, tension in her set jaw, and something else—apprehension? Worry? Was it fear? Was Meredith afraid?

Which scared me to death.

I enlarged it, trying desperately to see what had her attention outside the window, looking for clues as to exactly where they were, and found none. I showed it to Vree, who burst into tears. "I know, Vree." I let her sob on my shoulder. "I know." I let her get it out, then stopped the crying the only way I knew how, by asking her to talk. "Vree," I said. "We need to talk about dogs."

"Okay." She sniffed. "Sure." She mopped her eyes. "I love to talk about dogs."

Vree loved to talk. Period.

*　*　*

The waterworks stopped and the talking began, and Vree talking, as tired as my ears were, was better than Vree crying. My brain raced desperately for an easy fix to the hard problem I was facing, all the while I pretended to listen, nodding along, commenting when I had to, through her recitation of Bubblegum Howard's championship résumé: Miss Bow Wow Alabama; Little Miss Sweet Southern Sassy Paws; Miss Furry Personality; Miss Red, White, and Barking Blue; Miss Canine Cutie Alabama; Miss Southeastern Pup Glitz; Miss Southeastern Tail-Wagging Most Talented—the list went on. And on. And on.

I caught her taking a breath and dove in. "Bubblegum's titles don't sound like dog awards."

"Have you seen *Toddlers and Tiaras*? Or *Little Miss America*? Or *Pageant Princesses*? Just like that, but with fur."

Really?

"What—" I wanted to know "—is Bubblegum's talent?"

"She's a dancer," Vree said.

"She's a what?"

"She dances. Swing, foxtrot, and contemporary."

The dog danced?

"All I have to do is say 'Katy Perry' and she's up on her back paws killing it, Davis. I mean it, she's so good."

The dog danced.

"I'm her choreographer."

"So, this is a talent competition?" I asked.

"Not totally. But talent is twenty-five percent. I mean, there's also composite, eveningwear, swimwear, and interview too."

What?

"Vree, how in the world are the dogs interviewed?"

"Well, like, 'Are you a good girl?' 'Do you want a treat?' 'Do you love your mommy?' 'Do you want to go bye-bye?' Like that."

"What's composite?"

"Let's see." She tapped her chin with a finger. "Presentation. Wiggles and wags. Maneuvers. Grooming, training, general appearance, structure, coat, gait, teeth. I could go on and on forever."

Agreed.

"Where do we find a dog like Bubblegum, Vree? Where did you get her?"

"From a breeder. A championship breeder in Kentucky."

"That won't work." Bradley might notice if I commandeered one of the Bellissimo jets for the afternoon. "We're not going to Kentucky."

"It wouldn't do us any good anyway," Vree said. "Championship breeders place puppies years before they're born. And even if we were in line for one and she was ready to go home today, Hubba Bubba is four years old. I mean, I can't show a puppy! We need a show dog, Davis. A purebred. One with a championship blood line. Who loves Katy Perry! What are we going to do? I mean, what? Drive up and down the streets tossing Milk Bones out the window saying, 'Here puppy, puppy!' and hope a champion Westie wags her tail all the way up to us? Then we borrow her? We can't do that! What, Davis? What what *what* are we going to do?"

Blindly batting around for a dog would be a fruitless endeavor.

And dognapping was a terrible idea.

Awful.

What kind of person kidnaps a witch and a dog on the same day?

(A person who loves her sister.)

"No, Vree." I rubbed my forehead. "We can't go out and find a dog. We don't have time. We need a dog to come to us."

"How? Take out an ad on Instagram? Facebook? Twitter? Flickr? Google? How?"

"You're the one who knows about dogs, Vree. Not me. What situations do dog owners get in that they need outside help?"

"Like when they need their shots? Like the veterinarian?"

"That won't work," I said. "We can't set up a veterinarian office right here and right now."

"Obedience," Vree said. "Like obedience school."

We couldn't do that either. I had two babies. I couldn't bring a misbehaving dog into my home. "What else?"

"Boarding," she said.

"What?"

"Boarding. Like babysitting. Like when you can't take your baby with you and you have to find a sitter. I mean, I'd never ever stay somewhere Bubble Girl wasn't welcome. I've thought about starting a pet hotel for that very reason, because it's so much trouble to find sitters. But we don't even have a people hotel in Pine Apple. What would we do with a pet hotel? Who would stay there? It's not like we have strangers with dogs running in and out of town. When I leave Gummy Girl, which is just about never, I leave her with one person." She held up a finger. "One. And you know who that is."

Her best friend. Meredith.

I had an idea. "Give me a minute, Vree."

She followed me back to my office, where it took twenty.

Celebrities and such could bring anything they wanted to the Bellissimo suites—lions, tigers, or bears. The general-population guests in the seventeen hundred hotel rooms couldn't. No pets. I wiggled into the reservations block of the Bellissimo website and added an entry at the bottom of the dropdown menu under number of guests—*NUMBER OF PETS*. I slapped up a webpage that routed straight to me, linking the pet option, and just like that, the Bellissimo Resort and Casino was pet friendly. We were the largest casino resort east of Las Vegas, and the reservation page of the website took several thousand hits a day. All I had to do was wait for a pet to check in.

In ten minutes, my webpage had fourteen views, ten of those making pet reservations. Nine in the future, one arriving tomorrow. "We have a pet."

Vree picked up her head from the other side of my desk. "A Westie?"

I had no idea.

"A girl?"

I hadn't thought to ask for any details other than how many pets, the date they'd arrive, and names of the pets. It occurred to me, for all I knew, the pet arriving tomorrow could be a cat. Or a rattlesnake. Or a gorilla. "Yes," I said. "A girl." A girl what, I didn't know. "Her name is Princess."

"What are you two doing back here?" I jumped a foot when my husband appeared in the doorway, with a sleeping Bexley on one shoulder and a sleeping Quinn on the other.

* * *

Somehow, I made it through the rest of the day.

At least a dozen times, I got busy with the girls and forgot for three seconds, only to inwardly collapse with panic and guilt when I remembered. Another dozen times, I opened my mouth to tell Bradley everything. I stopped myself half of those times and he stopped me the other half. Either his phone rang, Bex or Quinn or both caught his attention, or Vree interrupted. Nervous energy coursed through me, and it was all I could do to maintain a semblance of normalcy. I had to believe Meredith wasn't in immediate or direct danger—Gully didn't have it in him—but at the same time, I was living and moving through a thick fog of fear, because with the proof-of-life picture, I realized there was a reason he had her. Not necessarily what I would consider a good reason, but a good Gully reason. What was it?

Something about the picture was bothering me.

I couldn't put my finger on it.

Not to mention I promised Fantasy I'd do my best to get Bootsy out of her bonus room as soon as humanly possible, by the next day at the very latest, and almost as bad as anything else, along with the dog library, Bianca sent down what she wanted me to wear representing her at the judges' table—horse clothes. They were horse clothes. Equine couture. English riding breeches and jodhpurs. Show coats, turtlenecks, ascots, gloves, boots, and top hats. I pulled off the lid of a white satin box, thinking there'd be a fox head stole in it, and found a nine-foot braided leather riding crop.

I could be looking at the worst week of my whole life.

I had one chance to get to my office late that afternoon, when a call came in from the front desk that Bradley was needed downstairs to meet and greet a VIP guest checking in. That only happened a handful of times a year, so that would make the guest an Extra Special VIP. The ESVIP was an oil baron; he and his entourage, including a first-time contender on the dog-show circuit, would be my neighbors for the next week, staying in the Jay Leno Suite, the other half of the twenty-ninth floor, with our home being the first. (Half.) Bradley stopped what he was doing. "I'll be right back, ladies."

"Aren't you going to change?" It was Saturday. Jeans and Nikes.

"Davis, our guest is blind."

That was a first.

"Back in ten," he said. "Or fifteen."

I could use twenty. Hours.

Bexley and Quinn were in their highchairs trading bananas and Cheerios, donating plenty to the floor, and while Vree had her head pointed in their direction, I don't think she was really seeing them. The sadness playing all over her face couldn't possibly have had anything to do with my daughters. Her heart, like mine, was in Houston. The second I heard the front door close with Bradley on the other side, I said, "Vree, watch the girls."

"I am watching them. Where are you going?"

I was already on the other side of the kitchen island. "I'll be right here," I said. "In my office." Staring at the picture of my sister.

What was the look of quiet resignation on Meredith's face? Why, despite the fact she was clearly uncomfortable, was her expression also one of acceptance? Why wasn't she mad? What was the passivity? What was Meredith's...conflict?

*   *   *

Later that night, after tucking in my tired girls, I didn't fall asleep so much as the fatigue and worry of the day got the best of me, effectively flipping my off switch. Or maybe it was Vree piping down after I plied her with red wine, giving me permission to let go for a few hours. Or that Bradley was so busy preparing to be out of town—non-stop phone calls, last-minute itinerary changes, and three quick trips downstairs to his office—he'd stopped asking when Meredith would arrive. When he had asked, I gave him my best answer, the one I hoped and believed was true—she'd be here soon. I remember him climbing into bed after me, gently rousing me to ask again if everything was okay. Half asleep, I told him it was. It worked, as much as lying to your husband ever worked. At the time, I didn't have the words to explain the lunacy of my hometown raining down on us again. We lived two hundred miles from Pine Apple and we might as well have lived on Main Street between Meredith and my parents, in terms of how often our lives were detoured by the small spot on the Alabama map that I called home. If it weren't my ex-ex-husband Eddie (long story) or his mother (longer story) it was, like now, my immediate family. I was weary of my past dominating Bradley's present—it wasn't fair to him—and at least until I had more to work with, I would handle it myself. Bottom line, Meredith wasn't where I wanted her to be, or where she was supposed to be, but I believed in my heart Gully meant her no harm. The situation needed a solution, no doubt, which would come in time, hopefully very little time, time I didn't want to take from my husband. Whatever craziness Gully had up his sleeve, one of us worrying about it was enough.

Thus the lie.

Maybe I'd find the words the next day.

Then it was the next day. By ten minutes or so, when Fantasy called.

"Davis?" Bradley clicked on the bedside lamp. "Fantasy needs to talk to you."

I sat straight up in the bed. "Meredith?"

"What? Davis?" He reached for me with a gentle shake. "Wake up. Fantasy needs to talk to you."

I took the phone. "Do you know what time it is?"

"I know exactly what time it is," she said. "I just left work. I'm in my driveway."

Consciousness crept my way. Slowly. "And?"

"Davis, there have to be at least a hundred blackbirds on the roof of my garage."

"Who?"

"Birds. Blackbirds. Maybe two hundred. In the middle of the night on my garage roof."

"If they're black, and it's the middle of the night, how can you see them?"

"Because there's a full moon."

It was on the tip of my tongue to ask why she was waking me to talk about full moons and blackbirds on her garage when I remembered who was in the bonus room above her garage. "What is it you want me to do?"

"I want you to tell me who I have locked in my bonus room."

"Fantasy, they're birds. Just birds."

"I want this woman off my property, and I mean it this time. Not that I didn't mean it the last time." She hung up on me.

"Davis?" Bradley, who'd been on the receiving end of my side of the crazy conversation, asked again, "What is going on?"

I mumbled a non-answer, mostly vowels.

"Obviously, something's going on. Is it that you don't want to tell me or that you don't want to bother me with it?"

"The second one."

He eyed me suspiciously. "You're sure?"

"I'm sure," I said. "Everything's okay. Let's get some sleep."

Everything was not okay, and sleep wouldn't come again for me.

An hour of insomnia later, I realized what it was about the picture of Meredith that was bothering me. It was the window. The window Meredith was staring out had a handle. A turn handle that cranked out in a single pane to create a wide glass awning. Why hadn't she cranked it out? Opened, two of her and two of Bubblegum could fit through, and it couldn't have been more than a four-foot drop to the ground. For that matter, why hadn't she locked or blocked Gully and Gina in the small back bedroom or tiny shower stall of the Winnebago, grabbed the dog, and made a run for it? And what was it I'd seen on her arm?

I made a dark run for my office.

Enlarging the picture, blowing it up to grains on the screen, I saw what my subconscious had seen hours earlier. It was the edge of a milky white vinyl wristband around her left wrist, which was tucked behind her right arm. Meredith was wearing the kind of wristband issued at amusement parks, festivals, and emergency rooms. I scrolled to the crook of her left arm and saw the edge of a clear Band-Aid.

Gully had my sister at a hospital.

I had to turn away from the screen, bent over double, to weigh my options. I could wake up my husband and tell him everything or leave him out of it. Either way, I had to save my sister. Immediately.

SEVEN

The Southern Gaming Federation, a division of the American Gaming Federation, was a trade group made up of casino operators, suppliers, and other entities with gaming interests. AGF had recently relocated its southern headquarters from Charleston, South Carolina, to Nashville, Tennessee. Founded in the late 1980s, the federation championed the two-hundred-and-forty-billion-dollar industry, supervised and protected it, and supported the 2.7 million casino jobs in forty-eight states.

Utah and Hawaii were gaming free.

Utah made sense. But Hawaii?

SGF promoted corporate and public responsibility, industry initiatives, and what my husband had more than a vested interest in, legislative and regulatory challenges faced by gaming. More than anything else, the gaming federation served as the industry's voice on Capitol Hill.

Bradley, a casino attorney before he was a casino CEO, loved everything about it, and never missed the annual symposium. I think he loved that it was his field: gaming, but without the gaming. No smoke. No liquor. No cash to protect. No bells, whistles, or angst. While it was easy, and fun, to watch a gambler bet five dollars and win a million, it happened very rarely, whereas he saw the darker side of gambling every day. And it wasn't easy, or fun, to watch a player donate his or her life savings to a Jumbo Lap of Luxury Double Deluxe Bonus slot machine. Gamblers seldom left the casino as happy as they'd arrived. And while Bradley had justified the moral aspect of gaming long before the girls were born—the players knew what they were doing—he was increasingly concerned about how we'd introduce and explain the ethics of his chosen profession to them as they grew. We both were. My concerns weren't as gambling centric as his were. It bothered me more that Bexley and Quinn would never play in their own backyard, because their backyard was a casino, than it bothered me they'd know what double down on aces meant before kindergarten.

All that to say this: The Talk was coming. We were quietly preparing. We loved Biloxi, we loved the Bellissimo. We'd met and married there. The view of the Gulf from every window of our home couldn't be beat. But did we really want to raise our daughters there? If not, where? Realistically, attorneys could work anywhere. And if it ever came to it, law enforcement, which was to say me, could too. But what would that look like? East Texas, where he was from and where his mother lived? No. Pine Apple, Alabama, my home? No. (NO.) Lately, it looked a lot like Nashville. Bradley was thrilled when SGF moved its headquarters—it would be, if we were to pursue it, a smooth move from casino CEO to SGF administrator—and as such, he'd been dropping Nashville nuggets on me for weeks.

"Davis? Did you know the driveway at Andrew Jackson's home in Nashville was shaped like a guitar decades before Nashville was known for country music?"

I didn't.

"Davis, listen to this. Nashville has a full-size replica of the Parthenon in Centennial Park."

Really?

An hour later, "Davis, Seabiscuit was from Nashville."

"The horse?" I asked.

"The horse."

In the weeks leading up to the symposium, Bradley's fascination with Nashville whittled down to one primary, three major, and three minor points of interest. Primary: it would be a great place for us to raise our daughters. Major: the Southern Gaming Federation, Harpeth Hall School, and Vanderbilt University. Minor: Brentwood (the suburb of), the Tennessee Titans, and the Nashville Predators. While some had a one-year plan and others a five-year plan, Bradley operated on a ten-year plan until we became parents, then he began projecting further. Now he planned twenty years into the future, all the way to our daughters graduating from Vanderbilt Law School. He had yet to speak the words, "We should think about Nashville," but I could hear them nonetheless. The day before Meredith didn't arrived, he'd said again he wished the girls and I could go with him, and asked me if I knew the closest casino to Nashville was almost two hundred miles away.

I did not.

I did know the draw of Nashville and thoughts of our family's future were on his conference agenda. And I didn't want to, nor did I want him to, change his plans. The next morning, it took everything I had to kiss him bye. But not only did he want to go, for professional and personal reasons, I wouldn't, and couldn't, make him part of what I was about to do.

*   *   *

I only had one interest in Nashville.

A son for us, a brother for Bex and Quinn.

Because that was a decision already carved in stone: no more casino babies.

Two was enough.

* * *

The first thing I did on the second morning of my sister's captivity was see my husband off. As hard as it was to keep a straight face when I told him all was well—I had this—what I really had was a feeling that letting him go wouldn't be the hardest part of my day.

Next, I sent out an SOS to the girls' nanny, July Jackson, to tell her I needed her ASAP.

"I'll be there in ten."

She could get to me in ten because, like us, July lived at the Bellissimo. In a condo on the twenty-fifth floor. She helped me with Bex and Quinn four days a week, Monday through Thursday, from ten until two. For the most part, she came to us, because we lived in ten thousand square feet, and that meant endless hide and seek. But with all that had happened and all that might, I thought it best for the girls to be offsite. So I asked July to take them downstairs to her Bellissimo home. Which, for the girls, was like going to Disney.

"Is everything okay, Davis?"

July, so cute, so smart, and part of our family in many ways, was sharp too.

I chose my words carefully. "I think so."

"You think so?"

Bex and Quinn were all over her. Tugging and pulling her to the elevator.

(Mommy who?)

"I do."

I did not.

I couldn't even hint at my predicament. And a Sunday predicament at that, which never happened. Thus July's suspicion all wasn't well. Sunday was Baylor's one day off. Baylor, as in

Bellissimo Spy Team Baylor, took up all the slack Fantasy and I left when we semi-retired to spend more time with our families. Baylor was the other half of July, and why she lived at the Bellissimo. Because he did. When Baylor wasn't working and July wasn't with my girls, they were glued together. July's New Orleans parents thought she lived with us. (She was twenty-eight; he was twenty-nine.) A secret I didn't think we'd have to keep much longer. I saw a ring in July's future. And I saw trouble from Baylor in my future if I even hinted at the trouble I was in. To let on to July would be to let on to Baylor. Everyone in our world had finely tuned radars.

"Everything's fine," I lied. It would be. It had to be. "I don't know how long I'll need you today. It could be several hours."

"You know where we'll be if you need us."

And there went my girls.

I braced myself for my third chore. Vree.

I found her in my living room, perched on the edge of a deep swivel chair, staring out the glass wall at the city of Biloxi. She was spilling out of a sleeveless floral top over denim capris. Her long blonde hair was pulled back in a tight ponytail. Her posture was ramrod straight, her hands balled into fists on her thighs, and she smelled like apple pie. I sat directly in her sights.

"Davis."

She said my name on a relieved sigh, so happy to have someone to talk to. (At.)

"Vree."

"Did you sleep? I didn't. I was awake most of the night. I mean, I'm so used to Gooch snoring. He's like an engine running, you know? White noise? The kind that keeps you asleep? I called him twice to ask him to put his phone on speaker, then lay it on my side of the bed, then I was going to put mine on speaker and lay it on his side of the bed, you know what I mean? The side of the bed that would be his if he was here? And thank goodness he's not? I called twice and he didn't answer either time. I got his voicemail and it said, 'Vreeland is out of town. Don't be bothering me.' Which I didn't appreciate one little bit, especially since I couldn't sleep. But I thought, well, maybe it's a good thing, because I'd probably end up telling him what his witchy aunt was up to, and we're not supposed to tell, or else. So I didn't get ten winks. You know those sound machines that have crickets chirping and ocean waves? They should add another song. Gooch snoring. I couldn't sleep because it was too quiet, and I couldn't sleep for worrying about Bubbles and Meredith. And you! I was worried about you! I mean, this has got to be killing you, Davis! I feel like I know what Bubbles is doing, because I'm channeling her with my brain. And I think she's either curled up on Mer's lap or she's found a hidey hole somewhere in the camper, like a tucked-away comfy place, and she's dreaming puppy dreams. As smart as Bubbles is, she still doesn't really know what's going on. I mean, she knows she's not with her mommy, but she doesn't know *know*, you know? I was awake wondering what Bubbly was doing wondering if you were awake wondering what Meredith was doing. And Meredith isn't a Westie, she's a person! My bestie best person! This is awful! This is the worst! This is a nightmare!"

Vree got in a full workout in with her Good Morning, Davis speech. I could've been wearing noise-blocking earmuffs and still picked up the gist of it, because she'd acted out every thought. Every time she'd said the word "sleep" she'd feigned nodding off. "Ocean" was accompanied with hula girl waves. When she'd said "Gooch" she made burly arms and took on a split-second caveman persona. When she said she was channeling Bubblegum with her brain, she rolled her eyes back in her head and pressed fingertips to her forehead. It was draining. And Vree's way of coping, the non-stop noise and action. She stayed so busy narrating her life she almost didn't give herself time to live it. She certainly didn't give herself time to think. I wondered again what it was she didn't want to think about.

"Vree, is Meredith sick?"

Her arms shot out, her eyes darted right and left, then she said, "Wait just a minute. What?"

"Is Meredith sick? Has she said anything? Have you noticed anything? Has she complained about anything? Headaches? Weight loss? Do her pinkie fingers hurt?"

"Davis." Vree glanced at the slim gold watch on her wrist. "It's so early. I mean, really, truly, shouldn't we be talking about going to Houston or robbing the casino or not killing Bootsy or finding a dog for me to show so I can win the money? All the things we talked about yesterday? All the halfway plans we made to get them back? Shouldn't we be talking about the other half of those plans? Why are you asking me about Meredith's pinkie fingers?"

I didn't answer. I sat there patiently. I'd decided to take a different approach with Vree that day in my efforts to elicit information. Instead of stop-signing her, I'd wait her out.

It didn't take long.

About two seconds.

"Sick? Like the flu? We had flu shots," she said. "We didn't get them from that idiot Urleen. Do you know Dr. Urleen? Leverette Urleen? He took Dr. Kizzy's place at Pine Apple a Day when Kizzy retired? You know how everyone thought Kizzy was crazy? Wait 'til you meet Urleen. Have you met Urleen? Sure, you've met Urleen. So, you know Urleen, and he's why we went to Greenville for our flu shots, because for all we knew, he might accidentally shoot us with straight-up Ebola. We had the salad bar at Ruby Tuesday after. Ruby Tuesday has the only salad bar left in the world that has pickled red beets. I love pickled red beets. Meredith, not so much, but she's had her flu shot for sure. And it's, like, spring. No one has the flu in the spring. Well, wait. Maybe some people have the flu in the spring. I mean, it's not like I'm the flu patrol. I do keep an ear to the ground, you know, I keep up, but that doesn't mean I understand the flu, or flu shots, for that matter, because, and you can tell me if I'm wrong, don't they make the shots from old flu? You can't get the old flu. You can only get the new flu. So what good does a shot of old flu do?"

I sat quietly.

"No," Vree said. "Meredith's not sick. She's not sick at all."

There had to be more.

"We had bloodwork done."

(More.)

"Who had bloodwork done, Vree?"

"Everyone. Everyone in Pine Apple. Even people from Yellow Bluff and Oak Hill. And we *did* go to Dingbat Urleen's office to get stuck for blood, when we didn't go for flu shots, because it wasn't Urleen doing the shooting or the sticking. It was Jenna Ray. You remember Jenna Ray? Kizzy's old nurse? All we did was stop by Urleen's for Jenna Ray to draw our blood. Because Jenna Ray isn't off her rocker like Urleen is. I don't think she's really a nurse either, but you know Jenna Ray, she'll do in a pinch. She's put two hundred stitches in Gooch, at least, and two thousand in his brothers. She sets bones and pops backs, and she even delivered a breech calf—did you hear about that?—so we all think of Jenna Ray as a nurse, and you know, no one minded her taking their blood."

An odd energy buzzed behind my eyes. "Vree?"

"Hmmm?"

"Why did everyone in town have blood drawn?"

"Gully's brother."

She said it so matter-of-factly. As if it had nothing to do with anything.

"He's sick," Vree said. "You know Gully's brother? Greene? Jesus Water Greene? Who Bootsy works for? He has a blood disease. Long name. I couldn't come up with it if you paid me. He needs a blood donor. Like, I mean, someone whose blood works with his. Preacher Gully's blood wasn't a match, even though they're brothers, same mother, same father, go figure? Bootsy was second in line, because she's sweet on him—you knew that, right? Not Preacher Gully, but Brother Gully. But you knew that."

(I did not know that. I most certainly did not.)

"Hers wasn't a match either," Vree said. "I guess not, since she has witch blood. Her blood wouldn't match anything but another witch's blood, right? They're the oddest couple in the whole wide world, Bootsy and Greene, especially since he's sick. He only has, like, half of the blood going to his brain that's supposed to be going there, so his eyes roll around, because of his blood disease, his skin has this green glow, like alien green, which, in a way, is funny, like Greene is green? You know? And then there's Bootsy, in her witch clothes. They're scary looking together."

I forced breath into my body. Then out.

"Davis?"

I stared out the window when I said, "Could you not have told me this yesterday when it was the very thing we were talking about?"

"Told you what? What were we talking about? Which time?"

"When I asked you repeatedly what the connection was between Bootsy and Gully, did you not think to mention they were a couple?"

"For one thing, Davis, you kept holding up stop signs. And for another thing, you asked me about Bootsy and Preacher Gully, Davis. Not Brother Gully."

I stood.

"Where are you going?"

"Give me a minute."

I took a walk, cooled off, pulled myself together. I poured us both a cup of coffee, and when I was sure I was past the point of throttling her, which wouldn't help a bit, I sat back down and passed her a cup. "Let's start where we stopped," I said. "Gully's brother is sick."

"Yes." She blew across the top of her coffee. "Sick sick. Bad."

"Tell me about it, Vree."

Her favorite words.

"He's sick with a blood disease. And worse, he doesn't have insurance. I don't think they pay attention to details at Jesus Water. I hope they pay their taxes. Surely they pay taxes. I mean, it's Uncle Sam, you know? And you'd think Jesus would be watching out after them. I just thought of something, Davis! They must not be drinking the Jesus Water! Otherwise, how could this happen? They're not drinking the water! You can't get the blessings out of the bottles if you don't drink them! Or maybe they are, and they think drinking Jesus Water takes the place of paying taxes. Which is ridiculous. I'd like to see them try to talk the IRS into that. Truth is, Davis, I don't know if they pay taxes or not, but I tell you one thing I know for sure they don't pay, and that's insurance. And how I know they don't is because Gully's brother doesn't have any. Not a lick. So the first problem is finding someone who has Greene's blood—"

That was where I could hear my own blood rushing through my temples.

"—or I should say a match for Greene's blood. And then the next problem is how are they going to pay for it? Because it's like, a million dollars—"

That was where I broke out in a sweat.

"—and if they ever find those two things, the blood and the money, then, they have to find a hospital to do it. To, I mean, move the blood out of the match person and into Greene. It's supposedly as expensive as a bone-marrow transplant, and I guess not many doctors do it. For sure, that crazy Urleen doesn't."

That was where a cool tear I didn't know was coming slid down my hot cheek.

"So, I think, there are like four hospitals who can do what Gully's brother needs done. Maybe fourteen or forty. None in Alabama, no doubt. It's a mess. I mean it, Gully's brother is in a bad way."

My mind raced around my little sister's incredible heart.

Vree scratched her neck.

Finally, she asked, "What was the question?"

It took me a beat to find my voice. "Why did everyone have blood drawn?"

"Oh, I answered that. To find a match for Gully's brother. Next question."

My mouth was so dry, my body on fire, my heart in my throat. I barely got it out. "Did they?"

"Did they what?"

"Find a match?"

"Yes."

I could see it coming. First, in her eyes.

"One."

Then her face.

"Meredith."

With my sister's name, every muscle in Vree's body walked off the job.

I caught her as she tipped forward, out cold.

I eased her to the floor.

I collapsed beside her, knowing it was a very good thing I'd let my husband go to Nashville and that my girls were safe with July. Because I truly might have to rob the casino.

EIGHT

Ten quiet minutes passed after Vree came to. We were side by side on the sofa, her sipping a Coke with one hand and holding a cold cloth to her forehead with the other, the two of us staring out the glass wall in silence, when the doorbell rang. My heavy heart and I didn't get up to see who it was—I didn't care unless it was Meredith—until my phone buzzed with a text. The caller ID said *No Hair* and the message was *LET ME IN*.

No Hair's real name was Jeremy Covey. My boss, and one of the first people I met when I came to work at the Bellissimo five years ago. He's the head of security, the size of a minivan, a true friend, and shiny bald.

The doorbell rang again, and again and again, until another text landed on the screen of my phone. *If you don't let me in, I'll let myself in. I don't have all day.*

I dragged my feet through the living room, down the hall, and around the foyer to the front door. I opened it, and there stood No Hair, holding the bunched knot of two ends of a Bellissimo hotel bath towel fashioned into a sling. Protruding from the bath towel sling were the front and back ends of what might be the ugliest dog I'd ever seen in my life. It might not have been a dog. It might have been a weasel. Or an armadillo. It was an animal, for sure, and if by any chance it had any dog DNA, it might have been chihuahua.

Maybe ten percent chihuahua, forty percent polecat, fifty percent baby dragon. It wasn't big, maybe ten or twelve pounds, had a severe underbite, inordinately long stick legs, all dangling from the towel sling, one small black eye, and one large yellow eye. The yellow eye stuck out. As in protruded. Its ears were larger than its head, and set at odd angles from each other, with one where it was supposed to be on top of its head, and the other misplaced, more on the side of its head. The animal was missing large patches of hair in some places, and others, like directly above the bulging yellow eye, sprouted thick white tufts. One back leg was completely bald. And purple. Whatever it was, it had purple skin. That was just what I could see. There was more of it in the towel.

I was ten feet away and I could smell it.

I couldn't identify the smell right away, because it was such an assault, it defied immediate recognition. I didn't know if I smelled garlic, swamp, or Doritos. Maybe all of the above. I pulled my shirt over my nose and mouth, while No Hair held his towel sling package as far away from his body as he could. Which was way too close.

With a low ominous growl, deep in its throat, the dog trained the yellow eye on me. Then all its legs got going in the air, as if it were trying to race my way. The dog wanted to eat me.

No Hair, towel sling first, stepped into my home with it.

I plastered myself against the wall.

Then, with no warning whatsoever, the towel started dripping. The dog was leaking. All over my travertine floor and No Hair's shoes. A vast amount of fluid. A fountain. At least a gallon. It went on and on. That whole time, the dog, head tipped back, eyes closed, audibly sighed, as in, "Ahhhh."

I was too stunned to speak, move, and I certainly didn't dare breathe.

No Hair looked at the ceiling and shook his head.

The dog finished its business from several feet off the ground.

No Hair said, "This, Davis, is Princess."

"So? Get it out! Look what it did to my floor!"

"Your floor? How about my shoes? These are Ferragamos, Davis, and I just broke them in."

The dog tipped its head back, which was to say its inordinately large ears disappeared for a second, and I swear to you, it laughed.

Its tongue was black.

Which was when, to my horror, I remembered.

I was expecting a Princess. I'd made the Bellissimo pet friendly, and a pet named Princess was checking in today. This couldn't possibly be her. Yet here we were: me, No Hair, and a creature named Princess. "Vree!" I yelled over my shoulder. "Get in here!"

No Hair was swinging the Princess sling like a pendulum. At me. "Take it."

I was slowly creeping away, willing to creep through my house, out a window, over the safety ledge, and down twenty-nine stories in a free fall, because I didn't want it. I crept all the way into Vree, who took one look at No Hair and the creature in the towel sling, then said, "What in the world?"

I didn't know if she was talking about No Hair, who made an intimidating first impression, because he's size XXXL, or the dog, or the lake on my travertine floor. Probably the dog. If it even was a dog. It had raccoon paws, as in opposable thumbs.

"Take this dog, Davis," No Hair said. "Do something with it, or I'll march it straight to your room and land it in the middle of your bed."

The towel was still dripping.

Vree tried to help. She took a brave step forward, and in a singsong voice, said, "Hey, there, good little...thing." She eased a hand in the dog's direction, and the dog spit on her. From several feet away. It reared its head back, hissed, and spit on her. Vree jerked back and we huddled, then started a slow retreating dance around my circular foyer. No Hair took one step forward with the dog for every two steps we took back. We were doing our best to put space between us and them. I wasn't about to take it from him, which would mean holding it. I couldn't believe No Hair was still holding it. He was going to need to burn his clothes, then boil himself.

I stopped with an idea. "The playpen!"

"Who?" Vree asked, her head snapping back and forth.

I made a run for the storage closet, Vree on my heels. I had two Pop N' Play playpens from when Bex and Quinn were infants. I had two of everything from when Bex and Quinn were infants. I tore open the door, then tossed, while Vree dodged, a double infant stroller, two bouncers, two activity centers, ten baby gates, and a double baby swing before I unearthed a collapsed Pop N' Play. From the foyer, we heard something that sounded like a cross between a fire drill and fingernails on a chalkboard. It got louder and louder. We left the baby yard sale contents scattered up and down the hall, then lumbered back to the foyer with the compact length of the Pop N' Play between us, the noise from the foyer growing more urgent. Over it, Vree yelled, "That's not barking."

"No Hair!" We dropped the Pop N' Play on the travertine floor. "What'd you do to it?"

"I didn't do a thing to it," he said over the noise. "And I'm not holding it one more minute."

The animal's head was tipped back, mouth wide open, and the noise kept coming.

"Hang on." A whiff of garlic Doritos wafted my way. My eyes watered, and I couldn't remember who I was, what I was doing, what my sister's name was, or how to make the Pop N' Play pop. I turned my head the other way, gulped what clean air I could, then tackled the playpen. The second I wrestled it open, No Hair suspended the towel sling over it, then let the animal slide out. I secured the safety latches, then the three of us watched it turn circles. From a safe distance.

It was missing a huge chunk of fur from the middle of its back.

No Hair pulled reading glasses from inside his jacket and perched them on his nose. From a different pocket, he produced a piece of paper. "This is an email from the front desk, Davis." He shook it open and cleared his throat. "'Mr. Covey, I'm not sure what to do with this animal. The couple checking in left it with me, claiming they had a reservation for it. I realize we have the pet show this week, and guests are checking in with pets right and left, but these guests, whose pet isn't in the show, insisted it had its own reservation. When I tried to explain our no-pet policy, the woman climbed over the front desk, backed me into the corner, took my picture, posted it on Facebook, and threatened me. At which point, obviously, I said we'd take the dog. I think it's upset, or maybe has issues, or honestly, it could be the owners. They were unusual, to say the very least. They said the dog's name was Princess and she's a six-year-old Mexican Hairless Chihuahua. I asked if she was up to date on her shots and they said yes, including a double dose for rabies. They said the dog only eats manicotti with extra sauce and thumbprint cookies. It doesn't like to be touched and they told me not to laugh, sing, or wear bracelets around it. They said it loves to watch YouTube videos of Madeleine Albright speeches, especially Madeleine's TED Talk. They said play it over and over. They claim she's sweet once you get to know her, but then said it was terrified of hangers, as in clothes hangers, and men with beards. They said they'd pick her up Friday morning and walked off. Actually, they ran. It was very disturbing and very confusing. I thought about calling animal control, but decided to check their reservation first. Mr. Covey, they really do have a reservation for their animal. I had the IT department look it up and they confirmed the reservation originated from an IP address on the twenty-ninth floor. Since that could only be Mr. Cole, and he's out of town, I thought I'd contact you. Can you help me?'"

Of all the bad news in the email from the front desk, the worst was the Friday morning part. Friday morning? It was Sunday. I'd signed up to keep it for the next five days?

"Do you have anything to say for yourself, Davis?" No Hair asked.

I shook my head.

I did not.

He shoved the note at us, then spun on his contaminated Ferragamo heels and left. From the open door, a red satin duffel bag slid in and came to a stop between the Pop N' Play and the puddle. Princess yelped at it. My front door slammed. Hard.

Vree and I looked at each other.

Princess sat down and began gnawing on herself, the purple leg, furiously.

"Get that end, Vree."

"Why?"

"Because it's not staying in my foyer."

We picked up the playpen. Princess gave her purple leg a break long enough to hiss at us, then went right back to it.

"Davis, this thing is leaking." All over my hall. "Where are we taking her?"

"This way." I led the charge to the guest wing, as far away as possible from where my children would be when they returned. We lumbered down the hall to the smallest of the three guest rooms, the one with twin beds, a rocking chair, and a perfect view of the Gulf. I opened the drapes and we pushed the Pop N' Play against the window. Next, I called housekeeping and told them I'd had a little nuclear waste spill, would they please send a cleanup crew with everything they had, and the cleanup crew should probably wear Hazmat suits. "Bring heavy equipment and plenty of straight bleach."

"There are twenty boxes of Stouffer's cheese manicotti and two huge jars of Ragu Thick and Hearty Roasted Garlic sauce in here." Vree was going through Princess's luggage, and that explained the garlic smell. "There's a muzzle, Davis, and pumpkin-scented dog perfume, a million dog toys, and what are these?" She held up long Kevlar gloves.

"Safety gloves, Vree. Those are safety gloves."

"*Why*?" Vree's eyes were wide.

It was ten o'clock in the morning.

I had things to do.

Save-my-sister things.

And I'd have liked to have her saved her by seven tonight, when I would take my seat at the judges table in the conference center for the first round of competition at the dog show. None of which would happen if I choked to death. "Vree! Stop!"

Vree was blasting Princess with the pumpkin juice.

I batted through the haze.

"I was just trying to help, Davis. She doesn't smell good."

"And now she smells worse!"

Now the dog, dripping pumpkin perfume all over the Pop N' Play, was mad. It charged us, teeth bared, bouncing off the mesh sides of the playpen every time, which made it even madder.

"Do something, Vree!"

"What? What? What?" She dove into Princess's duffel bag and came back with a tattered blanket. The minute she held it up, Princess quieted to a whimper and the room filled with a different noxious gas.

"This must be her blankie." Vree had it pinched between two fingernails.

Princess saw it, or maybe got a whiff of it, and was trying to vault out of the playpen.

"Throw it in there, Vree."

Princess, clearly happy to see the blanket, bunched it up, circled it, then fell on it.

"There's one problem." Vree pointed. The dog's fur, soaked in pumpkin perfume, parted in wet clumps to reveal a rhinestone dog collar digging into its neck. "Her collar is too small. It's choking her."

Vree was right. The collar was way too tight. "Take it off."

"I'm not touching it," Vree said.

I rolled my eyes. I pulled on the Kevlar gloves. I dove into the playpen and freed the dog from the collar. I held it by a silver buckle for Vree to see, and said, "Vree, you're a big chicken." I tossed the Kevlar gloves and the ridiculous collar, then sat down on one of the twin beds. "Where's the email?"

"What email?"

"The email from the front desk. We need the owners. We need their names. I'm going to call and tell them to come get their animal. There's no way we can put this dog in the dog show, and we can't keep it here."

Vree batted around and produced the email. She studied it. "The only name is Lauren Clark."

That wouldn't help. Lauren was the front-desk receptionist who sent the email. "Let me have it." Vree was right. No guest name, no guest room number. I called the front desk to hear Lauren had gone home sick. I wasn't surprised, because I was half sick myself. Had I linked the pet page to the guest page? Surely I had. If not, I was perfectly willing to page Princess's anonymous owners in the casino, on a loop, around the clock, until they showed up. Behind me, a grating noise erupted from the playpen.

"Aw, that's sweet." Vree had to raise her voice. "It's sleeping.

And it snores like Gooch."

I braved a look. Princess was sleeping flat on her back with the yellow eye wide open. The yellow eye was still aimed at me.

"Can you sit with it, Vree?"

Vree's face immediately registered terror.

"Can you stay here with it long enough for me to go to my office?"

"No."

"Vree. Do you remember what happened right before it got here?"

"No."

"Think about it."

She paled. She remembered. She surveyed the room, locating the nearest exits. "Go," she said. "Do your computer thing, Davis. Find Meredith. Find Bubbles. And please hurry."

Hurry, I did. Away from the dog.

Listening for the doorbell with one ear—housekeeping should have been there by then—I used my other ear to check in with my husband, who'd arrived in Nashville without incident ("Davis, it's beautiful! The mountains!") then July, for a Bex and Quinn report. All was well. I sat down at my desk and fired up my system. I passed on several emails from Bianca Sanders and two from Fantasy, one with the subject line *ANSWER YOUR PHONE*. I'd get back with them later. After I saved my sister. I had work to do. And if I didn't have it done in the next little bit, I would be boarding a Bellissimo jet on my way to scour hospital parking lots in Houston, Texas.

*　*　*

It took twelve minutes to find Greene Gully in Patient Records at the third hospital I tried, Jackson Hospital in Montgomery,

Alabama. It took fifteen more minutes to crack Jackson's firewalls and get to Greene's medical files.

You'd think a hospital would have a more secure system.

Greene was listed as a plasmapheresis patient. The documentation went back five years. Every three months, for five years, Greene had checked into Jackson and been hooked up to a big machine that removed his blood. (His *blood*.) (From his *body*.) The liquid was separated from the red and white cells, then the red and white cells were returned to him minus the plasma, so he could produce more plasma, plasma his body would reject, plasma that would become so toxic to his circulatory system that within three months' time, he had to have the plasmapheresis procedure performed again. Greene Gully had Idiopathic Thrombotic Demyelinating Polyneuropathy. A rare blood disorder that could be renamed, simply, Bad Plasma.

The quarterly procedure required a three-day hospital stay and cost upwards of ten thousand dollars. Out of pocket. Due at time of treatment. Not covered even if Jesus Water had insurance. The only cure was to find a one-in-a-million donor. Greene Gully didn't need my sister's blood. He needed her plasma. His was no longer working. He needed someone else's. Meredith's.

She was his one-in-a-million.

Meredith had to undergo the plasmapheresis procedure.

And give Gully her plasma.

To the tune of a million dollars.

I closed the excess of open blood screens on my computer, hoping to never see them again. I picked up the proof-of-life picture of Meredith and Bubblegum in the Winnebago I'd printed the night before, and it was a good thing it weighed a feather, because I was too weak from all the vampire reading to hold anything heavier. I studied her face again, giving the window she could have escaped from ten times only a glance, because I realized, at some point along the way, Meredith made the decision to go through with it. If she hadn't, she wouldn't still be there. And if my sister had enough compassion for a man we barely knew to let the blood be drained from her body, I had to find enough compassion to pay for it. With the one caveat—I didn't have a million dollars.

"*ABIS. OOK AT EEE.*"

The noise that made my broken heart stop was coming from the doorway of my office, and barely recognizable as human speech. No part of me wanted to "ook," because clearly, something was very wrong.

"*ABIS! OOK AT EEE!*"

I cut my eyes left and started at the floor.

As I feared, it was Fantasy. The feet in the doorway of my office were Fantasy's. I knew the canvas espadrilles.

"*ABIS!*"

I made it to her knees. Skinny white jeans. Still Fantasy. And I think she was saying my name. A version of it anyway.

"*ES OOH PONE BOKE?*"

As my eyes hesitantly traveled up, the hem of her cropped pink lightweight cashmere sweater came into view. The one with the V-neck and three-quarter sleeves. I made it that far. And she might have been asking me if my phone was broken.

I couldn't help it, I slapped my hand over my eyes. I didn't want to see above her sweater. Maybe she'd just come from an emergency trip to the dentist and things hadn't gone...as planned. Maybe she was chewing rocks. Maybe she bit her tongue. Off. But if it was anything else, I just didn't want to know.

"*ABIS. OOK AT EEEE.*"

I peeked between my fingers.

All I could see were lips.

NINE

Bexley and Quinn had Crayola Double Doodle boards. Scribbling ruled, but they were getting better at horizontal lines and lop-sided circles. They always wanted me to guess what they'd drawn, and I guessed until I got it right. Mostly, they drew Daddy. When they wanted to mix it up, they'd draw moons, or spiders, or their best girl, July. At their stage of budding artistry, everything looked the same, the lines and loops, but I snapped pictures of each and every masterpiece anyway. I led Fantasy to my kitchen table, sat her down, then from the toy drawer, I pulled out a Double Doodle board and three My First Crayons: red, blue, and black. Everyone loved options.

Do you not have a pen and paper?

She'd chosen the red crayon, a subliminal message: red was for rage. I wasn't about to add fuel to that fire. I stepped back into my office, emptied the paper tray of my printer, and grabbed a pen. "Fantasy?" I could finally look at her without shrieking. "What happened?"

Talk about scribbling—she went at it. I didn't think she'd ever stop writing. When she finished, she shoved it at me.

I don't know what happened. I woke up like this. My fifty-pound lips woke me up. DO NOT ask me if this is collagen.

(It hadn't occurred to me.) (Not a bad guess, but it hadn't

crossed my mind.) (And if it had, I wouldn't have asked.)

I want that woman out. She's still in my bonus room, and I'm not going anywhere near her. I want her GONE. Right now. This minute. Look at my LIPS. I woke up with THESE on my face. Every light in the house is flickering on and off. I poured myself coffee and my favorite cup exploded in my hands, not that a drop of it would have made it past my lips if my cup hadn't blown up. I just wanted to hold it and smell it. Then my car wouldn't start. I can't talk, I barely have electricity, my favorite coffee cup spontaneously detonated, then my car wouldn't start. Yesterday, the fire, last night, the birds, now look at me. And this all started the minute I left here with that woman. What is WRONG with her? I want her off my property. Now. And your ceiling is leaking in the foyer. Something foul. What is going on? Start talking.

Start talking was underlined three times.

She watched me read. When she knew I'd finished, she spilled out a string of angry unrecognizable gibberish, poking the kitchen table for emphasis, slapping it once, and while I didn't catch a single word, I got the gist of it. She wanted a full explanation. I pushed away from the table. I filled a Tommee Tippy insulated sippy cup with coffee, secured the lid, and put it down in front of her.

"*UT ES TIS?*"

"Coffee."

She made several unsuccessful attempts to get the coffee past her enormous lips before I suggested she tip her head back and shake the coffee into her open mouth.

She said, "*I ATE OOH.*"

I patted her arm. "No, you don't."

I passed her a dishtowel, because coffee was dribbling down her cheeks, and I placed the proof-of-life picture of Meredith and Bubblegum in front of her. Her head came down, coffee dripped on

Meredith, then Fantasy swung her lips my way. "*Abis?*"

"Let me get Vree," I said. "We'll try to explain."

I turned the kitchen corner, and from a mile away, could hear Princess. Her fire-drill bark. I picked up the pace. When I reached the guest-room hall, I yelled, "Vree?" She didn't answer. Maybe she couldn't hear me over the dog yapping. Louder, I called her again. "Vree? Are you okay?"

Vree was not okay.

Princess had tunneled out of the Pop N' Play and had Vree trapped in the closet. She'd scratched the paint off the closet door in long thin streaks in her efforts to get to Vree. And chew her up. I quietly closed the door and ran. I wasn't abandoning Vree. If I'd distracted Princess to free Vree, the dog would have come after me. And then been loose in the house. Closer to my own bedroom than anything else, I ducked in, ran around the bed, yanked open the drawer of my nightstand and grabbed my laptop, praying it was charged. When I made it back to the guest room—Vree still in the closet, Princess having clawed down to the bare wood—I had YouTube pulled up on Google Chrome. My shaky fingers somehow found Madeleine Albright's TED Talk. I cranked up the volume, slid the laptop across the rug, and held my breath. Princess's top ear perked. She stopped screaming. Her paws slid down the closet door for the last time as she turned to find Madeleine. When she located the laptop, in front of the destroyed Pop N' Play, she stretched out on her belly, crossed her front paws, and sighed.

I counted to ten. "Vree? You can come out now."

"No!"

I barely heard her.

"Seriously, Vree. Come out."

The closet door cracked. I could see one of Vree's eyes. It was wild.

Finally, she worked up the nerve to put one toe out. She leapt on the twin bed closest to the door, then almost knocked me down clearing the six feet from the foot of the bed to the hallway. We flattened ourselves on either side of the door. "If you can just stay here long enough for me to get a baby gate, Vree, I'll be back in two seconds."

"No," she said. "You stay here and *I'll* get the baby gate."

"Fine."

"And I'm taking my time," Vree whispered. "That dog is crazy." She opened her mouth to explain, and would probably, before she finished, throw in a few Crock-Pot recipes and give me her thoughts on naval ships, when my arm shot out and I pointed. As in, *go*.

I would be guarding the dog alone—me versus it—for several minutes, so I prayed. I had two daughters to raise and a sister to save. I needed the dog to let me live long enough to get those two things done. There was nothing between me and it but a thin wall and an open door, and I didn't want to distract the dog by closing the door, just to distract her again when I opened it after Vree returned with a gate. And who knew how long that would take, because she had to go down the hall, through the foyer, to the other side of our house to get to the storage closet where I hadn't found the time to return any baby equipment. Vree could very well find a wall to talk to at any point along the way. I cautiously poked my head in to check on Princess, and couldn't believe what I was seeing. Hearing, rather.

The dog had Madeleine Albright's TED Talk memorized. Which was not to say the dog was talking. But she was nose to laptop screen imitating Madeleine Albright's words. Tone, inflection, modulation, and delivery. In dog language, yips and yaps, Princess was vocalizing along with the speech.

What in the world?

I observed until Vree returned lugging a baby gate. I stopped her with a hand motion, then pointed at Princess and the laptop, then to my own ear, as in, *listen.*

Vree cocked an ear, shrugged, then made *what?* hands.

I made binocular hands over my eyes, as in, *look.*

Vree whispered, "Do you want me to look or listen?"

"Both!"

She peeked. "Oh my gosh!" She clapped her hands to her face. "What is she doing?" she whispered. "What is she watching?"

"Madeleine Albright's TED Talk."

Vree's mouth dropped open. I could see her molars.

I latched the baby gate, effectively trapping Princess, but still able to hear or check on her without having to set foot in the bedroom, then led Vree to the kitchen. I said, "Don't overreact when you see Fantasy. Pretend like nothing's wrong." We stepped into the kitchen, Vree took one look at Fantasy and screamed bloody murder.

Soon to be matched by the scream that escaped Fantasy when she met Princess.

And still, no housekeeping.

No sister, no million dollars, and no housekeeping.

*   *   *

The first Pop N' Play was wrecked. We set up the second one in the living room, just off the kitchen. Fantasy kept making suggestions I couldn't understand. In a huff, she grabbed my laptop and recorded the TED talk, then set it up to run on a loop. When the recording stopped, fourteen minutes and fifty-nine seconds in, it started again. Princess patiently waited out the Ancestry and Cialis commercials.

Fantasy, Vree, and I returned to the kitchen table, where I was gearing up to tell all, but just then the doorbell rang. Finally. Two big burly housekeepers greeted me with blank stares. One had a thick beard that hit him mid-chest and the other was wearing a green-eyed skull and crossbones nose ring. Past the facial hair and the piercing, they had enough industrial scrubbing equipment to clean up a crime scene. They were armed with everything. I think I saw a jackhammer. I know I saw a multi-purpose floor cleaner the size of a riding lawn mower. Maybe I shouldn't have used the words "nuclear waste spill" when I called it in.

I pointed at the puddle. Then I pointed down my guest-room hall.

They circled, examined, and peered down the hall.

"I'll be through there if you need me." I pointed again.

Thirty minutes later the nose-ringed housekeeper poked his head in my kitchen door and said, "You're good to go, Mrs. Cole. You got anything else? We're scheduled here for two hours."

I opened my mouth to say no, thank you, take your lawn mowers and hit the road, when a piece of paper landed in front of me.

Send them to my house to get the witch.

I wrote her back. *We don't know these men.*

She wrote back. *They're Bellissimo employees and they're only going to the garage. It'll be fine. Have them jump my car off while they're there.*

While they didn't look like ninety percent of the housekeeping staff, the ones in starched uniforms who pushed cleaning carts in and out of guest rooms, they did look like they could handle Bootsy Howard. Not only did I need to get Bootsy out of the bonus room, I needed her for bartering purposes too, and her phone wouldn't stop buzzing with texts from Gully. *Sister Bootsy, has the Lord moved in mysterious ways yet? Sister Bootsy, have God's blessings from the casino rained down on us yet? Sister Bootsy, has the righteous hand of God struck Davis Way about the head yet?*

I paid the housekeepers cash, retrieved from my cash-stash

cookie jar, two hundred dollars each, then called transportation to tell them I was sending two men to pick up a sturdy vehicle. I asked them to throw in jumper cables. Then I gave the housekeepers Bootsy repo instructions and directions to Fantasy's house. Fantasy said, "*ANK OOOH*," to the nose-ringed housekeeper.

I said, "Be careful. She bites."

"Bring her back here?"

"Yes." (No.)

I saw them out, then it was back to the kitchen, where Vree and I told Fantasy everything. The first time Vree got sidetracked, I said, "Maybe I should tell the story."

We didn't have all day.

Fantasy responded with gestures, jotting specific questions in writing. In the end, she wrote at length. When she finished, she flipped the paper around. I bent over it and read.

I agree, tell no one, act as normal as you can. But first things first, you can't rob the Bellissimo. If you're going to rob a casino, rob the Slipper. Or Last Resort. Or even Hard Rock. Don't bite the hand that feeds you. Second, everyone knows Bradley is in Nashville nosing around about a job with Southern Gaming because he's convinced Bex and Quinn are going to grow up to be degenerate gamblers if you stay here one more minute. Forget it, Davis. You'd hate Nashville. You don't even like country music, or barbeque, and that's all they have in Nashville. This is your home. Third, you can't put that dog in the show. Look at it. I don't care if it could wag its twiggy tail all the way to the White House gate and pass itself off as Madeleine Albright, talent is only part of the competition, and that dog's obsession with Madeleine Albright is hardly a talent. Forget it. I'm not sure it even IS a dog. It might be a ferret. Finally, and most importantly, get the witch's phone and call the preacher. Stop texting him back with glory hallelujahs. He'll answer, because he'll think it's the witch calling. Just level

*with him. Tell him you know everything, and you're working on
the money, but you want Meredith and Vree's dog in a nice hotel,
not stuffed in his ratty camper under lock and key, and tell him
you want open communication with her. Tell him nothing happens
unless Meredith convinces you she's going through the procedure
by choice, with no undue influence. Do you have any Benadryl?
I'm positive this is a spell your witch cast on me, but on the off
chance it's not, I need an antihistamine. Either that, or I'm going
to have to go to a doc-in-a-box for a shot. I can feel my lips getting
BIGGER.*

I said, "Fantasy, she's not a witch. There's no such thing."

Vree said, "She most certainly is—"

"Vree," I said, "stop with the witch business. Just stop."

The house phone ringing scared us to death.

We were so on edge, with Madeleine Albright yammering in
the background, the unexpected noise almost did us in. It was the
bearded and pierced housekeepers. It had been well over a half
hour; I'd forgotten all about them. They called to say no Bootsy.
The bonus room was empty. And they didn't jump off the car in the
driveway because there was no car in the driveway. No woman, no
car, sorry.

Having held it together since the morning before when I
realized my sister wasn't coming, I gave up. I was terrified for my
sister; I missed my husband; I missed my daughters, who I hadn't
seen or held in hours. Vree wouldn't shut up, Fantasy had balloons
for lips, and I had to rob the Silver Slipper. I'd saddled myself with
a Democrat dog that smelled like carnage and hated me, I was a
nervous wreck from living on coffee, and I had to wear horse
clothes and judge a dog show that night. Now Bootsy was gone?

It was too much.

I laid my head down on my kitchen table and was on the verge
of coming undone.

A slip of paper joined my pity party. On it, Fantasy had written, *Davis, the preacher isn't going to touch a hair on Meredith's head. He needs her. And the witch is still in the bonus room. I have no idea where my car is, but the witch is there. She hid somewhere and the housekeepers didn't look hard enough. Come on, and we'll go flush her out. Do you have any way, shape, or form of antihistamine?*

Then, patting her chest, Fantasy said, "*I ILL ELP OOO.*"

A very good thing, because I needed "elp."

*   *   *

Fantasy's lips still took up half her face, but the bottle of Children's Benadryl she chugged reduced her swollen tongue enough for her to speak somewhat clearly. We were stuffed in the cab of her husband Reggie's beat-up work truck, Fantasy driving, Vree riding shotgun, me bouncing off both from the middle seat.

"If the Benadryl is working, Fantasy, that means you've had an allergic reaction to something. Bootsy didn't voodoo you."

"You two need to get on the same page," Fantasy said. "Is she a witch, or isn't she?"

"She is." Vree leaned past me. "One time she turned the water black. For three days, all the water in Pine Apple was as black as ink. Our grocery store, the Pig, ran out of bottled water. And it was all Bootsy's fault—"

"It was not," I said. "It was manganese."

Vree said, "It was Bootsy."

"What is manganese?" Fantasy took a right off Beach Boulevard. We were less than a mile from her house.

"Manganese is like iron," I said. "And like iron, it can make its way into a water supply from groundwater runoff. When it does, the water turns black. Which was what happened."

Vree said, "Also if a witch puts a spell on the water it turns black."

We passed a Coast Electric Power truck. A big truck. A bucket truck. And two men were sky high in the bucket, repairing a transformer. I said, "There's your power flickering on and off. It was a transformer. Not Bootsy."

"It was Bootsy if Bootsy was the one who blew the transformer," Vree said. "Do you remember when Orange Bennett cut line in front of her at the Gas 'n Go? And ten minutes later he broke out in hives all over his body? Even his privates?"

I did remember that. Orange wore nothing but Wolverine boots, calamine lotion, and a spray-painted wooden sandwich board with BOOTSY HOWARD IS A WHICHY WHICH on the front and BURN BOOTSY HOWARD AT THE STEAK on the back. For a month. And the month was January. When the tip of his nose turned black, Daddy told him if he caught him walking up and down Banana Street one more time wearing nothing but his sandwich board he'd lock him up. Free speech was one thing. Frostbite was another.

"Why are so many people in Pine Apple named after foods?" Fantasy turned into the driveway and drove past the house. "Orange? As in juice?" I didn't have time to answer—his daddy was a Tennessee fan—before Fantasy said, "Where in the world is my car?"

The housekeepers were right, the car was gone. The garage was still there, and so far, so good. No shooting flames, no bats, no National Guard. Fantasy shifted the truck into park and killed the engine. "Where's my car?"

"Maybe Bootsy witched it somewhere," Vree said.

"Where would she have witched my car to, Vree?"

"Let's go in and ask her," I said.

"What if she's really not there?" Vree asked.

"She's there," I said. "And if by some chance she's not, surely she left us a few clues."

*   *   *

She wasn't there.

And there were no clues.

Clues? No.

A solid black Standard Poodle guarding a dead body? Yes.

TEN

Fantasy and I opened our mouths at the same time—in all fairness, Fantasy couldn't close her mouth because of her lips, still bee-stung swollen, by a whole hive of bees—to tell Vree not to touch anything, but we didn't need to. Vree swooned again. We were three for three: She hit the floor yesterday when we shot Bootsy with the tranquilizer gun, then again that morning, when she connected the bloody dots between Meredith and Greene Gully, and just then, when she realized the woman in the easy chair behind the big black dog was dead.

The dog was glad to see us. It rushed us, clearly seeking help. I tried to calm it; it tried to pull me by the sleeve. "I know." I patted the huge fluff ball on its head. "I know."

Fantasy checked the body for a pulse. She shook her head. "Davis, she's still warm."

I stepped around the eat-in kitchenette bar and rifled through the drawers for something to use for a cold compress for Vree. Vree needed to buck up. There were no pools of blood, no gaping wounds, no signs of trauma. If it weren't for the woman's gray pallor and glazed dead stare, she might be asleep.

I found a Saints t-shirt.

I dragged a moaning Vree farther from the body, put a throw pillow under her head, then positioned the wet t-shirt across her brow, while Fantasy poked the dead woman with a rolled magazine. It looked like a gamer magazine.

"What are you doing, Fantasy?"

She was poking a dead woman with a magazine was what she was doing.

"No purse," she said. "No keys, no nothing except a dog leash. I'm seeing if she has anything in her pockets. What should we do here?" she asked. "Call the police?"

"And say what?" I asked. "Our witchy prisoner escaped and in her place we have a dead woman we don't know?"

She patted her swollen lips and thought about it. She could see where calling the police too soon might not be the best idea. She stepped past the dead woman, around the corner to the small room with the bunkbeds, then I heard tapping.

"What are you doing?"

She reappeared. "I turned the air down to popsicle."

Good idea.

We searched high and low, over and under, above and beyond, for Bootsy Howard or any sign of her, and the only thing we found was her tapestry bag full of witch clothes. The housekeepers were right—no Bootsy. No sign of her and not a single clue. Our search stopped where it started. In front of the dead woman.

"What happened to her?" I whispered.

"I don't know," Fantasy whispered back.

"Should we pray?" I asked.

"Yes, Davis. We should pray. But at this point, I think we should pray for ourselves."

"Her necklace," I whispered.

"I know." Fantasy crossed herself.

We stared at the pendant around the dead woman's neck. It was a cameo in an antique silver setting. A hummingbird fluttering above morning glories on a powder blue stone. I wasn't even

Catholic, but crossed myself too.

The big black dog, between us, paying his own respects, woofed, snapping us out of our death trance and back into the here and now.

"Do you want the dog or Vree?"

Fantasy looked from one to the other. Clearly not wanting either. "I'll take Vree."

It was a morbidly quiet ride out of Fantasy's subdivision, other than the dog barking at thin air.

* * *

The plan had been, once we returned to the Bellissimo with our Bootsy leverage, to get Preacher Gully on the phone and hammer out a deal. We had no Bootsy, we had no leverage, so we had no plan. A dead woman in Fantasy's bonus room, another dog, a missing car, but no plan. We were three miles from the Bellissimo, and Vree was coming around. Again.

"This is a real dog."

The real dog was big. Standing, it was two feet off the ground. Nose to tail, it was three feet long. It weighed maybe fifty pounds, but the real story was the haircut. The trunk of his body and his legs were almost shaved. Everything else was cut into huge fluffy balls. Like pompoms. His head was a giant pompom, it looked like he was wearing pompom bracelets above his paws, the tip of his tail was fashioned into another perfect fuzzy ball, and he was getting sand all over the truck.

"The woman had the dog at the beach."

"Clearly, Fantasy." I swiped sand off my leg.

"How did she end up in my bonus room?"

"How did she end up dead?"

Vree said, "This one looks like a dog, acts like a dog, and

smells like a dog. In a good way. Does that make sense? Do you know what I mean?"

We were stuffed in the cab of a truck with it on a warm April day. The dog was straddling me, his long legs on either side of mine, his head out the window on Vree's side, and Fantasy was trying to drive over his...other end. None of us were gagging. So we knew what she meant.

"This guy's fur is like wire." Vree was petting his head from crown to neck in long smooth strokes, comforting him, and in the process, comforting herself. "Bubblegum's fur is coarse. I mean, I go through the conditioner like nobody's business, and if I don't brush her out three times a day she gets—"

Vree stopped talking for a second. It was glorious.

"—there's a collar in here."

"What? A what?" I reached for the dog's neck too, but didn't find anything but fuzz. "Get it."

"It's way down in this fur ball."

"Find the hook thing," Fantasy said. "Unhook it."

"From what?" Vree asked.

"Unhook its collar. The hook, the clasp, the buckle, whatever." Fantasy moved his tail out of her way.

I dove in from underneath. I ran my hands along his chest— were dogs supposed to have way faster heartbeats than humans?— and hit pay dirt. "Got it." I held up the second dog collar I'd removed in my life in as many days.

"You're so good with dog collars, Davis."

"I've been dressing babies for almost two years."

"Right," she said. "Baby clothes."

"Read it." Fantasy was trying to turn into the Bellissimo over the backend of a large dog. "What does it say?"

"Harley." The engraving was impossibly small. "His name is Harley." I held it above his back. "There are three numbers. Short, medium, and long. The short one starts with the letters S and D. No owner's name, and neither of the others look like phone numbers."

"SD means he's a service dog," Vree said. "That's his service dog number. The other two numbers are probably rabies and microchip."

"Service dog? What kind of service dog?" Fantasy asked. "Is it a police dog?"

He didn't look like any police dog I'd ever seen.

"There are so many kinds of service dogs," Vree said. "There are guide dogs, seizure dogs, autism dogs, diabetic dogs, and emotional support dogs. There are even gluten dogs."

"Are you saying this dog has autism? Or he's diabetic?" Fantasy asked. "How in hell do we take care of a dog with diabetes?"

I was still nose to collar. "Tell us about the microchip." Because that sounded promising.

Vree took a deep breath to tell us a long story, and Fantasy stopped her before she could start. "You know what a microchip is, Davis. Finish with the diabetes, Vree. Is the dog diabetic?" She parked at an angle, spreading the truck out over two parking spaces, and batted Harley's wagging tail out of her face again. "Do we look like we have dog insulin? Where do you even get dog insulin? CVS?"

"How would Vree know if this dog is diabetic?" I asked. "And I'm not asking her to explain microchips to me, thank you. I want to know what we're supposed to do with the microchip. I can't see us taking the time to find a dog doctor, dragging in a dog we clearly don't know, and saying, 'Scan this dog, please.' The vet would be questioned. 'Yes, Detective, they were here,' he'd say. 'Three of them. Like Moe, Larry, and Curly. And not one of them said a word about a dead woman.'"

Fantasy's face said, good point.

"You wouldn't believe how many owners don't microchip their pets," Vree said. "You'd better believe Bubblicious is microchipped. Of course, I had to turn around and cover my whole head when they shot it in her, I'm squeamish like that—"

"For real, Vree?" Fantasy asked. "You're squeamish?"

(Bubblegum had a microchip—another detail Vree didn't think to tell me the day before when I was desperately trying to locate my sister.)

"I know!" Vree said. "Go figure!"

"Vree, you pass out every ten minutes," Fantasy said. "We know you're squeamish. Here's some advice for you." Harley's tail pom hit her in the face again. She swatted. "Don't even think about having kids. You won't be able to take it."

Vree's head dropped.

"Let's talk about your dog's microchip later and this dog's microchip now," Fantasy said. "Can we get information about the dead woman in my bonus room with it? I have a husband, Vree, and three sons, who'll be home tonight. As in my husband will park his car in the garage. And I'd like to get the dead body out of the bonus room before he does."

Vree sniffed. "I don't see how the microchip will help get the dead body out."

Harley barked.

*   *   *

Fantasy's car was equipped with Volvo's On Call service.

Bootsy, as far as we knew, was still alive, and had taken off in the Volvo. More evidence she was just mean and spooky. If she were a real witch, she wouldn't have carjacked the Volvo. She'd have gone to the broom closet for transportation. Witch or not, we'd find her first. Kinda needed to know where she was before I got on the phone with Gully and started making demands.

"How does Bootsy Howard know how to hotwire a car?"

Fantasy and I were in my office. Vree was on dog duty in the living room.

"I left the keys in it," she said.

"Why would you leave the keys in it?"

"My plan was to send a tow truck after it, Davis. You have to leave the keys if you want it towed."

"How in the world did Bootsy start the car if you couldn't?"

"Maybe she witched it."

Surely not. "Call Volvo."

"We can't call Volvo," Fantasy said.

"Why not?"

"Because when an owner asks Volvo to find their car, Volvo assumes it's for no good reason. On Call will only give the information to the police. The car owner has to get the information from the police."

Yeah, that wouldn't work.

"Plan B," I said. "We'll leave Volvo out of it and track down the car ourselves. What's your VIN number?"

"Are you kidding me, Davis? Who knows their VIN number?"

"Your lips aren't big."

In the course of finding a dead body, losing a car, and welcoming a second dog into my home, Fantasy's lips had returned to normal.

"My iPad."

"What?"

"My iPad is in the car. We can track the iPad."

Five minutes later, we had a bead on Bootsy. She was near the Ponchatoula, Louisiana exit on I-12, pointed straight for Baton Rouge, on her way to Houston, no doubt. Which meant she'd made her escape after Fantasy left and before the hairy pierced housekeepers arrived. We didn't know where or how the dead woman fit in, but we knew the timing was tight. The three events had to have happened almost simultaneously.

Had Bootsy Howard actually killed someone?

And if so, who had she killed?

The website was www.petmicrochiplookup.org. I typed the fifteen-digit number in the box, hit enter, and the next screen was a search engine asking for the microchip's manufacturer. Which I didn't know. I searched for pet microchip manufacturers, thinking there'd be three, and as it turned out, there were three hundred. At least. The only way to the microchip registration information, and thus the dead woman's name, was from a veterinarian, or by loading microchip manufacturers into the search engine until it found a match. Which we didn't have time for.

"Is Vree good with computers?" Fantasy asked. "Put her on it."

"Then who will watch the dogs?"

"Not I."

We looked at each other over Bootsy's phone—the lifeline to my sister.

"I turned the air down to forty, Davis. The dead woman isn't going to get any deader. Put the witch, the dead woman, and the microchip business on hold and make the call." She pushed Bootsy's phone an inch.

While it was never a good idea to put a dead body on hold, I couldn't take it one more minute, and with shaking hands, I clicked the Sharing and Caring icon on Bootsy's phone and found Gully's number. It rang three times.

"Sister Bootsy," he answered.

"Wrong, Gully. It's Sister Davis. And I want to talk to my sister."

* * *

We slept in my bedroom that night. All over my bedroom.

Bexley and Quinn had been toddling their way into our bed two or three nights a week since they graduated from baby beds to big-girl beds. When Bradley traveled, I didn't want to sleep alone, and chances were high the girls would wander in anyway, so we skipped the preamble and had all-girl slumber parties. The girls were sweet little sleepers. Wiggly, I woke up feeling like I'd slept with baby octopuses, but warm and cuddly too.

Fantasy's oldest son's basketball team won in the loser's bracket, whatever that meant, and the last time she heard from Reggie, he said the wildcard game would end too late for him to drive home. They'd see her tomorrow. Unless the boys won again. In which case, they'd advance to the finals and see her whenever.

Hopefully, we'd have the dead woman out by whenever.

The dead woman was why Fantasy didn't want to go home.

I couldn't say I blamed her.

I slept on my side of the bed, she slept on Bradley's, with Bex and Quinn between us.

Harley, the big black poodle, slept at the foot of the bed.

Princess wasn't sleeping in her Pop N' Play beside the chaise lounge.

Vree was on the chaise lounge.

One would think two twenty-month-old girls would keep the room awake, but having missed their afternoon naps because they were having too much fun with July, then the excitement of getting dressed up and going to the first round of the dog-show competition to sit on the front row with Aunt Vree while I, in jodhpurs and spurs, passed out Bianca-worthy low scores at the judges' table, had worn them out. They fell asleep before their curls hit the pillow.

It was Princess who kept us up.

She was the noisiest dog in the world.

Could she not get comfortable?

"Toss her another thumbprint cookie, Vree," Fantasy whispered.

"She's eaten a whole box already," Vree whispered back. "Have you seen her stomach? Listen to this." It sounded like Vree thumped a watermelon. "This dog will blow up if I feed it one more bite."

"Princess!" Fantasy loud-whispered. "You see Harley? This is how dogs do it. They lay down and go to sleep. They don't gnaw on themselves and whine all night."

I said, "If we start talking about Harley, we'll never get to sleep," I said. "You two put pillows over your heads and try. We have a big day tomorrow."

"We're going to have plenty of time to sleep when No Hair finds out we have this black dog," Fantasy said. "Because we'll be unemployed."

Vree said, "I wish we could call Meredith again."

We'd talked to Meredith four times. Twice at length, twice just to hear her voice.

"We'll call her again in the morning, Vree," I whispered.

"Right after we get the dead body out of my bonus room."

Fantasy spoke the words over my dreaming babies.

I would talk to Bradley early tomorrow. He'd call before his symposium day started. I planned on telling him to find us a house in Nashville. Then buy it. Then move in. The girls and I would meet him there at the end of the week. After I helped hide the body of Harley Al Abbasov's caregiver and returned him to his owner, Hiriddhi Al Abbasov, oil baron, blind from birth, and my neighbor.

Hiriddhi Al Abbasov was the VIP next door to me on the twenty-ninth floor in the Jay Leno suite. His beloved dog Harley, a first-time contestant in the Southern Canine Association's competition, was missing from the Bellissimo Resort and Casino. His beloved dog Harley's caregiver was missing too. Al Abbasov's secretary and spokesman, Rod J. Sebastian, announced Sheik Al Abbasov was offering a million-dollar reward—the exact amount of money we needed—half a million for information leading to the whereabouts of Harley's caregiver, sixty-two-year-old Doris Harrington, and another half million for the safe return of his seeing-eye dog, Harley.

Who was sleeping on my feet.

ELEVEN

It was a Bellissimo housekeeping supervisor who innocently let me know just how much trouble I was in. At first it didn't register, how bad things were, because I'd finally spoken to my sister. I had to go through Pastor Gully to get to Meredith, and my first conversation with him the day before had gone as expected. He hung up on me.

As if that would make me go away.

I dialed him back immediately; he didn't answer.

"Give him a minute," Fantasy said. "He's processing."

A calling-all-cars email from Bellissimo Security hit my inbox with a click, and at the same time, a notification flashed across my phone. I ignored both. I was so far past ready to make contact with my sister. *Give it up, Gully,* I texted. *I know where you are and I know Greene is sick. I want to help you, but only if you let me talk to Meredith.*

I put the phone on my desk where Fantasy and I could watch it. We could hear Vree in the living room, talking the dogs' ears off. Five minutes later, nothing back from Gully, I texted again.

Your brother has Idiopathic Thrombotic Demyelinating Polyneuropathy. He needs my sister's plasma and you need a million dollars to pay for the procedure. I know all this, Gully. Let me talk to her.

More clicks and Bellissimo notifications on both mine and

Fantasy's phones. Something was going on in the hotel or the casino. Something urgent.

Finally, Bootsy's phone dinged. *Where is Sister Bootsy?*

I shot back, *I'll tell Meredith. Give her the phone. Let me talk to her.*

From Gully: *Who else knows?*

Me: *No one. Let me talk to Meredith.*

Gully: *Who told you?*

Me: *I figured it out. I want to talk to my sister.*

My thumbs were shaking. I dropped the phone. Fantasy's nose was to hers.

What did people do before smart phones?

"Davis." She looked up. "We have a problem."

Bootsy's phone rang on the word "problem." I grabbed it. "Gully." There was a pause, then a breath. A breath I'd known all my life. My sister said, "Davis."

There were tears.

In the end, she said, "All I have to do is lay on a table with a needle in my arm to save a man's life. His whole life, Davis. You and Daddy are in the life-saving business. Look at the people you've dragged out of burning homes and wrecked cars. Look at Daddy's long career. How many lives has he turned around? And even what you do now, you help. You make a difference. I don't like how Gully ambushed me either, and Gina is about to drive me up the wall, but the fact remains I have a chance to help. To save a life. If you ask me, mine isn't the hard job. Yours is. Because you're the only person any of us knows with access to that much money. Money Gully plans to pay back. His plan is for every penny of tithes and offerings for the rest of his life to go to you. They're going to sell Jesus Water to pay you back. So it's more like borrow the money, if you can figure out how to loan it to him, because Davis, Greene is dying."

It was while I was on the phone with my sister that Atlanta oil sheik Hiriddhi Al Abbasov reported his black standard poodle and the poodle's caregiver missing. With that, things went from bad to worse. Much worse. We were harboring a wanted dog. Wanted to the tune of a million dollars. The exact amount of money we needed. And all this went down at exactly three o'clock. Which was exactly when the front door burst open and the pitter-patter of two pairs of Mini Melissa Mary Jane flats raced my way, then my daughters dove into my lap. Bex said, "Mama, mama, mama!" while Quinn said, "Dog, dog, dog!"

They pulled me into the living room to show me not one, but two dogs.

I held them back. A very safe distance. "I know!"

Harley, the nice dog with the crazy haircut, who we'd just learned belonged to the blind bazillionaire next door, wanted no part of Bex and Quinn. He eyed them curiously, then quietly stepped behind Vree. To hide.

Princess, the yellow-eyed terror, sensing a change in the air, looked up from Madeleine Albright. She sniffed. She stood and turned in circles, accidentally stepping on the laptop and quieting Madeleine—a relief—until she found what she was looking for. She marched in our direction, then pressed a rolling yellow eye against the mesh of the playpen wall and zeroed in on my girls. Who I had a firm grip on.

Princess did a little dance, whined, and yipped a greeting. She stretched as tall as she could, her long black fingernails curling over the padded edge of the playpen. She plopped her head between her paws. Then she smiled. I'd never seen Princess smile. I'm not sure I'd ever seen any dog smile. Her head tipped back, her mouth dropped open, she bared her crooked nubby teeth, then her black tongue flopped out of the left side of her mouth. Her eyes lit up, the black one and the yellow one. She pointed the yellow one at Bex and Quinn. Then the back half of her started twitching. Furiously. Princess was wagging her...body. From her thick neck down, she wagged her oddly shaped middle, whimpering eagerly the entire time. Black tongue flapping. Bex and Quinn strained against me.

No way.

I held on tight.

"Would you look at that?" Fantasy said. "Princess likes little people."

*   *   *

I closed the space between Bex, Quinn, and Princess in minute increments. An inch at a time. Even at that, it wasn't long until their noses were pressed against one side of the playpen and hers against the other. Bex and Quinn didn't judge. They were too young to see, care about, or smell anything different about Princess. To them, she had no...disadvantages. They saw little dog and they wanted little dog.

"Honestly, Davis," Vree said. "Princess loves them. It's like she speaks their language. I can tell you right now she won't hurt them."

She who wouldn't hurt them started showing off for them. She rolled over, begged, played dead, and did a full back flip.

They roared.

We all did.

Meredith was trapped in Houston, we had a dead body on ice in Fantasy's bonus room, Bootsy was missing, and we were harboring an oil sheik's seeing-eye dog. We had no plan, solid or otherwise, to scare up a million dollars for Greene Gully's procedure, and there we stood, laughing at my girls, who were laughing at a crazy dog, who was laughing back.

It was like a miracle and a horror movie at the same time.

Fantasy broke the spell when she said, "We need to call housekeeping."

"Why?" I asked.

"We can't take this one out." She pointed at Harley, still watching from his safe place behind Vree.

"Take him out is exactly what we need to do," I said. "We need to take him out, down the hall, and return him to his owner."

"You think? What are we going to say when his blind owner asks where the caregiver is? Are you going to tell him she's dead, or am I?"

"Couldn't we just say we found his dog and get the half-million dollars?" Vree asked. "Then we'd only need the other half-million. Which, when I say it out loud, sounds crazy. I mean, I've never even seen a million dollars in my life, or a half million either. I can't believe I'm even talking about that much money. How would we get it here? I mean, would it be a check? Or cash? If he gives us cash, would we need a suitcase or a forklift? I have no idea what a million dollars looks like. If you add up all the money I've ever seen, like *seen* seen in real life, with my own eyes, it probably wouldn't even be ten thousand dollars. I'll tell you what I have seen. Those money trucks. You know the ones? The bank trucks full of money? Gooch says that's his dream car, one of those money trucks. He says it all the time. 'Get me one of those for my birthday, Vreebee, fully loaded.' Then he punches me in the arm to make sure I got the joke. Which I always do. Fully loaded, like, he means, full of money."

Fantasy and I had been using the time to think.

She said, "We have to figure out what happened to the caregiver before we hand over the dog. Which means we need housekeeping."

"How is housekeeping going to help?" I asked.

"They can bring turf. A mile of it."

"You know what I think would be a good idea?" Vree asked.

"Find one of those money trucks, steal it, then drive it to Houston."

"Vree," Fantasy said, "keep your day job. You'd never be a good criminal. We wouldn't make it ten feet in a bank truck."

"What are we going to do with turf?" I asked.

"I don't really have a day job," Vree said.

"Set it up on your balcony or something," Fantasy said. "This is a big dog. He's going to need to go out."

"For sure," Vree said. "There's this service in Montgomery just for dog owners who live in apartments with balconies. I think most apartments have balconies. Newer apartments do for sure. The company is PupPup Lawn—"

Fantasy stopped her. "Has anyone ever hit you over the head with a shovel, Vree?"

"What? No. Why would someone hit me over the head with a shovel? If someone was swinging a shovel, I'd get out of their way. A shovel! That's it! We could bury the lady in your backyard, Fantasy. Take turns digging, drop the old lady in there, then take Harley back and get the money."

Fantasy asked me if I had a shovel.

"No, I don't have a shovel. Why would I have a shovel?" She was right, though, and not that we should hit Vree over the head with a shovel. She was right that we needed to know what happened to the caregiver before we returned Harley. We needed a little time, and time was something we had very little of. She had to clock in and be downstairs for the first round of the Deputy Dog slot tournament, followed by the first round of the dog-show competition, which I also had to be downstairs for. Either of us not being where we were supposed to be would be the same as dragging No Hair and Baylor into it, and two of us hiding a dead body and a wanted dog were enough.

Turf on the balcony it was.

"Mrs. Cole," the housekeeping supervisor answered. "How can

I help you?"

"I called yesterday."

She clicked on a keyboard. "I see that."

"The two men you sent? I need them back. And I need them to stop by landscaping on the way."

"I didn't send any men," she said.

"You did. They were here."

"I see where you called, Mrs. Cole. Nuclear waste spill, straight bleach. But I also see where the work order was transferred."

"By whom to where?"

"That, I don't know."

"Two men from housekeeping came to my home."

"They weren't my men," she said. "I'm not sure what happened. I show the work order transferred to another department, but I don't know which one. I have you calling and placing the order, then twelve minutes later, before I could dispatch anyone, the work order was gone."

If those men weren't from housekeeping, where were they from? Where were they, period? The last time I saw them, they were on their way to repossess Bootsy. Had Bootsy Howard done something to those men?

In the two minutes it took the housekeeping supervisor to unravel my life just a little further, Princess did it again. She tunneled out of the Pop N' Play. One minute she was in it, the next she was out. And between Bexley and Quinn.

I held my breath; Fantasy held me back.

They sat across from each other on the floor, four Mini Melissa Mary Janes touching, their little legs forming a diamond. Princess ran in it. From one to the other. They raced. They played hide and seek. They traded toys. I drew the line at thumbprint cookie sharing. The three of them were having the time of their lives.

The three of us? Me, Fantasy, and Vree?

Not so much.

Then Princess kept us up half the night.

It was going to be a long week.

*   *   *

Monday morning, bleary eyed, we gathered over breakfast on the terrace. Three women, two toddlers, one Harley, and one Princess. Fruit parfaits, whole grain waffles, K9 Natural Lamb Feast, and manicotti, extra sauce.

"She's been dead twenty hours." Fantasy checked her watch. "That we know of. There's been a dead body in my house for twenty hours. We've got to do something."

"Do you think she'd fit in the refrigerator?" Vree asked.

Fantasy and I just looked at her.

"If you took out all the shelves and vegetable bins? Like when you clean your refrigerator? I mean—"

Still, we just stared.

Vree shrugged an apology.

"We need to call the police before they call us," I said. "Our prints are all over that room."

"It's my house, Davis." Fantasy poured more coffee, then passed the carafe to me. "We can explain our prints."

"You checked her for a pulse, Fantasy. How are we supposed to explain your prints on her neck?"

"All the more reason to get her out of my bonus room."

I poured, then passed the coffee to Vree. "We need to know if she died of natural causes or...something less natural."

"Like Bootsy." Vree poured.

Bex and Quinn said, "Boo, boo, boo."

"Bootsy must have cast a death spell on her," Vree said. "How will we know? I mean, it's not like we can ask her. 'Lady, did you have a stroke or did Bootsy do this to you?'"

"Which is why we need a doctor," I said.

"A doctor we have dirt on," Fantasy added.

"A dirty doctor?" Vree said. "How about a crazy doctor? Would that work? Don't come to Pine Apple sick, Fantasy. I'll tell you that right now. Our doctor is deranged. One time—"

"Let's say we had a dirty doctor," I said. "What would we do with him? Her? It? The woman's already dead."

"We'd have him, her, or it determine the cause of death," Fantasy said. "That way we'd know which direction to take. If she died of natural causes, we call it in and be done with it. If she died of unnatural causes, well, that's a different story."

"Altogether," I said.

"What would be so different?" Vree asked. "Isn't she dead either way?"

"The difference is, if she was murdered, we'll be suspects numbers one, two, and three," Fantasy said.

"How's that?" I asked.

"Because there's a price on her head, Davis. And we have the dog. Which makes us look twice as guilty. It will look like we killed her for the reward money. The police will start digging and figure out fast we actually *need* the reward money." She pointed at me. "Suspect." She pointed at Vree. "Suspect." She turned her finger on herself. "Suspect."

Vree said, "Then we should blow up your bonus room."

Fantasy and I looked at her again.

"I mean, you know, get rid of the evidence."

Still, we just stared.

"Don't you watch *CSI*, Vree?" Fantasy asked. "There is no getting rid of evidence. The woman has teeth. You can't blow up teeth."

Vree ran her tongue along her teeth. "Well, how can I help?"

"You're helping with the dogs," I said. "That's enough. Let us worry about the rest. Unless you have a million dollars."

Vree sighed. Fantasy tapped her chin. I wondered what my life as a divorced single parent would be like after Bradley found out.

"Let's do this," Fantasy said. "Let's deal with the dead woman first. After that, we'll go straight to work on the Meredith situation. I say, as far as priorities go, the dead woman in my bonus room trumps the live sister in Houston."

It was familiar territory for me. I was the mother of twins, who often needed my immediate attention in the exact same way at the exact same time. I was torn the same way then, forced to choose between concentrating my energy in my sister's direction and giving the woman in Fantasy's bonus room the respect she deserved.

"What about Bootsy?" Vree asked.

Bex and Quinn said, "Boo, boo, boo."

"We'll get to her after the dead woman and Meredith," Fantasy said.

I covered my face with my hands and talked through them. "We're in so much trouble."

"We're not in trouble yet," Fantasy said. "We didn't kill the lady. All we did was find her. We're just not going to say *when* we found her. And we'll hit the Slipper for the money to save Meredith, at which point, Davis, we'll be in trouble."

"Who are we going to hit?" Vree asked.

"What," Fantasy said. "What are we going to hit. We're going to hit Silver Slipper. A casino up the street."

I came out from behind my hands.

"We don't even have time to hit the Slipper. We'd have to do surveillance first. It would take days of watching how they move the money to find a way in, if they even have one. I haven't heard of a Slipper heist as long as I've been in Biloxi, which says to me they know what they're doing."

"Then we hit The Last Resort," Fantasy said.

"The Last Resort probably doesn't even have a million dollars."

"What is The Last Resort?" Vree asked.

"The name says it all," Fantasy said.

"Are we really going to rob a casino?" Vree asked. "Like machine guns and ski masks? Why don't we talk Meredith out of giving her blood away instead? Would that be cheaper? Like, not cost a million dollars?"

"Meredith doesn't want to be talked out of it," I said. "She wants us to come up with the money and loan it to Gully. She's convinced he's going to pay us back."

"Where is Meredith?" Fantasy asked.

"In a suite at the Four Seasons close to the hospital."

"Bubbs." Vree collapsed into a sob.

"Go." I'd made the offer nine times the day before, and I felt certain my tenth offer just then wouldn't be the last. "I can make one phone call and have you in Houston in an hour, Vree."

"I can't leave you like this, Davis!"

"She's right," Fantasy said. "Who'd take care of the dogs? I don't know a thing about dogs. What do you know about dogs, Davis?"

"I have to stay and help," Vree said. "At least until we find Bootsy. Because if we don't find Bootsy, Gooch will be furious with me. One time Bootsy—"

Bex and Quinn said, "Boo, boo, boo."

"See, Fantasy?" Vree pointed at the highchairs. "They're babies, and even they think Bootsy is a witch."

"No, they don't," I said. "They're trying to say her name."

And we were right back where we started. In forty-eight hours, the only thing we'd really accomplished was relocating Meredith and Bubbles, so we were breathing, but we still had no idea what to do about or with the dead body, what to do about or with the dogs, where Bootsy was, who the housekeepers worked for, and we certainly didn't have a million dollars.

TWELVE

Bradley called a half hour later. He sneezed, I blessed him, then he said, "How are things?"

"Quiet." I didn't lie. It was quiet in the kitchen pantry. Which was where I hid to take his call. It was anything but quiet outside of the pantry.

After breakfast, we made a chore list. Locating Bootsy was the easiest, so we tracked Fantasy's iPad again only to find Bootsy had turned the Volvo around. Fantasy's Find My iPad app pinged a dot in Mandeville, Louisiana, headed east. We were east. Was Bootsy coming back to Biloxi? Was there someone here she'd forgotten to sprinkle death dust on? If she wasn't on her way to Houston, where in the world was she on her way to? Since we didn't have a clue, we moved on to our next item—the procurement of a refrigerated storage unit for temporary dead-body storage until we could determine cause of death, because at the time, it seemed like the right thing to do. We couldn't just leave the poor woman in Fantasy's easy chair. Nor could we find a refrigerated storage unit that wasn't smackdab in the middle of downtown Biloxi, where there were webcams on every corner, and we didn't need documentation of us hauling a dead body into a refrigerated storage unit, so we started a new search for a refrigerated truck. ("Like an ice cream truck?" Vree asked. "I love ice cream trucks. Remember when we were little, Davis, and—") We'd wasted the half hour before that racking our brains for a doctor, a medical examiner, an EMT, a mortician, or even a Girl Scout with her Corpse Badge who owed us a favor, couldn't drum one up, which looped us back to temporarily relocating the caregiver's body. Just until we could take care of a few other pressing matters. The vote was two-to-one. Fantasy wanted the dead woman out of her bonus room, and Vree sided with her. ("I mean, gross.") I didn't want dead body charges on my record, so I voted no. Fantasy said, "Not reporting her death, if we're caught, is a misdemeanor. A fifty-dollar fine at most, unless she's a public threat, and I don't see a dog's caregiver as any kind of public threat. I see it as a private threat. Very private. Like in my bonus room private."

I argued not reporting the body was one thing, but moving it was quite another. Moving it would constitute abuse of a corpse. Far past a misdemeanor, very against the law, up to a year in prison, not to mention wrong, just wrong, using phrases like "...everything good and decent and right in the world," when my phone rang. "It's Bradley." I jumped up and made a run for the pantry. "Everyone try to be quiet."

"Quiet? It's never quiet," he said. "It couldn't possibly be quiet with Meredith's friend there, Davis. What's going on?"

Blood swaps, dead bodies, witches, lost dogs, and ice cream trucks. I thought it best to steer our conversation in a different direction. "The dog show is going on, and Bex and Quinn love it."

"Jeremy tells me two dogs didn't register, Vree's is one of them."

I should have chosen a different direction. If No Hair told him Vree's dog wasn't in the show, then he told him Hiriddhi Al Abbasov's wasn't either. A subject I most definitely did not want to discuss with my husband, considering Hiriddhi Al Abbasov's dog was in our living room. "Vree's dog missed the deadline."

Totally true.

"Davis, I talked to Baylor. Have you seen him? Have you talked to him?"

"No," I said. Another true answer. I hadn't seen or talked to Baylor and I didn't want to see or talk to him. Fantasy and I had spent years teaching Baylor everything we knew, and now all he did was use it against us. Baylor would take one look at us and know we had the oil sheik's dog. "Why?" I asked Bradley, knowing why. If No Hair hadn't told him there'd been a dognapping, Baylor would've.

That was it. My marriage would soon be over.

"Because they're running in circles," Bradley said. "There are dogs all over the property, including a missing dog surveillance can't find, and between the missing dog and the dog show, I've taken no less than ten dog calls. I don't know how I let marketing talk me into a dog show at the Bellissimo, but I can tell you this, Davis, it will be item number one in my exit interview. Don't let a dog in the door. Not only the dogs," he said, "a couple checked in yesterday."

What did a couple checking in have to do anything? Where was he going with this? Hundreds of couples checked in every day. "And?"

He sneezed again. "Hold on." I heard two distant sneezes. The first faraway sneeze made me wonder why he was sneezing. Bradley never sneezed. The second one gave me the split second I needed to jump through the safe-subject window he'd opened.

I blessed him two more times, then said, "A couple checked in?"

"Jeremy keeps calling them schmucks."

No Hair divided casino guests into one of three categories: lucky ducks, cat ladies, or drunks. Schmucks was a new one.

"Davis, these people are raising hell all over the casino. Have you seen the incident report?"

The incident report listed, well, casino incidents: disturbances, underage gambling, medical emergencies, security threats. And I hadn't looked at it in months.

"Apparently, they had reservations, a room for themselves and a room for their bodyguards—"

"We have guests who brought bodyguards?" I asked. "Who?"

"Schmucks. Other than that, I have no idea who," he said. "But after raising hell at the front desk, they ended up in a Magnolia Suite."

Magnolia Suites, of which there were six on the twenty-seventh floor, had four bedrooms, indoor pools, and private poker rooms. Serious gamblers, who had twenty-five hundred a night to blow on a hotel room, stayed in Magnolia Suites. The schmucks causing trouble were either serious poker players, super rich, or they'd raised so much hell checking in, the only way to appease them was to put them in a Magnolia.

"The guests have been there a day," Bradley said. "Maintenance has had to repair two walls, replace a room of carpet, and the police have been called three times. That I know of. No telling what Jeremy and Baylor aren't telling me."

"Why the police?" Honestly, I didn't care why. I took it for what it was: No Hair and Baylor were busy. Which was very good news for me.

"One of the calls was for indecent exposure." He sneezed. "I don't have any other details." He sneezed again.

"Bradley, is it dusty there?"

"No," he said. "Why?"

"Why are you sneezing?"

"I have no idea. Where was I?"

"Schmucks and details."

"Right," he said. "I don't have details and I don't want them. Davis, I'm tired of the details. Keep Bex and Quinn as far away from the public venues as you can until Jeremy and Baylor take care of the schmucks."

"I won't let the girls out of my sight, Bradley."

When the whole story came out, and it would, Bradley would remind me of this conversation. The conversation in which I could have told him about Meredith, about Gully and Greene and Bootsy, about Princess and Harley, not to mention the dead woman in Fantasy's bonus room, and didn't.

"Tell me about judging the show," he said. "Then I need to let you go."

I used my sleeve to mop my brow. There was no air in the pantry. "The dogs marched around the ring in a circle, then stopped at the judges table to give us dirty looks, and we gave them points."

"For?"

"Presentation? But I wasn't really sure what they were presenting."

"How did you delegate points?"

"Bianca," I said. "She was watching close-circuit, and she texted. 'That one is hideous, David. It looks like a monkey. Zero points.'"

"Bex and Quinn were where?" he asked.

"In the front row. With Vree. Bradley, I wish you could've seen what Bianca had me wearing."

"I did."

"How?"

"You're on the front page of the Life section in *USA Today*."

Surely not.

"What was up with the hat?"

"I didn't have time to go blonde."

"Ah."

"Tell me about Nashville."

"It's beautiful. The new SGF offices are in a part of town called the Gulch, between downtown and Music Row. I wish you could see—" He sneezed again.

What was up with all the sneezing?

"Are you coming down with something?"

"No." He sneezed again. "I feel great. It would be hard to be in this city and not feel great."

He was still on his Nashville kick, planning his exit interview already, just as I was beginning to think we'd need to be farther from Biloxi than Nashville. We would need to move to Tibet. Or Niue. Or Point Nemo, the oceanic pole of inaccessibility.

*   *   *

We split up at ten 'til ten Monday morning.

Fantasy walked Bexley and Quinn to July on the twenty-fifth floor. Vree went on dog patrol, and I, in tweeds, riding boots, and a black felt derby perched sidesaddle on my Bianca blonde ponytail, judged the obstacle-course round of the dog show.

Arriving two minutes early for the second round of competition, I took one of the minutes to see what I'd missed in my haze of trauma the night before. The ballroom, the center of the conference facilities, was directly above the casino. Other than the massive crystal chandeliers, everything else had been dogged. The competition ring colors were Mardi Gras—green turf, purple stages, and gold boxes identifying the different breeds—Neapolitan Mastiff, Newfoundland Labrador, Boykin Spaniel, and several more boxes touting dog breeds I'd never heard of, and had no chance of recognizing—it's a good thing they wore numbers. The ring was fenced in, surrounded by spectator bleachers, and the overwhelming smell was that of buttered popcorn. I spent the second minute before the first dog jumped and jogged around the obstacle course talking to Bianca.

I rolled my eyes as I answered my clone phone. "Good morning, Bianca."

"David. Take my hair down or twist it into a chignon. I look like I'm in eighth grade." She must have thought about what she said and decided looking like she was in eighth grade wasn't all bad. Because she followed with, "On second thought, I'll let it go this one time. But cross your ankles, not your legs. How many times do we need to go over this?"

I spotted the close-circuit cameras as the announcer stepped up to the podium.

"Gotta scoot, Bianca." I muted my phone.

The dogs did their thing for almost an hour.

I thought I'd lose my mind for fifty-nine minutes of it.

The split second I entered the last score for the last hurdle, I slipped out the back, then ducked and dodged my way from the convention center to my office, where Fantasy was ticking items off our to-do list. She put her pen down and said, "You look ridiculous."

"Thank you."

Her? With the lips the day before? I hadn't said a word.

She was in my chair, so I sat down to the unfamiliar view from the other side of my desk. "Where are we?"

"I tried Operations, Maintenance, and Engineering. No one has seen the housekeepers. And that's not the bad news."

It was plenty bad.

Where had Bootsy stashed those men?

"No Hair called," she said.

Three phones were lined up between us. My uncloned phone, Bootsy's, and Fantasy's. She said No Hair had called her phone, and when she didn't answer, he dialed mine.

"Why?" I pulled the derby off and sailed it. "What'd he want?"

"He wanted to know why I didn't answer my own phone but

answered yours."

"What'd you say?" I loosened the ascot choking me.

"I said, 'No Hair, what do you want?'"

"And?"

"He wants us to find the oil sheik's missing dog." She pointed in the general direction of next door. "He said someone in the Leno suite called for a limo to drive the caregiver and Harley to the dog beach. Which explains why they were in my neighborhood. But the caregiver and the dog never showed up for the limo. So we don't know how they ended up in my neighborhood. Then he said if we didn't find the missing dog in the next thirty minutes, we need to sit down with the oil man and look at security footage."

"How long ago was that?" I asked.

"Right after you left."

I left an hour earlier. Our thirty minutes were up thirty minutes ago.

"How are we supposed to look at security footage with a blind man?"

"I asked the same question, and No Hair said stop being cute."

"We can't."

"Right? And why would we want to? What's left after cute?"

I wrestled out of the tweed jacket. "We brought Harley in through the back door and up the freight elevator. No security cameras, there's nothing to see. And why us? Why can't Baylor look at nothing on security footage with the blind oil man?"

"No Hair's busy being Bradley because Bradley's out of town, Baylor's busy being No Hair because No Hair's busy being Bradley, and both are busy chasing schmucks in the casino."

"Bradley mentioned schmucks in the casino when he called this morning."

"There are always schmucks in the casino." She waved it off. "No Hair wants to know what we're busy doing, because someone needs to find the oil man's dog. He said they needed help, and for us to get off our lazy butts and help."

I searched for buttons through the ruffles of the blouse I was wearing.

"Are you going to strip, Davis?"

"Did you tell him you're busy with the Hair of the Dog tournament and I'm busy with two little girls and judging the dog show?"

"He hung up on me before I could. He said get to work, then...click." She took a deep breath, then clasped her hands on my desk. She leaned in. "There's one more thing."

We didn't need one more thing.

We needed three or four less things.

"He wants one of us to—" she used air quotes "—'stop watching soap operas and eating bonbons long enough to take cage at four.'"

My hunt for lost buttons in the sea of ruffles on my horse blouse ended.

If one of us needed to take cage at four, it meant it was still Monday. Which sounded impossible, but if someone had to take cage, it was indeed, one of the longest days of my life, and still Monday. Monday meant the cage audit, where one of us—No Hair, Baylor, Fantasy, or me—oversaw the transfer of the weekend's casino cash haul to the vault. Usually we drew straws, because no one really wanted to be in the windowless basement count room alone for an hour counting stacks of money. Then verifying the count. And signing off it. It being tens of millions of dollars.

If one of the million dollars were to, say, be misplaced, it wouldn't be caught until another one of us took cage the next Monday. At which point, Greene Gully's blood business would be completed. And my sister would be home.

* * *

Between one Monday's cage count and the next, a misplaced million could be replaced.

* * *

Fantasy, in her navy-blue security blazer, left for round two of the Dog Days slot tournament at eleven fifteen. I picked up the house phone and dialed the Leno suite. The sheik's secretary answered. I identified myself as a Bellissimo internal security operative, then set up an appointment for one of my coworkers and me to go over security footage with the oil sheik at three o'clock. "If you don't mind me asking, how will this go?"

"What do you mean?"

"How will we watch surveillance video with a man who can't see?"

"You'll be surprised at His Excellency Al Abbasov's skills," the secretary said.

I'd been surprised enough in the past two days to last the rest of my life, thank you very much.

(His what?)

"Thirty percent of our brains are devoted to vision," he said. "From birth, His Excellency has redirected his untapped visual cortex function to his other senses. He can smell a lie. He can hear you blink. He can source a wine to its geographical origin by tasting a drop. He's more than capable of processing what you describe. Without his dog, though, he's bumping into walls. He needs the dog. We'll see you at three."

Which gave me a few good hours to check in with my sister, track Bootsy the Witch, and make some kind of, any kind of, progress with the dead problem in Fantasy's bonus room.

"How long should we plan on meeting with Mr. Al Abbasov?" I asked.

"Address him as His Excellency."

Sure thing.

"And I've scheduled you for fifty minutes. Until 3:50."

Which would free me up to take cage at four.

If I were so inclined.

Then Vree's smiling face filled my office door. "Davis!"

She was more than smiling. She was beaming.

And she wasn't alone.

Leverette Urleen, MD, Pine Apple, Alabama's resident physician, was with her. Wearing one of his signature seersucker suits, slack bowtie, and exhausted wingtips, he looked like Albert Einstein, smelled like Sunday morning at the frat house, and had a wide smug smirk on his face. He was absentmindedly scratching his chest. "Hey, Davis. Long time no see. Vree says you need my help with a stiffie."

"Excuse me?"

He said, "A stiffie. Cadaver? Carcass? Dearly departed?"

* * *

In as far as how much trouble I could potentially be in with my marriage, my job, and felony theft charges when I waylaid a million dollars during the cage count that afternoon, which would land me in the pokey for years to come, heaviest on my heart, with my sister as safe as she could be for the time being, was the dead body at Fantasy's. And not so much that we walked off and left her there—at the time, it was our only option—but the fact that the woman, who looked like Mrs. Doubtfire, had to have a family somewhere. Was there a husband pacing a floor? Probably not. Who would leave a husband to live and travel with a blind oil baron to take care of his dog? What about children? She had to have children. At her age, they'd be grown. Which meant we walked off and left someone's dead mother in an easy chair. And what if her children had children? The dead woman could have grandbabies who adored her, or a sister! She, like me, might have a sister with whom she shared a bond like no other. So as sorry as I was to see Urleen, the quackiest of all quacks to ever take the Hippocratic Oath—and I was so sorry to see him—even I had to admit, he was my best option.

Leverette Urleen could tell the story all day long and no one would believe him.

The dead woman needed my help. She deserved it.

Those two truths pulled me up from my desk. My limbs felt leaden. It was half past eleven. I had a meeting with His Excellency at three and the cage count at four. Which left plenty of time to get to Fantasy's with Urleen the Idiot. I said, "Let me change clothes."

The horse clothes were killing me.

THIRTEEN

The talented team of designers and installers from the Bellissimo theater department had turned the conference-center slot-tournament room into a dog house. Because of the proprietary nature of the game inside, cell service was blocked. To talk to Fantasy I either had to call on the security channel of the casino's two-way radio system and let everyone else in security listen in, or walk in the dog door. Urleen and I walked in the door of the Hair of the Dog slot tournament under the pitched roof of a massive redwood dog house. Directly above our heads was a crooked white sign with hand-painted letters: FiDO. The lower-case I was dotted with a pawprint. Urleen made a beeline for the open bar to our right. I caught him by the back of his wrinkled jacket. "What's wrong with you?"

"A little libation is just what the doctor ordered. And I'm the doctor."

I gave him a shove. Away from the bar. Where the bartenders were wearing furry dog-ear hats and the drinks were being served in stemmed glass dog bowls. Just past the bar was a gated fence with a security guard dressed as a dog catcher.

"Your badge?"

Urleen puffed up. "I'm a doctor."

"So?" the security suit said. "Where's your badge? This is a private event."

"I'm a private doctor."

"You need a badge, private doctor."

I peeked over the Balenciaga sunglasses covering half my face.

"Mrs. Cole." The dog catcher recognized me. "Welcome."

I grabbed Urleen by the seersuckered sleeve. "Come on."

The first year Bradley and I were married, we kept my identity secret. We tried to, anyway. I worked undercover, and the best way to blow that cover would've been to walk around on Bradley's arm waving my wedding band. It wasn't long, a year, maybe, until our marriage was the worst-kept secret throughout the three million square feet of Bellissimo property. When a graveyard shift of blackjack dealers took it to the next level, the payout on their "Is He or Isn't He?" pool topping five thousand dollars, one of the dealers, wanting his ex-wife off his back for unpaid child support, laid in wait behind a giant schefflera tree in our vestibule, then snapped a picture of a welcome-home kiss Bradley and I shared just inside the open front door of our private residence on the twenty-ninth floor. The problem was, at the time, I'd just finished a round of Bianca Sanders duty—I was temporarily blonde, green-eyed, and head to toe Givenchy. So the blackjack dealer took, and distributed, a picture of what looked like the casino president sharing a sloppy kiss with the owner's wife.

At which point, we had to come clean.

Bellissimo President Bradley Cole was, indeed, married, to a woman who did, eerily, favor Bianca Sanders.

The blackjack dealer won the five-thousand-dollar pool, but lost his job before he could be fired for using such poor judgement when he was arrested for failure to pay the back child support.

The photograph floated around for months.

By then, I was pregnant with the girls, and present day, most of the Bellissimo knew Mr. Cole was married to the seldom-seen mother of the twin girls, who were often seen with him on Saturdays, and that his wife looked a lot like the mean woman who lived in the Penthouse. I was no longer the lead story in the employee break room, but still, I didn't parade around the property toting a Boss's Wife sign. I hid under a hat or behind sunglasses when I went out my front door. Like then. As soon as security recognized me and let us in the fence, I was back behind my sunglasses. And being barked at.

I loved slot machines, and I loved tournament slot machines the best. Rather than the usual cherries, diamonds, and flaming sevens, tournament machines were themed. Heavily. Inside the dog house were two rows of twenty-five gigantic bone-shaped Double Dog Dare slot machines, every seat I could see occupied, and every machine barking as the players tried to line up the dogs by breed. A lady directly in front of us was playing the bonus round, Puppy Love. She was tapping the screen, selecting from a sea of dog biscuits that flipped to reveal fire hydrants, tennis balls, postal carriers, and diamond collars. Four diamond collars paid five thousand dollars. I watched until she turned over four ripped-panted mailmen, winning one thousand dollars. Someone tapped me on the shoulder. The someone was Fantasy. "Davis."

Urleen—a drama king to begin with—took one look at Fantasy and clutched his heart. His mouth dropped open. He took a dramatic step back. He used his best game-show host voice. "You are the most beautiful creature on God's green planet. I adore you. You're Venus and Serena without the bulk. You're Rihanna without the umbrella-ella-ella. You're Diana Ross without the Supremes. May I please examine you?"

"Fantasy, this is Urleen."

"*Doctor* Urleen." He reached for her hand. She jerked it away. Urleen wasn't discouraged. He straightened his bow tie, then swept into a low bow. He rose slowly, looked into her eyes, and said, "I'll have you know I completed my gynecological residency at the top of my class. And I'd surrender my substantial wealth to see your fallopian tubes up close and personal. Scoot down just a little more."

"Take a step back, fool." Fantasy kicked him in the shin. "You're disgusting." She turned to me. "What the hell?"

I sighed, closed my eyes, and put a palm to my throbbing forehead. "Fantasy, he's all we've got. And I need to know how to get into your bonus room."

She still had a lip curled at Urleen, who was dancing in a small circle, flapping his hands like a bird's wings, singing a warped version of "Pretty Woman."

"Where'd you get him?" she asked.

"Vree. She was trying to help."

Urleen was still bird dancing and singing. He was attracting an audience. I kicked him in his other shin. "Take it down a notch, Urleen."

"How are you going to get there?" she asked.

Urleen perked an ear. "My chariot awaits, fair lady. I'll take you anywhere. Everywhere. The moon! Moon over Miami! Bad moon rising! Fly me to the moon!"

"I wouldn't go to a landfill with you," Fantasy said. She pulled her keys out of her pocket and asked me, "Are you okay to drive the truck?" I nodded. "You're sure?" I held my hand out. "Get him in and out as quickly as possible."

I grabbed Urleen by the seersucker. To Fantasy, he yelled over his shoulder, "Until we meet again, tall maiden!"

* * *

I didn't drive much. I didn't leave the Bellissimo property often, and when I did, I rode in the backseat of a Bellissimo town car, and my driver, Crisp, well, drove. I turned the key in the ignition of Fantasy's truck, and with that simple act, it shot forward three feet, leaving half an inch of air between the front end and a concrete parking bollard.

Urleen slapped around for a seatbelt. "I'd drive," he said, "but I had a few nips on the way this morning."

"You drink and drive, Urleen?"

"Past tense," he said. "I drunk and drove. I don't anymore. Now I drink and ride. My nurse, Jenna Ray, is also my driver."

"Jenna Ray is here? In Biloxi?" Had I known, I'd have her in the truck. She wasn't even a registered nurse, but knew more about healthcare in her sleep than Urleen knew at eight in the morning after a pot of strong coffee.

"Oh, a sinner of the worst sort." Urleen's jowls shook with disapproval. "A loose woman, a gossipmonger, and, it would seem, an addicted gambler too. She's somewhere in the bowels of your casino. Donating her life's savings to the one-armed bandits, no doubt."

"And this horrible sinner Jenna Ray drives you around why?"

"My authorization is in question."

"Your authorization to drive? Do you mean you lost your license, Urleen?"

"A bone I pick with your father daily."

"Let me get this straight." I put the truck in reverse, remembering to engage the clutch that time, but let it go too soon. We shot ten feet back, kissing the bumper of a Gulf Coast Laundry truck.

"Lordy, help." Urleen crossed himself. "Our Father. God bless us, every one."

I put it in D and lurched forward. Urleen gripped the dash with both hands. "Explain this to me, Urleen. Daddy arrested you for driving under the influence, you lost your license to drive, but you still practice medicine?" Maneuvering the parking lot, I was getting the hang of the truck, which was to say I didn't plow into anything, and thank goodness, because Bianca would have a cow if I showed up at the dog judges' table wearing a whiplash collar.

"I don't practice medicine, Davis. I excel at it."

"Whatever."

Navigating Beach Boulevard traffic was tricky, and I was honked at heartily from all directions.

"How far are we going?" Urleen asked. "Is the raving beauty's home within walking distance? Walking is the medicine of life, you know, and it occurs to me I need a dose. Walk this way? Walk the line? A little walk on the wild side?"

"We only have two turns left, Urleen, and the raving beauty is twenty years younger than you, a foot taller, and married."

"What a lucky man." Urleen smacked his lips. "Those long brown legs."

We finally made it to Fantasy's.

The security door to the bonus room was wide open.

Doris Harrington's body was gone.

In its place, Bootsy Howard's dogeared book: *The Tale of the Body Thief*, by Anne Rice.

Bootsy had the dead woman.

She'd cooked up a new plan that involved the body and returned for it. Either she had witchcraft business with it, or the dead woman was Booty's new bargaining chip, which she intended to sell to me for a million dollars.

Great. Just great.

* * *

Jenna Ray, Urleen's scandalous chauffeur, was nowhere to be found. She didn't answer her phone, a zip through the main casino didn't turn her up, and neither did a loudspeaker page. I didn't have time to track her through the surveillance system, nor did I have time to babysit Urleen until she surfaced, so I checked him into a Bellissimo guest room, telling him to wait there, quietly, until it was time for him to go. He asked when that might be, and I said as soon as I found Jenna Ray. He said he was in no big hurry; I told him his patients in Pine Apple needed him. He asked when he'd see tall, dark, and gorgeous again—dinner, perhaps? I said he'd see her never, then pointed him to the guest room's minibar and ran. To July's. On the twenty-fifth floor. Where I gathered Bex and Quinn, telling July I'd bring them back in an hour. The girls and I rode the VIP elevator to the mezzanine level, where I waited at the back door of Snacks for a to-go picnic lunch for three. The waitress asked me what we'd like, and I was so tired of making decisions, I told her to think Lunchables. The girls and I played the Quiet Game through our front door on our way to the playroom, sneaking in without Vree knowing I'd returned—I wasn't ready to share the latest devastating development—or reminding Bex and Quinn of Princess, who was probably busy with Madeleine Albright anyway. I spread a quilt on the playroom floor, then watched the girls trade squares of peanut butter and jelly sandwiches, stack orange slices, and blow milk bubbles through straws.

In the quiet safety and haven of the playroom, I reminded myself I didn't have anything to do with Doris Harrington's death or disappearance. That was all Bootsy.

Then I dialed my sister.

I didn't want to drag her into it, but at that point, I had to.

"Are you comfortable?"

"Are you kidding, Davis? This hotel is as nice as yours. And you should see this dog. She has her own bed, her own blanket, crystal food bowls, and every two hours, a pet concierge takes her for a walk in the pet park. She has her own room-service menu from a restaurant downstairs called the Barkery."

Bubblicious.

In the excess of dogs—dogs, dogs, and more dogs—I'd forgotten Vree's.

"I sent her to the spa yesterday."

"Four Seasons has a dog spa?"

"It's so cute. If Vree saw it, she'd move here."

"Meredith, I've lost Bootsy Howard."

Bex and Quinn said, "Boo, boo, boo."

"What?" Meredith said. "Under what circumstances did you have Bootsy Howard to lose her?"

"She showed up ten minutes after I read the email from Gully Saturday morning." I went on to hit the highlights. "I had to get her out of here, Mer. I couldn't think with her witching around. At the time, it seemed like a good idea to lock her up at Fantasy's until I could trade her for you, but the next thing I knew, Fantasy's car was gone, there was a dead woman, and the housekeepers were missing. I think Bootsy Howard killed a woman and made off with two housekeeper hostages. For all I know, she might have killed them too, if she didn't turn them into lizards."

After the longest pause, Meredith said, "Davis? Have you been drinking?"

"No!"

"Start at the beginning. Slower this time."

I went through it again in more detail. In the end, Meredith had three things to say: "Why are you just now telling me this?" And, "Did you let Bex and Quinn have the carnival suckers? We've heard it all our lives, Davis. Skip Bootsy's house on Halloween and don't eat anything she brings to potluck unless it's straight out of a Kentucky Fried bucket." And, "Why do you think the book in the chair was some kind of message from Bootsy? What if the dead woman had been sitting on the book the whole time?"

"Meredith? What does it matter if the dead woman sat on a book? I'm going to prison for the rest of my life. My husband will divorce me, then my mother-in-law will move in and have my daughters in saddle oxfords until they're old enough to run away from home. And you're defending Bootsy Howard?"

"I'm not defending her. I'm just saying you're assuming a lot. I can't see Bootsy doing all that. She's odd, she's creepy, and there's no denying strange things happen when Bootsy's around. But kill a woman, make off with the body, and turn housekeepers into lizards?"

Well. When you put it that way.

"Where do you think she is?" Meredith asked.

"I thought she was on her way there, but it looks like she turned around to come back here. She's either here, there, or somewhere in between with a body strapped on the roof of Fantasy's car with housekeeper hostages and I need to find her."

"Davis. This is horrible."

"Meredith, this is worse than horrible."

"How can I help?"

"Get in touch with Gully. See if she's made contact. Ask him if she's there or on her way."

"She's not. He calls me every hour on the hour. He says he's calling to pray with me, but he's really calling to make sure I haven't flown the coop. He hasn't said a word about Bootsy except that he hasn't heard much from her. Between hospital visits with Greene, he writes sermons. So far today, he's written, 'Stop, Drop, and Roll Doesn't Work in Hell', and 'If You Would Shut Up You Could Hear Jesus', and 'If You Don't Sin, He Died for Nothing.'"

"Nice."

"Nervous energy," she said. "He's writing sermons to keep from writing his brother's eulogy."

"What's Gina doing?"

"Praying. Out loud. Very loud."

"Anything about safe travels for Bootsy?"

"Just Greene. If you could see him, you'd be praying out loud too. He has so little time left, Davis. His skin is ghost gray. His lips are blue. His toenails are black."

"I'd cover up those toenails."

"I covered up my eyes."

"When was the last time you saw him?"

"This morning. Visiting hours. From ten until ten twenty."

"And Bootsy wasn't there?"

"Tenth time, Davis. Bootsy isn't here."

Where was that witchy woman?

"Davis, you don't really believe she killed anyone, do you?"

"I don't know what to believe," I said. "I know she helped kidnap you. I know she wants your blood pumping through her boyfriend's veins, and she wants it bad enough to have triggered a spiraling crime spree. If that's the case, there'll be no witching her way out of it, and I have to find her before anyone else gets hurt."

Meredith and I shared a moment of spooky sister silence.

She broke it. "Davis, do you feel bad about Mother and Daddy?"

"Of course I do. What if, down the road, our children kept something this big from us?"

"You know they will," she said. "But in a way, don't you look at it like we're protecting them? Mother would have a stroke. I don't know what Daddy would do. Lock Gully and Bootsy up, for sure."

"Gully and Bootsy need to be locked up."

"If Bootsy's gone off the deep end and actually taken a life, yes. But not Gully so much. The only thing Gully is guilty of is trying to save his brother's life, and this is how far he's willing to go to do it."

An orange slice landed in front of me.

"I'd do it for you, Davis."

Which put an entirely different spin on things. Because I'd do it for her too. In a heartbeat. I looked at my own daughters, willing them to love each other the same way.

*   *   *

At two o'clock, I tiptoed out my front door and returned Bexley and Quinn to July. On the short ride from the twenty-ninth floor to the twenty-fifth, they fell asleep, Quinn, then Bex. I kissed their warm blonde curls goodbye, passed them one at a time to July, who kissed their warm blonde curls hello.

I knew one thing Nashville didn't have—July.

Another thought that flew through my brain as I parked the girls' double stroller to the left of July and Baylor's door—I'd have to take Bex and Quinn with me to the cage count at four that afternoon. Because the stroller would be the only way to get out with the money.

*   *   *

No.

I'd have to think of something else.

I couldn't let my daughters watch me steal a million dollars.

FOURTEEN

There was no avoiding Vree when I walked back in my own door five minutes later. I had less than an hour before my blind date with the oil sheik, and I needed to spend it online. Which meant my office, and there was no other path to my office than through the doggy daycare that was my living room. And I wasn't trying to dodge her so much as I didn't have time. Saying good morning to Vree took until afternoon. Asking about lunch took until dinner. She could talk about sunset 'til sunrise.

I caught a break. They were asleep—Vree on one end of the sofa, Harley on the other, and Princess was snoring in the patched playpen.

I tiptoed.

First, I checked the three phones on my desk—my two, original and cloned, and Bootsy's confiscated phone. I had a text message from Bradley. About eyedrops. (What?) I put on my everything-here-is-just-fine hat and dialed. His phone immediately went to voicemail. Before I could leave a message, another text dinged in.

I'm in a Responsible Gaming Awareness breakout session. So far, nothing I haven't heard before. Davis, my eyes are red and they itch. The only thing they have in the lobby shop are Blink Better eyedrops, which I've never heard of. How are you and the girls?

Blink Better? I'd never heard of it either. I googled. They were lubricating drops for contact lens wearers, of which, Bradley wasn't. *Don't get the Blink Better drops. What's wrong with your eyes? Is it one eye or both eyes? If it's one eye, maybe you scratched it? Accidentally? Do you need to go to an eye doctor? We're fine. The girls are being little angels. We miss you.*

From him: *I don't need to go to a doctor. It's just irritating. Both eyes. It's probably the 1,000 watt LED lights all over this hotel.*

Me: *So your eyes don't hurt outside?*

Him: *Now that you bring it up, they're worse outside. Although, that might be the humidity.*

Me: *Bradley, first the sneezing, now your eyes. Either you're coming down with something, or you and Nashville aren't a good match.*

Him: *This session is ending, on my way to the next. Talk later? I love you, Davis.*

I rubbed my eyes.

*   *   *

There was nothing on the surface of the internet about Hiriddhi Al Abbasov. And by nothing, I meant not one thing—no Facebook, no Instagram, no Snapchat. I couldn't find public records of a deed in his name, a divorce, or a DUI. Either the man lived an unusually quiet life, or obscure immigration laws allowed him to keep his business to himself. A deeper dig netted me the basics. He was forty years old, single, a graduate of Riverdale Academy for the Blind in Buckhead, a suburb of Atlanta, where he'd been an international boarding student from the age of eleven. He was granted dual citizenship at age twenty-one. He had a BBA in Financial Analysis from the University of Georgia, go Dogs, and an MBA from Harvard

Business School. Go...Harvards. He was president of the United States operations of SourceOil Petroleum, producing the equivalent of two million barrels of oil per day.

Impressive.

But all facts. No insight. Nothing that would give me an edge. I didn't know if I'd need one, but always be prepared. I was on my way to his Bellissimo portfolio—we'd have some dirt on him—when a text hit my phone from No Hair.

Do you and/or Fantasy have the cage covered?

I replied, with shaking thumbs, *Yes.*

Unnerved by being reminded of what I had ahead of me, I clicked the wrong casino marketing tab. Instead of searching for Al Abbasov specifically, I pulled up the inhouse VIP list. Available to casino management—hosts, pit bosses, and floor supervisors—the inhouse VIP list was a who's who of current guests, ranked by importance, either fame or fortune. Which would work, because Al Abbasov, at two million barrels of oil per day, would surely be at the top of the list. But he wasn't. He was in the number two spot. We had a guest with more money than Al Abbasov? We did. Their names were Cleavon and Candy Smucker.

Who?

Smucker? As in schmucks? Were these the people causing so much trouble?

Curiosity got the better of me. I clicked on their joint portfolio. The Smuckers weren't tenth-generation jelly money, they were lottery winners. Cleavon and Candy, of Marietta, Georgia, another suburb of Atlanta, won a record-shattering 1.7 billion dollars with the single winning Mega Millions lottery ticket purchased less than a mile from their mobile home ten months earlier.

Good grief.

I couldn't help myself; I took a quick look.

And there they were with a big check. And their yellow-eyed

dog.

Princess.

*   *   *

I didn't see or hear Fantasy until she was standing beside me tapping her watch. I was too busy being appalled by the wealth of information, both personal and financial, in front of me.

"Are you on Facebook?" Fantasy asked. "What are you doing? Watching someone decorate meatloaf? We have to be next door in two minutes."

I tilted the screen.

It was a closeup of Princess Smucker, yellow eye blazing, crooked teeth bared. Candy had captioned it, *GARD DOG!*

"You found her owners?"

I clicked Candy Smucker's profile picture.

Fantasy said, "She's the naked dancer. That's the woman who was dancing on a craps table in red panties. She's one of the schmucks. Her husband is the other."

We scrolled. And found everything. By everything, I meant every single thing. Candy Smucker documented her life, her whole life, in images and narrative, on social media—every thought that passed through her brain, every bite of food she consumed, every move she made, and every penny she spent. Candy's video library was endless, and all the same show—Princess, guarding a bag of Cheetos, a Cadillac CT6, or the husband, Cleavon. Candy pointed, said, "Guard!" then laughed hysterically as wild-eyed Princess got her warrior on. Candy's last post was ten minutes earlier from the high-stakes room of the casino, where she'd taken a selfie with a five-hundred-dollar Ole Jalapenos Hot and Spicy slot machine. The caption she wrote above her pouting face was, *This slots took my 70 thou $$$s. I'm fixin to get Cleave to shoot it. JK! Our guns R N the* *room!*

We scrolled through Candy's life quickly, but came to a screeching halt at a post from two weeks earlier, when Candy made a worldwide web appeal to her five thousand plus followers for a bodyguard-slash-dog-sitter to accompany them to the Bellissimo Resort and Casino. *We R takin big $$$s to the casinos and we need somebody to go with us to watch it and take care of Miss Priss. I pay GOOD.* The applications for temporary employment in the comments below the job-offer post went on and on and on. It looked as if half of Facebook's two billion subscribers wanted to accompany Cleavon and Candy Smucker to the Bellissimo and watch their $$$s. It had been shared to other Facebook walls more than sixteen hundred times. At the very end of the feed, for all the world to see, Candy struck a deal with the brothers Sebastian, Butch and Brutus. I clicked on Brutus Sebastian's name. Facebook took me to his personal page.

I knew him.

He was one of the missing housekeepers.

His brother Butch was the other.

Those men weren't housekeepers.

They were bodyguards-slash-dog-sitters.

Did Cleave and Candy Smucker send them to my home to check up on their dog? On me? Were the Smuckers that paranoid? And what kind of bodyguards intercepted internal work orders and impersonated housekeepers? Were they former CIA operatives?

Bradley was right. Our world was too dangerous to raise children in.

I let those men in my home.

Then I sent them to Fantasy's.

Where they met Bootsy Howard.

If I hadn't had Bootsy's phone, I'd have called her and said, "Have your way with the fake housekeepers, Boots. When you're finished with them, send them my way."

We scrolled to see the employment contract, including time, place, and salary details—anything and everything the world might want to know—posted above a picture we hadn't seen yet. It was Princess, gnawing her purple leg, sporting her new Harry Winston dog collar. Candy's comment accompanying the shot was, *Aint Miss Prisss new necklace cute? It otta be. I paid 2 milion $$$s for it.*

I looked at Fantasy.

"What, Davis?"

"Princess had that collar on when she got here."

"She did not."

"She did."

We ran.

*   *   *

Princess's collar wasn't in her red duffel bag or anywhere else in the small guest bedroom. And we tossed it good.

"Is there any chance Vree put it back on her? Could she be wearing it?"

"I don't know, Fantasy. I try not to look at her." I was halfway under one of the twin beds. "The last time I remember seeing it was when I took it off her. And that was in here."

"How did you not know it was a Harry Winston?" Fantasy was stripping the other twin bed.

"How could I have known it was? What dog in the world wears a Harry Winston collar?" I crawled to the closet on my hands and knees, checking every square inch of carpet on the way.

"Well, it's not here." Fantasy had the first ruined Pop N' Play flipped over. Banging it. "And who drops off a dog wearing a two-million-dollar collar with total strangers?"

"Crazy rich people," I said. "That's who."

"Schmucks," she said.

We ran back to the living room. Vree and Harley were still asleep. Princess was busy with Madeleine Albright.

No collar.

"Vree." Fantasy snapped her fingers in her face. "Nap's over. Get up."

Vree startled. "What?" She sat straight up. "Gooch? Is that you? Bubbs? Where am I? Are we on fire?"

I checked my watch. We were already fifteen minutes late to our sheik meeting, which meant we were forty-five minutes from cage count. Time was slipping away. "Vree," I said, "we have to go. We have a meeting. You need to wake up and find Princess's collar."

"Her what?"

"Her collar, Vree," Fantasy said. "You know, her dog collar. The one that goes around her neck."

"The rhinestone collar?"

"That's the one." And those weren't rhinestones. I turned for the front door. "Find it, Vree. We have to find it. We'll be back as soon as we can. I have my phone with me. Text me as soon as you have the collar in your hands."

"But where am I supposed to look? I mean, Davis, this is a big house."

"She's only been in a few of the rooms," I said. "Look everywhere she's been. Please, Vree. This is important."

One minute later, huffing and puffing, I knocked on the Leno Suite door. Fantasy was tugging her blouse, fanning herself. "It's a good thing this man can't see," she whispered. "Because you look like you've been digging ditches, Davis."

I smoothed my hair just as Hiriddhi Al Abbasov opened the door.

It had to be him.

His two-thousand-dollar Tom Ford sunglasses gave him away. Our mouths dropped open.

He was baseball and apple pie. I don't know what I was expecting, but it wasn't what I got. I pictured a man named Hiriddhi to be dark-skinned, wearing a thobe with a keffiyeh headdress. Not hardly. The man at the door could have been ripped off the pages of *Southern GQ*. He was in top-athlete shape, with chestnut hair, cut close, a five o'clock shadow on a sturdy jaw, and all that above jeans and a perfect white oxford shirt, starched sleeves rolled almost to his elbows.

He offered a hand. Fantasy and I looked at each other. She pointed at me. I stabbed a finger back at her. Hiriddhi said, "Don't fight over me."

No accent whatsoever.

I reached out. He held my hand with both of his. "Do you have red hair?"

"Almost," I stammered.

"And children. Daughters, perhaps."

"How—"

"Ivory Snow Gentle Care," he said. "Mothers of young sons use stronger detergents." His thumb gently grazed my wedding band. "And someone loves you very much."

He dropped my hands and reached for Fantasy's. He laughed. "You're a tall drink of water. And of French Creole descent, with an Ivy League education."

Fantasy and I looked at each other, wide eyed.

How perceptive was this man?

We exchanged overly polite introductions for the next minute, and just when I was wondering if he'd ever ask us in, Fantasy said, "We're ready to go over the surveillance video if you are, Your Excellency."

He casually leaned against the doorframe, knowing exactly

where it was. "We don't need to watch the footage, because you have Harley. Please return him," Al Abbasov said. "I need his help."

My breath caught in my throat, certain the next words out of his mouth would be, "And I can smell Mrs. Harrington's dead body on you two. Sit tight while I call the authorities." But he didn't. Instead he called out over his shoulder, "Rod? Will you accompany these ladies?" He didn't say it loud enough for Rod, whoever he was, to hear it, and he didn't give Rod, whoever he was, time to answer either. "On second thought," he said, "I'll accompany you."

Hiri didn't trust us.

Imagine that.

FIFTEEN

My skill level for lying through my teeth when the occasion called for it, like then, was expert. Any other time under those particular circumstances I'd have lied my head off. But I proceeded cautiously with this Harvard man who knew the brand of laundry detergent I used to wash Bex and Quinn's clothes. I had a feeling it would do no good to lie. Had I been so inclined, the one on the tip of my tongue was that the Bellissimo was full of dogs, we'd been around dozens, and I had no idea who or where his dog was. Instead, I said, "Please don't bother. I'll bring Harley to you, Your Excellency."

"No need for the formality. Call me Hiri." He hesitated, just a beat, engaging an internal sonar, before he took a step out the door. "After you."

"Not necessary, Your...Hiri," Fantasy said. "Wait here. Davis, stay with him. I'll get Harley. I'll be back in two shakes."

I looked at my watch. Two shakes to return Harley to his rightful owner, but only three shakes until one of us had to report for cage duty. It took ten shakes to get there, unless one of us had wings. And if I had wings, right about then, I'd scoop up my daughters and fly to Nashville.

"Am I keeping you, Mrs. Cole?"

"Listen, Mr. Hiri." I didn't know if I should apologize to the man, then tell him the whole story of how we came across his big black dog, which I could never tell without exposing Bootsy for the killer witch she was, then he'd think I was crazy, and instead of stealing a million dollars from the Bellissimo or finding a fence who would front me a million for a Harry Winston dog collar I couldn't find, I'd be in a straitjacket trying to explain it all to the good people at Gulf Oaks Psychiatric Hospital. Before I could decide what to say or how to say it, Hiri's big black dog was between us, overjoyed to see everyone.

In a smooth and practiced way, Hiri said, "Slow."

Harley quieted.

Hiri said, "Sit."

Harley circled to Hiri's left and sat.

Hiri said, "Blow the ladies a kiss."

Harley raised a paw to his lips, then threw us a kiss.

We were about to make our awkward exit when Hiri looked over the rims of his Tom Ford sunglasses, as if to look us in the eye, which he did. Back and forth, his dark eyes sought and somehow found ours. "I realize you need to go," he said. "The adrenaline pouring from you both is remarkable. You've checked your watches five times that I know of. Obviously, you have a pressing responsibility elsewhere." He settled his Tom Fords back on the bridge of his nose. "I'd like a little of your time after whatever it is you're late for. I want to know the circumstances under which you came in possession of Harley and I want to know exactly what happened to Mrs. Harrington."

I did too.

"One more thing. Your dog has canine atopic dermatitis. Thus the odor. Take her to the veterinarian."

Princess. Dermatitis, no collar, and not our dog.

Fantasy sniffed the lapel of her jacket.

* * *

We took cage together.

After a smallish argument.

"I'll do it," I said.

"No, Davis, I will."

"No, Fantasy, *I* will."

"Oh, no you won't. I'm taking cage."

Already late, we stood at the elevator doors rocking, papering, and scissoring. Deadlocked three times in a row, we stepped into the elevator together. She didn't want me to steal the money, and I didn't want her to steal it. If we could find the collar, we wouldn't even need to, but then we'd be stealing a collar.

We fished our phones out of our pockets as the elevator doors closed.

I started with Vree. "Have you found the collar?" "No, but—" "Keep looking." I hung up on her and dialed Bradley, who said his eyes were better, but now he had a brick between them. "What?" I asked. "A brick between your eyes? What?" He said, "It feels like there's a brick between my eyes, Davis." Beside me, Fantasy whispered, "Allergies." I flipped the phone upside down and whispered back to her, "Bradley has never had an allergy in his life." She said, "He does now." To Bradley I said, "Is there any chance it's allergies?" He said, "I've never had an allergy in my life." Then I called Pasta, an Italian restaurant on the mezzanine level, and ordered dinner—salad, spaghetti, and cheese bread. "For how many, Mrs. Cole?" I told her ten. (You never know.) Fantasy said, "How can you order spaghetti when your house smells like Little Italy already?" I told her because Bex and Quinn wouldn't stop asking for Princess's food. ("Bite, bite, bite.") My last call was to July. I told her I was on cage duty until five, and asked her to take the girls home, where there'd be spaghetti. She said she'd bathe and pajama the girls, have them ready for spaghetti, and see me after cage.

What would I do without July?

Fantasy called her husband. She didn't even have the chance to say hello. He started in on her before she could. After half a minute, she held the phone away from her head. I could hear Reggie through the small speaker. She put the phone back to her ear and interrupted, "Listen up, Reggie. I've been working myself stupid with this dog show while you've been watching layups and eating loaded potato skins at TGI Friday's. I haven't even been home. I stayed with Davis last night because my shift ended at midnight and Bradley's out of town. No one stole your truck. I'm driving it because I had...car trouble. I did not delete your SEC spring football games, or throw away your toothpaste, and there's nothing going on in the bonus room that I know of." To me, she said, "He hung up on me." Then, "He's mad because the boys lost the game. I think he's projecting his anger on me." I said, "You're probably right." Then she called No Hair. "We're on our way to take cage." Poor Fantasy was yelled at by two men in a row. "No, we're not joined at the hip, No Hair, stop calling us the Bobbsey Twins, and I don't appreciate you suggesting neither of us can count high enough to take cage alone." To me, she said, "He hung up on me." Then, "He's mad about the Smuckers. I think he's projecting his anger on me." I said, "You're probably right."

When the elevator doors parted on the casino level, heads ducked, we fought the lobby crowd, then the casino crowd, until we reached the main cashier cage, where we had to wait for retina scans before the next set of elevator doors parted to take us to the vault. On the way down, Fantasy said, "Reggie asked about the bonus room."

"Asked what?"

"If I'd taken an ax to the door."

"You didn't, did you?"

"What happened to the door, Davis? Did you tear it up getting the dead woman out?"

"Not so much."

"She's out, right, Davis?"

"She's out."

"What did Dr. Delirious say? How'd she meet her maker?"

"He didn't." The doors opened to a security-scan booth. "She was gone."

Fantasy turned white. "She was what?"

"Gone. No body."

Fantasy slapped the sides of the scan booth and gasped for air, which brought the cage guards running. One put a hand on his holster. The other raised an eyebrow at two of us showing up for cage, late, and obviously, Fantasy at least, shaken. It was a standoff, both sides waiting it out, until the guards decided they didn't want to challenge Mrs. Cole. We stepped through the body scan and into the vault, then heard the clicks of vault imprisonment with relief. For the next forty minutes, we wouldn't get any bad news.

For the first few, we did nothing but pant.

"Let's get the count over with, then we can talk."

"Good idea," I said.

We verified seventeen million dollars.

We did not sign off on it.

We had another ten minutes in the vault.

Plenty of time.

We pulled metal stools from under the count table, then perched on them, the seventeen million in wrapped stacks on the table between us. We talked over it.

"Davis, where's the dead woman?"

"I don't know."

We contemplated our bleak futures.

We verified the seventeen million dollars without stealing one of them.

I couldn't do it.

I'd have to find another way, because I couldn't bring myself to take a million dollars from the Bellissimo.

*   *   *

"I miss Harley."

It was six thirty Monday night. The sun was setting on the Gulf. Another search of my home hadn't produced Princess's Harry Winston collar, we left the vault without a million dollars, we didn't know where Bootsy was because the iPad was dead, as dead as the AWOL caregiver, plus we hadn't done what we'd said we'd do, which was get back with His Excellency Hiri for a tell-all. On top of all that, my husband had cancelled his dinner plans with the general manager of our sister casino, Jolie, also at the SGF Symposium, because now he had three bricks between his eyes. Fantasy, Vree, the girls, and I were having dinner on the veranda because Bex and Quinn were spaghetti slingers. Vree was crying in hers. "I miss Harley so much."

I poured her more red wine.

Bex and Quinn, tangled in noodles, said, "Dink, dink, dink."

Vree took a big dink of the wine and said, "I mean, first I missed Meredith and Bubble Bath." She pushed her salad away and pulled her wine closer. "And it's not like I don't miss them anymore, I do, even though they don't miss me a bit. It's like this was supposed to be our vacation together, but they're the ones who are having fun—I guess it won't be fun when Mer has to go to the hospital—but for now, they're having fun. The hotel they're staying in has a doggie pool. Meredith sent a video of Bubbs in her bikini swimming with two beagles from California, but she didn't know their names. They were sister and brother, so you know they had cute names. Can you even believe it? A doggie pool?"

Bex and Quinn, covered in red sauce, said, "Dog, dog, dog."

"Then Harley came." Vree dabbed her eyes with a napkin. "He filled the hole in my heart. He was so sweet. He stared into my eyes like he knew me. And that was one thing about Harley that reminded me of Gooch, like how Gooch was when we first started dating, because he stared into my eyes like that too. Like looking all the way into my soul. Harley did the same thing, and I have a feeling Harley would love me like that forever, while Gooch hasn't even called me one time. Can you believe it? Not one time? I was thinking that if we didn't give Harley back he could come home with me, like, I'd walk in the door with him and tell Gooch there was a new man in my life. One who would love me forever, even if I was the biggest disappointment in the whole wide world, and Harley wouldn't go fishing all the time, because, for real, dogs don't fish, but I'm not saying I'd pretend like I had a dog husband. Wouldn't that be funny? A dog husband? That would be a good Hallmark movie. I love Hallmark movies. Especially at Christmas. Those are the very best. I mean, it would be more like Harley would be Bubblegum's husband, but, you know, they could never have puppies."

Vree went silent.

Fantasy and I looked at each other.

"I mean—"

Vree snapped back.

"—Meredith and Bubbs are having the time of their lives, Gooch won't answer the phone, Harley is gone, and I'm stuck with Princess."

From the Pop N' Play under the cherry tree, Princess, deep in a dish of manicotti, yapped. I turned my head for one second to look at her, and when I looked back, Bex and Quinn had donned spaghetti bowl hats.

"Davis," Fantasy said, "your children need another bath."

Bex and Quinn said, "Bath, bath, bath."

"Then what?"

Good question.

"Then we face facts." Fantasy checked the time. "Vree can't win the money at the slot tournament because she's not in it. We didn't steal the money from the Bellissimo vault because we thought we had the dog collar. We don't have the dog collar."

I said, "We don't have Bootsy either."

Bex and Quinn said, "Boo, boo, boo."

Vree said, "What are we going to do with the collar when we find it?"

Another good question.

Fantasy stood and tugged the sleeves of her Bellissimo blue security jacket, on her way to the evening round of the Three Dog Night slot tournament. "What are we going to do if we *don't* find the collar?"

The million-dollar question.

SIXTEEN

Rain slapping the bedroom windows in sheets woke me before dawn Tuesday morning. I rearranged Bex and Quinn, who slept through everything, thinking about Bradley, wondering if he felt better or worse, and thinking about Atlanta.

The dog-show judge with the toothache who didn't show—Atlanta.

Hiriddhi Al Abbasov—Atlanta.

Princess, the Smuckers, the fake housekeepers, the dead caregiver—Atlanta.

I wondered why Southern Gaming hadn't moved their headquarters to Atlanta. Home Depot, Coca-Cola, and UPS were based out of Atlanta. And if Bradley was so dead set on raising the girls away from a casino, well, Atlanta was away. There wasn't a casino in or near Atlanta. Atlanta gambled in Biloxi.

I wondered if there might be a dot to connect all the Atlanta people.

I couldn't see His Excellency running in the same circles with the Smuckers.

So, probably not.

I reached for the phone, dialed, and whispered, "Are you awake?"

"I am now," Meredith said. "Are you waking me up to tell me

you have the money?"

"I'm working on it." I tucked a corkscrew curl behind Quinn's baby ear. "Did Greene live through the night?"

"I don't know." I heard the click of a bedside lamp. "It's still night," she said. "I'm assuming he did because I haven't heard otherwise. How's Vree holding up?"

"She lived through the night," I said. "I'm assuming she did because I haven't heard otherwise."

"Where is she?"

"In one of the guest rooms with the worst excuse for a dog I've ever seen in my life." Speaking of dogs. "What's Bubbles doing?"

"She's curled up in her velvet bed. Dreaming dog dreams. It's six in the morning, Davis, everyone's dreaming. What about Bootsy? Has she surfaced?"

"Not here. What about there?"

"No Bootsy."

"She could be anywhere."

"Instead of looking for Bootsy, why don't you try looking for the fake housekeepers?" Meredith said. "If Bootsy has them, even if she turned them into lizards, you'd probably still be able to track their phones. Surely she didn't voodoo their phones."

"Meredith, you're brilliant." I told her I loved her, we promised to stay in touch, then I gently eased out of bed, propping pillows in my place. I tiptoed to the coffee pot. I'd go to Candy Smucker's Bellissimo guest profile, find her phone number, hack her phone, then find the fake housekeepers' phone numbers. They'd surely reported to her after they misrepresented their way into my home. I'd get their numbers, track their phones, and maybe find Bootsy. On the off chance Bootsy didn't have them bound and gagged in the backseat, or hiding under rocks in a lizard cage, I wouldn't mind finding them anyway. I had a few questions for those two. One was whose idea was it for Candy Smucker's bodyguards to pretend to be housekeepers and waltz into my home? What was the point and what was the purpose? Next, I'd ask how they intercepted an internal call to Bellissimo housekeeping. Then, I'd ask them the question I really wanted an answer to—when they were at Fantasy's, did they see or hear anything related to the caregiver's death?

One thing at a time, Davis. One thing at a time.

I poured a cup of coffee, sat down at my desk, fired up my computer, and found the Smuckers' Bellissimo portfolio. Two clicks later, I had Cleavon Smucker's cell phone number, not his wife's. His was listed on the guest profile, hers was nowhere to be found. Instead of taking the time to hack his phone to get her number, I logged onto Facebook, because finding her number there, and I was sure I would, would be faster than hacking his cellphone provider's database. I pulled up her page and didn't find her phone number, because I found his toe. Her last post, from the casino, twelve minutes earlier, was a stomach-flipping close-up of her husband's bare and beleaguered foot propped on a blackjack table. Above it, her heartfelt plea: *Cleavs ingrowed toe busted wild open!!! I danced on it by accidint! We need a doctor rite NOW. Were waitin here cause he cant walk.*

I had to act fast, before I passed out.

I phished and cloned Biloxi Urgent Care's Facebook page, then posted a comment on Candy's page under the picture of Cleavon's nasty nasty nasty nasty toe: *On the way.*

Candy, nose to phone, responded immediately, *Thank U! Hes hurtin. Free drinks for U and I pay GOOD!!!!*

I pushed my coffee aside. I was finished with food and drink for the rest of my life. I picked up the house phone, dialed the Bellissimo operator, and asked for Leverette Urleen's room.

He answered on the fiftieth ring. "Who is this?"

"It's Davis. Get up, Urleen. You're needed in the casino."

"By the Amazon goddess?"

Fantasy would kill him if she knew he called her an Amazon goddess.

"No, Urleen. It's a medical emergency."

"Let me put my pants on."

And there was an image to replace that of Cleavon Smucker's ingrowed toe.

I had to put my head between my knees.

When I came up for air, I covered my eyes, leaving myself a sliver of vision, just enough to get to the corner of Candy Smucker's post and hide it without seeing it again. Then I scrolled. I scrolled down, and down, and down, past the endless documentation of her life to her "Help Wanted" post of two weeks earlier. I clicked through the comments thinking I'd stumble on her phone number—she'd surely posted it somewhere—and before long I'd scrolled to the thread of correspondence between her and the fake housekeepers, sealing the deal. Then I saw, in the early light of a new day, what I hadn't seen in the frenzied haze of the afternoon before. The initial response to Candy's ad hadn't been from Brutus Sebastian. It was from someone who tagged Brutus Sebastian. Someone following Candy Smucker's social-media misdeeds saw the Bellissimo opportunity and led Brutus Sebastian to it by typing his name in the comments, tagging him, thus alerting him. The fake housekeepers would have never known about the Smucker job had someone not led them straight to it.

Who was that opportunistic someone?

That opportunistic someone wasn't a someone at all. It was an organization. The Atlanta Council for the Blind. The Council for the Blind led the fake housekeepers to the Smuckers, the Bellissimo, my home, and ultimately Fantasy's home too.

This was a big Atlanta con. The question was, who was conning whom?

There wasn't a shred of useful information about the Atlanta Council for the Blind on the world wide web. Nothing. I found a single webpage with directions to their facilities, lean office hours, and links to additional resources. I didn't find a phone number, email address, board of directors, list of donors, officer's names, or a membership roster, any of which could've helped. To tie the Atlanta Council for the Blind to the fake housekeepers, I'd have to go next door to Leno's and do it myself. I seriously doubted it was His Excellency. How could Hiriddhi Al Abbasov be on Candy Smucker's Facebook page when he wasn't on Facebook? Someone with His Hiri was the link to the fake housekeepers.

I texted Fantasy. *We might need your tranquilizer gun again.*

She texted back. *What's this "we" business?*

Vree appeared in the doorway, yawning, stretching, and wearing baby-blue shortie pajamas with matching fuzzy slippers. "Davis?" She yawned again. "I can't find Princess. She got out of the playpen. Have you seen her?"

*   *   *

If someone had told me that one day I'd try to talk my sick husband into staying at a strange hotel five hundred miles away instead of coming home to his wife, his daughters, and his own bed, I'd have said they were crazy. That day came, and I was the crazy one when Bradley called at eleven Tuesday morning to say he was seriously considering calling it a Nashville day, boarding the Bellissimo jet waiting for him at the airport, and seeing me in an hour. "I want a bowl of chicken soup from Chops."

"They don't have chicken soup in Nashville?"

"What are you saying, Davis? Don't come home?"

He sounded awful, and that was exactly what I was saying. He couldn't come home. I'd rather him be sick in Nashville than divorced in Biloxi.

"Of course not," I said. "I'll get in the car and come get you myself." When what I really meant was what he said—don't come home. Not yet, anyway.

"You don't have a car."

"I'll drive yours."

"Please don't."

I let it slide, but only because he was sick. "Do you have a fever?"

"I don't think so," he said.

"Does your hair hurt?"

"No."

"Then you don't have a fever."

"Again, Davis. It sounds like you're trying to talk me out of feeling bad."

I was.

"I'm not trying to talk you out of it so much as I hate to see you cut your trip short when, if you give it a minute, you might feel better."

We were on the terrace again—me, Bex and Quinn, Fantasy, Vree, Leverette Urleen M.D. (yes, Urleen the Idiot)—and Princess, who was back in the Pop N' Play, but this time we had the playpen upside down and over her. She could still see out the mesh walls, but she couldn't tunnel out, like she had earlier that morning, then nestled her garlic Dorito self between my two babies in my bed. Which was where we found her. In the bed I sleep in. In the bed my sick husband wanted to come home and crawl into. Urleen the Idiot was there because I called him. For the second time in a single day. He'd hospitalized Cleavon Smucker, much to the delight of each and every one of the Bellissimo's four thousand employees, diagnosing him with a bacterial infection approaching mutilated abscess that would hit his heart chambers any second and kill him dead. Candy posted a selfie on Facebook taken from the interior of the ambulance, accompanied with this explanation: *Cleavs toe is fixin to kill him. We need blessins and prayers.* I had to call Urleen again because Fantasy refused to touch her pink tranquilizer gun. She said I didn't need her pink tranquilizer gun to go next door and connect the housekeepers to the Council for the Blind, and if I did, I was on my own, because Hiriddhi Al Abbasov would smell her on it, and she didn't want to go to prison. I knew less about knockout drugs than Fantasy did, so once again, Urleen was my only option.

Fantasy waved to get my attention and mouthed, *"Bradley can't come home until we steal the money."*

I mouthed back, *"I know that."*

"Let me talk to him." Urleen's hand was in my face. I smacked it away.

"Who was that?" Bradley asked.

"Nothing. No one," I said. "I didn't hear anything. Do your ears hurt too?"

"My ears, my eyes, my throat, my head. If it's above my neck, it hurts."

I mimed writing. Fantasy dug in her purse and tossed me a small spiral notepad and a pen. I scribbled. *Ears, eyes, throat, head.* I shoved the note under Urleen's nose.

He read it, then sat back, tapping his chin. "Could be brain cancer."

"Hold on, Bradley." I kicked Urleen under the table. "What else? Do you have any other symptoms?"

"I can't taste anything," Bradley said.

I scribbled it down. *Can't taste.*

Urleen's bushy eyebrows closed in on themselves. He leaned too close to Fantasy and whispered in her ear. The look on her face would have been no different had a boa constrictor had its lips to her head. She shoved Urleen away and started scribbling again, then passed me another note. *This moron says if he can't taste, it's a brain tumor. Not brain cancer. Is there even a difference in a brain tumor and brain cancer?*

I wrote back, *You're not helping.*

"What have you tried to taste?" I had to keep Bradley on the phone long enough to talk him out of coming home.

"What have I tried to taste? Davis? Was that a real question?"

"It was." (It wasn't.) "What I meant—"

"I know what you meant. I tried to taste hot Jack Daniels with lemon."

Fantasy and Urleen were in the middle of an aggressive low-volume exchange. She was the aggressive part, slapping Urleen twice. She shoved another note in front of me. *This fool has decided it's a brain aneurism and insists I tell you Bradley should get his affairs in order.* I wrote back, *Tell him one more word out of him and he gets a bullet in his brain.* I let her read it, then wadded it and let it sail. It landed close to the Pop N' Play. Princess yapped at it.

Bex and Quinn said, "Woof, woof, woof."

"Was that a dog?" Bradley asked.

"That was Bex and Quinn. You're hearing things," I said. "How hard did you try to taste the Jack Daniels?"

He didn't answer right away.

"Bradley, you have a hangover."

"You think?"

"How many drinks did you have?"

"I don't remember."

"Call the front desk. Have them bring you ice water, Gatorade, and Advil. Sleep a few hours, then if you don't feel better, come home."

"You'll get me soup?"

"I'll get you soup."

I'd barely ended the call when my name was bellowed from the terrace door. Or, rather, not exactly my name was bellowed from the terrace door.

"DAVID!"

Urleen the Idiot's chair shot back and rocked on two legs, while he clutched his heart and ogled Bianca. "Davis! Do you have a defibrillator?"

Fantasy shot out of her chair, offering it. "Bianca! Please join us. Meet Dr. Urleen."

"Doctor?" Bianca tossed her hair over her shoulder.

*   *   *

She stood in the open door and gave a ten-minute dissertation about my lack of consideration for her reputation and valuable time. I'd missed a dog-show judge's meeting. Her first attempt to chew me out was a call to my cloned cellphone, sitting alone on the desk in my dark office. Then she tried the house phone, which was in the house, while I was on the terrace. I'd forgotten about the dog show entirely, including the meeting.

When she finished, Urleen the Idiot tsk-tsked me, shaking his head. "David. How could you? It's deplorable. *You're* deplorable. It's wretched. *You're* wretched. It's despicable—"

"I get it, Urleen."

In the middle of all that, Fantasy took a call from No Hair, who asked her if she wouldn't mind making an appearance at the Hot Dog slot tournament, well underway.

Bianca looked at Vree, who she'd never met. "You. Buxom girl. I need a tall glass, and by glass, I mean barware, of sparkling water on three cubes of ice with one squeeze of lime. One." Then she turned to Urleen. Bianca loved doctors, all doctors, any doctor. She asked if she might have a moment of his time.

"I'll oblige you anything." He stood as she sat. "Everything."

Her head wobbled. "What is that foul odor?"

Princess woofed.

Bex and Quinn said, "Banka, Banka, Banka."

Bianca, dropping all pretenses and all posturing, turned to my daughters and said, "Hello, darling girls."

There was that side of her.

Then she held an upturned hand above Urleen's seersuckered lap. "Do you see this?"

He cradled her hand in both of his and put his nose in it. "Yes, my dear. I do."

"The anomaly?"

"A slight discoloration. Horrors." Urleen licked his lips.

"What should I do?"

"Well, lovely lady—"

I grabbed Bex, Fantasy grabbed Quinn, Vree grabbed Princess, and we ran.

SEVENTEEN

I nervously tapped an ink pen against the gold linen covering the judges' table, waiting for the talent competition to start at noon. The other judges weren't too impressed with me to begin with, I think it was the horse clothes, and they were outright irritated at me for missing the meeting. They already didn't appreciate that I knew nothing about dogs, clearly didn't want to be there, and since the first round of competition, after Bianca stopped badgering me about scores, had given every dog the highest score—five, as soon as the score screen was ready to accept it. What little love my fellow judges might have had for me left completely when the competition finally began, and I spent it head down, phone-in-lap, returning messages from the first talented dog until the last.

I didn't plan it that way.

The first act was a French bulldog wearing sunglasses flipping around on a mini skateboard, and he hadn't flipped twice before a message hit my phone from the preacher's wife, Gina Gully. I couldn't help but look. It said, *Do you have a soul?*

I shot back, *Of course I do.*

Do you have the joy, joy, joy, joy down in your heart?

What do you want, Gina?

He who giveth and taketh life has bestowed his almighty power on you. You are on the throne.

I was on a banquet chair.

Thou must accept the job our Lord, God, and Savior has given you, Davis.

And what is that, Gina? To steal money for him?

To save a life.

I let that one sit there.

Otherwise, it's eternal damnation for you.

I gave a white dog the size of a black bear five points for her yoga poses.

Let me get this straight, Gina. You're telling me God wants me to spend the rest of this life in prison so I can avoid hell in the next?

To die is to gain, Davis.

What's that supposed to mean? Steal the money, then jump off a bridge?

You were always a willful, insolent, disrespectful child.

And she'd always been off her rocker.

I delicately clapped for a Tibetan spaniel who finished a double jump rope routine. I had to relinquish my phone to clap. It buzzed on the judges' table, and I got dirty looks from both sides. I dropped it in my lap to see what additional heavenly wisdom Gina had to impart, only to see it was a text from Baylor.

Davis. I'm in the emergency room of Biloxi Regional.

The Smuckers.

Rather than wait to hear the news Baylor had to report, because he poked text messages slowly with his right index finger, I clicked the Facebook icon on my home screen to get it straight from the horse's mouth. I found the worst selfie of Candy Smucker yet. She'd been awake and in the casino for forty-eight hours that I knew of, could have been seventy-two, and it showed. Behind her, Cleavon, in a hospital gown, was on a gurney, grinning from ear to ear and giving his wife, his pain pills, or his life in general two thumbs up. The caption: *Who wants to come to my casino? Me and Cleves goin to get a lawyer and soo the stew out of the Bullshitsio casino. There DR tried to saw Cleves toe off his leg. Come to SMUCKERS casinos for FREE DRINKS!!!*

I had bad news for them. Urleen was not the Bullshitsio's doctor.

And why Baylor was (blaming) bothering me with it was anyone's guess.

He wasn't.

A woman drove herself here in a hotwired Bellissimo truck. She told the admitting nurse she'd been knocked over the head, then bound, gagged, and thrown in the bed of the truck. The truck has been parked behind a boarded-up Long John Silver's on Bayview for three days. They're keeping her. She's dehydrated and has exposure exhaustion. Which I've never heard of. The truck was signed out to YOU. Come take care of this woman.

Who is it? What's her name?

She's talking gibberish. I couldn't tell you.

What does she look like?

A witch.

The rude judge beside me deliberately and dramatically cleared his throat in my direction. I looked up from the devastation in my lap to see the small screen in front of me waiting on my score. I pushed five, having not even looked up once to see who or what I was scoring, then went straight back to my phone. I texted Gina Gully. *I'll wire the money. I'll get it there in time.*

She texted back, *God's blessings on you and yours.*

It was my fault.

Everything was all my fault.

I had to make it right.

*   *   *

Vree and I took the long way through the parking lot and lobby of Biloxi Regional Hospital. Neither of us complained about the painfully slow elevator. Our walk past the nurse's station to Bootsy's hospital room matched the pace of condemned prisoners being led to the gas chamber. The door to room three-sixteen was cracked.

"Maybe she's sleeping," Vree said.

"We shouldn't bother her," I said.

"Vreeland? Is that you?"

Vree's neck turned beet red. The color crept up her face. She fanned herself with her hands. I took a deep breath and pushed through the door, dragging Vree with me. Bootsy's bony arms flailed in our direction. "Vreeland."

Two fat witch tears rolled down her hollowed cheeks.

*　*　*

Then she fell asleep. A nurse stopped by fifteen minutes later. "Oh, good," she whispered over Bootsy. "She said she wasn't closing her eyes until her daughter-in-law got here. I'm glad you're here. She needs rest. Which one of you is the daughter-in-law?"

Vree raised her hand.

We were on the other side of the bed, sitting side by side on a small plastic sofa under a window with a glorious view of the hospital's heat and air system.

"Boy, she's a snorer," the nurse said.

"How long do you think she'll have to stay in the hospital?" I asked.

"That's up to the doctor." She flipped through Bootsy's chart. "It says here she works for Jesus Water?" She looked up from the chart. "Jesus Water?"

"You don't want to know," I said.

"Well, she doesn't have insurance," the nurse said. "The doctor will probably let her go as fast as he can. Probably one more round of fluids, then he'll release her when he makes rounds this evening. Her vitals are good. She's a tough old bird, but she'll need round-the-clock supervision for the next little bit."

"Has she said anything?" I asked.

"What do you mean? Like what?"

"Like what happened to her."

"She was hit upside the head then tied up in the back of a truck for three days is what happened," the nurse said. "Any idea who did this to her?"

I knew exactly who did it and wasn't about to explain it to the nurse. "That's why I asked if she said anything."

"She was waiting on her daughter-in-law."

"I'm not really her daughter-in-law," Vree said. "You see—"

I zoned out.

Fifteen minutes later, when the nurse knew all she never wanted to know about Gooch Howard, and had backed up, inch by inch, all the way to the door, I interrupted Vree. "Did she have anything with her when she got here?"

"If she did, it would be in the closet."

The nurse made a run for it.

I pushed off the low sofa, walked to the closet, and opened the door. A large clear bag greeted me. In black marker, someone had written "Jane Doe" across a white panel. I carried it back and dumped it out beside Vree. She scooted out of the way. A witch boot and Bootsy's bloomers fell to the floor. I shook out her witch dress. I stuck my hand in the deep pocket on the right. Nothing. I stuck my hand in the deep pocket on the left and pulled out a green-eyed skull nose ring.

It hadn't been given up willingly.

Safe from the elements in the deep folds of Bootsy's canvas witch dress, there was plenty of DNA left.

Vree passed out.

*   *   *

Bex and Quinn watched me dress.

They said, "Shiny, shiny, shiny."

I stopped, put down my can of B Blonde, and kissed four chubby cheeks and two pink noses. "Thank you. You're shiny too and I love you."

They said, "Mama, Mama, Mama."

I wondered how their daddy, daddy, daddy was. Their daddy who needed to be home, home, home in his own bed, bed, bed. The last time we talked was at five as I was racing home from Biloxi Regional. He said he was catching a cat nap before Gaming Commission cocktails, of which he planned on having few to none. I told him I loved him, and told him if he wasn't any better in the morning, he'd have to come home (there went my happy marriage), then I made cocktail plans of my own. I called Cork, the wine bar in the casino.

"What's the most expensive bottle of wine you have on hand?"

"That would be Screaming Eagle Cabernet, Mrs. Cole."

"How much?"

"Three thousand a bottle."

"That'll work," I said. "Send one up."

Then I called Fantasy. "What are you doing?"

"I'm hiding from No Hair and Baylor until eight o'clock."

"What's at eight?"

"The next round of the Dogs Gone Wild slot tournament."

"Want to hide at my place for an hour?"

"Sure," she said. "What's up?"

"I need you to stay with Bex and Quinn. They've been with July since noon and I don't want to ask her. I've played the dog show card as many times as I can."

"What about Vree?"

"For one, she stayed at the hospital with Bootsy. For another, I don't know if you've noticed, but Vree doesn't do babies."

"You're the one who hasn't noticed, Davis. Vree gives it all to dogs because she doesn't have babies to give it to."

The thought had never passed through my brain.

"What about the witch?" Fantasy asked. "How's she doing?"

"They're releasing her later."

"Why?"

"She has no insurance," I said.

"Who's going to take care of her?" Fantasy asked.

I didn't answer.

I didn't want to say Urleen's name out loud one more time.

"Oh, hell," Fantasy said.

"Can you stay with Bex and Quinn while I go next door for an hour or not?"

"Sure," she said. "But I don't understand why you're going next door. We need to find the housekeepers, Davis, if for no other reason, I want my car back, but I doubt they're next door."

"We went over this earlier, Fantasy. The housekeepers found the Smucker job through the Atlanta Council for the Blind. There isn't a doubt in my mind someone next door represents His Hiri on that council. We need to know who."

"Can't you look it up?"

"I tried," I said. "I got nothing."

"And your plan is what, Davis? Knock on the door and ask His Hiri? He already knows you had his dog and probably suspects you know where the caregiver is. You need to find another way to connect the fake housekeepers to the Blind Center in Atlanta other than knocking on the sheik's door.''

"This is the fastest way, Fantasy. And besides, I'm going in undercover."

"Which is ridiculous," she said. "It doesn't matter how undercover you go in, he'll smell you."

"No, he won't. Can you stay with the girls or not?"

"I can. But if Urleen shows up, I can't promise I won't kill him."

"Have at it," I said.

Then I called my neighbor. Hiriddhi Al Abbasov. Who said he'd be delighted to clink a glass with Mrs. Sanders. I told him I'd come to him and I'd bring the wine. At five 'til six, dressed and ready, I backed ten feet away from the girls and all but bathed myself in Guerlain Le Bouquet de la Mariée, Bianca's signature fragrance. At a thousand dollars an ounce, I must have squirted nine hundred dollars on. I dared His Excellency to smell me through it. I checked Fantasy's pink tranquilizer gun. It was locked, loaded, and tucked in my Chanel clutch. I told my babies to be good for Aunt Fantasy, and I'd be right back. I picked them up. They coughed, "Banka, Banka, Banka."

I might have gone a little overboard with the perfume.

* * *

The problem wasn't His Excellency recognizing me. The problem was Harley. I didn't fool the dog for a minute. And it took me ten minutes to figure out how to get His Excellency on the balcony. I wanted to speak to him outdoors because for one, we were choking on my perfume and for another, I wanted to talk to him privately. He answered the door himself, and I hadn't seen anyone else, but that didn't mean someone else wasn't there. It was a big suite.

I stood as far away from my host as I could, in a living room as large as my own, eyeing the balcony. The last strains of sun setting over the Gulf meant nothing to him. The budding neon of casino row on Beach Boulevard at dusk, not a draw. The crescent moon that would soon appear? Didn't do a thing for Hiriddhi Al Abbasov. I was at a loss as to how to get him outside, when he, reading my mind, said, "How about the balcony?"

Too much perfume.

As it turned out, I could have saved nine hundred dollars.

His Hiri, in a golf shirt, slacks, and the Tom Ford sunglasses, expertly opened the wine at the bar, while I cased the place. Without moving his head, he said, "Who are you looking for, Mrs. Cole? And who are you hiding from?"

Hiriddhi Al Abbasov saw through everything.

He poured, not missing a drop. We followed Harley through the balcony doors. We settled, me downwind, his question and my perfume between us.

"I'm waiting." Not so patiently. His crossed leg was going a mile a minute. "What do you want? Why are you here?"

Might as well get it out there. "I have children."

"Yes," he said. "The daughters."

"I believe someone with you sent two dangerous men to my home, endangering my children. I, in turn, sent them to my friend's home, where your dog's caregiver died. If the men weren't directly responsible for her death, they are certainly responsible for her missing body. Last straw, Your Excellency, they almost killed a woman I've known my whole life. It started here. In your suite. I want to know who in your party is responsible."

His Excellency adjusted his Tom Fords and mulled my question over a sip of excellent wine. "What makes you think someone with me is responsible?"

"Because the men in question wouldn't be at the Bellissimo had they not been led here by someone associated with the Atlanta

Council for the Blind."

"So this is about me being blind."

"Not at all."

"But you just accused someone on the Council of endangering your children and hiding a body. Look around. I'm the only blind one."

Look around—an odd expression for a blind man to use. "I didn't accuse you," I said. "I'm accusing whoever represents you on the Council."

He put his wine glass down. On the very edge of the table. "And you want a name."

"I do."

"First, Mrs. Cole, let me congratulate you on putting two and two together."

There was a sharp edge to his voice. It set off an alarm in me.

"I'll tell you what." He sat back and laced his fingers behind his head. "Give me the dog collar and I'll give you the name."

Several hundred dollars of wine slid from my hand and spilled to the balcony tile in a Waterford crystal explosion. His Hiri wasn't His Anything. And he wasn't blind at all. He could see perfectly fine, but he didn't have X-ray vision. I had the pink gun out of my clutch and a dart in his neck before he could cross the perfume divide and stop me.

Fantasy was right. A dose of tranquilizer to the neck worked right away.

The only reason I shot him was because I didn't have the collar to trade for a name.

And I should have known when he adjusted his sunglasses.

EIGHTEEN

"You got me." Urleen scratched his head over the comatose man Fantasy and I dragged by his legs, one each, big black poodle bringing up the rear, out of Jay Leno's suite, down the hall, through my front door, the foyer, and down the guest-wing hall to the smallest bedroom, Princess's old room. Neither bed was made, not that it mattered, because His Fakeness's comfort wasn't a concern. We left him on the floor. Urleen gave him a prod with his foot. "I've never seen anyone this passed out."

"You are the sorriest excuse for a doctor ever."

Urleen winked at Fantasy. "It is my goal in life to win you over, beautiful maiden."

"How about your goal in life be to keep this guy alive, Urleen."

He turned to me. "I must insist you shower, Davis, doctor's orders. You're destroying the optic nerves of my left eye, distorting my image of the exquisite Bianca, while burning the cornea of my right eye with overwhelmingly fragrant chemicals. If I can't see this man, I can't save his life."

"Yeah, go change, Davis. You're killing me too," Fantasy said. "I'll watch the prisoner."

"Can you lock down Leno's place first?" I asked her.

"Sure. Is the expensive wine still there? Did you drink it all?"

"No. Why?"

"I'll grab it for later."

"By all means," Urleen said. "Grab the wine."

She ignored him, checked her gun, then said, "Be right back."

Urleen watched her leave. "Don't you just love a pistol-packing woman who appreciates a good wine?"

"Urleen, have you ever met a woman you didn't love?"

A wheelchair appeared in the doorway. Vree was driving. Bootsy Howard, in a hospital gown built for two lumberjacks, slid out of the seat into a passed-out puddle at Urleen's feet. She wasn't wearing much under the hospital gown, which was pooled around her head.

"Indeed," Urleen said. "I have."

*   *   *

I stepped out of the fastest shower ever, having washed a can of B Blonde and nine hundred dollars of perfume down the drain in record time, to my waiting babies, who asked to go to bed. Four little arms reached for me. "Night, night, night." I tucked them into my bed, propped pillows around them, wishing there was someone I could ask to put me to bed. I locked the bedroom door with a keypad security code we'd never used.

I hustled down the guest-wing hall and relieved Fantasy. "Anyone up?" I asked.

"No one's moved a muscle," Fantasy said. "And I'm late."

It took me, Urleen, and Vree to cuff His Fakeness to the bedframes. Spread eagle. If he came to, he wasn't going anywhere unless he took two beds with him. I hooked a portable baby video monitor up on him, then took a picture of his right index finger to run his print. Vree put a pillow under his head.

We put one of Vree's t-shirts on Bootsy, a Westie wearing a bright red clown nose, then piled her into Meredith's bed. Biloxi

Regional had spiked her final dose of fluids with Ambien. They said when she woke up, she'd be fine, but not to expect a peep out of her for hours. I placed an audio baby monitor on the nightstand; Vree clipped the receiver to her belt.

Princess was in her overturned Pop N' Play in the living room yammering along with Madeleine Albright, and Harley was following Vree, every step. We were barely situated in the living room—me, Vree, Urleen, and the dogs—when Fantasy joined us again.

"Aren't you supposed to be at Wag the Dog?"

"Davis, it's ten o'clock."

Time was (running out on me) flying.

"Who'd like a little libation?" Urleen's head bobbed between our blank faces. "No? No takers? A nip? A tuck? Get it?" He slapped his seersuckered leg, laughing at his own joke, then chuckled all the way to the bar where he poured himself a tall glass of whiskey. He sat back down with it, then rubbed his hands over it. "What's next, ladies?" His bushy eyebrows danced. "What other adventures do you have in store for your faithful servant, Leverette Urleen?"

"Lookit, Urleen," I said. "You're here because we have two half-dead people. Your only job is to keep them alive. Sit there and sip your drink while we talk."

"Has anyone seen Jenna Ray?" Vree asked. "She drove you here, right, Dr. Urleen? I mean, shouldn't we check on Jenna Ray? Has anyone talked to her? Has anyone seen her? If I were here by myself and I knew someone else was here from Pine Apple, I'd want to hang out with them. Like dinner, maybe, or what's that game where you pick a number? No. It's a color. You pick a color. Wait! I've got it! You pick a color and a number! One time Gooch—"

I barely tipped my head at Fantasy, who barely acknowledged. She slipped away first, then I made my escape. We stepped out to the terrace with what was left of the Screaming Eagle Cabernet. For the first five minutes, we did nothing but breathe and pass the bottle.

"Where's the real oil sheik, Davis?"

"That, we don't know."

"Who's the fake oil sheik?"

"We don't know that either."

I pulled my phone from my pocket. I swiped past four Bellissimo security alerts without reading them. I had enough alerts of my own. I opened Safari and entered Hiriddhi Al Abbasov. Still no images. We didn't even know who we were looking for.

"Where do we think he might be?" she asked.

"We have no idea."

"Do you have the energy to go to your office and watch the surveillance footage of him checking in? Maybe it was the real sheik who checked in. At least we'll know what he looks like."

"And if he checked in, he's somewhere close."

"Should we go look?"

"No." I would end up in my office before the night ended, if the night ever ended, but not to look for the sheik. "For all we know, the real sheik is the one pulling the strings."

The only answer we had was three-thousand-dollar Cabernet. Worth every penny.

We could hear the faint strains of Vree from the living room.

"Are you going home tonight?" I asked.

Fantasy took her time checking the time on her phone. "I'm waiting until I'm sure Reggie's asleep." She spoke slowly, reading and talking at the same time. "He's mad about my car, refusing to believe I misplaced it."

"So harsh."

"He spent the morning at the dentist and the afternoon boarding up the bonus room so no one would wander off the beach and set up camp above our garage. He blames me for everything."

"So unfair," I said.

She was still looking at her phone. She put it down, then held out her hand for the bottle. "You know what we really need to find?"

"What?" I asked.

"The dog collar."

That too. The real sheik and the dog collar.

"Not to mention the fake housekeepers and the dead caregiver are still in the wind." She poured three-thousand-dollar wine down her throat, chugging it like water, passed what was left to me, then stood.

"Where are you going?"

"Downstairs. Security says a loud woman accompanying a man with a bandaged foot sledgehammered into the dog hotel part of the conference center. They let the dogs out. The dogs are all over the casino. Then the same people and their sledgehammer went to high limits and took out the five-hundred-dollar Wheel of Fortune. I'm going downstairs to help No Hair and Baylor." She yanked the bottle out of my hand and polished it off. "Get some sleep, Davis. We're going to have another long day tomorrow."

I walked her to the door, then checked on everyone and everything, starting, then looping back and ending, with my daughters. I still didn't feel safe enough, with whoever it was I had cuffed to twin beds in my guest room. I called security and ordered myself two armed guards for the vestibule. I brewed a pot of coffee, then went to my office to steal a million dollars.

*   *   *

I'd never stolen anything in my life.

Maybe Bradley's heart?

That wasn't theft. He gave me his heart, just like I gave him mine. I dreaded the day, and it could be soon, he gave it back. I'd miss him terribly when I went to prison. I sat down at my computer, wondering if he'd visit me. I wanted to believe what Meredith believed—I was borrowing the money. But when you take something that isn't yours, even if you have every good intention of replacing it, it's still stealing. It's theft, robbery, burglary, larceny. I was on the verge of being a larcenist. A felony larcenist.

The one framed picture on my desk was of the four of us. Bex and Quinn's first birthday—frosting everywhere. I turned it over so my family wouldn't see what I was about to do.

I remembered reading about the greatest bank robbery of all time. It was at least a dozen years ago; my police officer's badge was bright. A gang of Brazilian thieves rented property in downtown Fortaleza, then posing as landscapers, spent three months tunneling two hundred and fifty feet to a bank. A bank they relieved of seventy million dollars. My first thought when the story broke? Brilliant. The thieves were brilliant. It was August, my first summer on the job, and my police-chief father and I watched the drama unfold on the television in the air-conditioned comfort of the police station while waiting on a domestic disturbance, traffic, or cat-in-a-tree call. I remember cutting my eyes at Daddy, wondering if he caught the look of admiration on my face before it occurred to me I should be, or at least pretend to be, appalled.

The Brazilian bank money was never recovered.

Which made the exit plan even more brilliant than the heist.

I needed a brilliant heist with an equally brilliant exit plan.

I gave myself points for not holding a Silver Slipper cashier at gunpoint. In spite of me telling Fantasy we'd need a week to hit the Slipper, the truth was it would have taken me ten minutes to get in and out with a million Slipper dollars. One minute to disable their surveillance and nine to wait on the cashier loading the money. But I didn't. I didn't help myself to one of the seventeen million sitting in front of me when Fantasy and I took cage either. And I hadn't fenced Princess's collar.

Well.

There was a reason I hadn't fenced Princess's collar.

I couldn't find it.

There I was at midnight. Alone at my desk. About to commit a million counts of larceny with my babies asleep in the bed, a hall away from a con man impersonating a blind oil baron, who was a wall away from a doped witch, who was a door away from Urleen, on self-appointed sentry duty, outside the twin bedroom with two taser guns and a cast-iron skillet, who was down the hall from Vree, a big black poodle, and Madeleine Albright's number one fan. My home was stuffed, and I'd never felt so alone.

The computer screens in front of me were dark. I knew as soon as I powered up, I'd cross the line, so I put it off. Just to put it off another minute, from my phone, I checked baby monitors—the one on my sleeping children and the one trained on the man between the twin beds who shouldn't be under the same roof with my sleeping children. Which was when it occurred to me—why should I risk getting caught stealing a million dollars? Why not let him risk getting caught stealing the million?

Digging through my desk drawer, past pens, paperclips, and baby girl bows, I found my Bellissimo passkey. It gave me access to seventeen hundred hotel rooms, including Jay Leno's. Chances were high His Fakeness had a laptop. Everyone had a laptop, and they were never far from it. Instead of taking the chance I'd leave a trail, why not let him take the chance? The only problem was, I couldn't and wouldn't leave my daughters unprotected with him in the house even to walk next door. If the man left his laptop in the foyer and start to finish I was gone less than three minutes, I still wasn't going to take the chance. I wouldn't ask the security guards to stand at my bedroom door. I couldn't call Fantasy; she was in deep enough. I wouldn't call Baylor and ask for help, because he'd tell No Hair before he did anything else. I wasn't about to call No Hair.

I could easily put Bex and Quinn in their stroller and take them with me—they'd sleep right through it—or I could wake up Vree and put her on patrol at my bedroom door with a taser gun. Then I could run next door, toss the place, find a laptop, and be right back home.

How was it, in a house so full, there was no one I could trust to watch over my daughters?

I thought of someone.

Carrying a thick play quilt from the living room with me, I stepped over Urleen, who had passed out in the hall with one of the taser guns an inch from his own head, his finger on the trigger, the skillet between his sprawled seersuckered legs. I eased open Vree's door. Harley's head popped up from the foot of the bed. "Shhhh," I said. By the light of the hall, I lifted a corner of the flipped Pop N' Play and dropped the quilt over Princess the second she escaped. The quilt smelled like Bex and Quinn; she didn't protest. My package and I dodged Urleen on the way back to my bedroom. When I got to the door, I dropped the quilt, then spread it out. Princess turned circles on it, then glared at me with her yellow eye. I showed her the door. "Guard." She spread her long skinny legs, the three with patchy fur and the bald purple one, and a growl erupted from her thick middle. She showed me her teeth.

I ran like the devil was chasing me. It took four minutes to find two laptops: one on the coffee table of the sitting room outside of the master bedroom, a MacBook Pro, and one askew on the floor of the solarium adjacent to the indoor pool, a BrailleNote Apex BT 32. I went with the MacBook, and it only took one minute to grab it and run to the front door, but two more minutes to run back to the solarium and take a second look at the BrailleNote. It took three minutes to bust through the barricaded pool door and find Hiriddhi Al Abbasov. It took seven minutes to rescue him, and another minute to dial 911.

Princess was right where I left her.

Good dog.

NINETEEN

With emergency services on the way, I stood in the hall between my open front door and the Leno suite soaked to my bones and freezing to death. I called No Hair. "I have a situation."

"At this time of night, Davis? You have a situation? Too bad, because I have a situation of my own."

"The Smuckers?"

"They're gone. I'm watching them leave now. Separate squad cars. Lights blazing."

I didn't say, "Stay right where you are. There'll be more blazing lights in a minute." Instead, I asked, teeth chattering, "What'd you get them on?"

"Destruction of property."

The sledgehammered Wheel of Fortune slot machine. "It won't stick, No Hair. They'll be out before sunrise."

"No, they won't," he said. "IGT is charging them with loss of income."

Wheel of Fortune was a multistate progressive game. Cleavon and Candy Smucker hadn't just taken out the Bellissimo's Wheel, they must have shut down the game nationwide. That meant more than two thousand Wheels in Las Vegas alone, no telling how many coast to coast. I hoped the Smuckers had set aside a little of the billion and a half dollars, because they were going to need it when

International Gaming Technology rained down on them.

"What is it, Davis? I'm dead on my feet. I need sleep. I don't want to hear about your witch."

Baylor. That rat.

"Hiriddhi Al Abbasov?"

"Your neighbor?"

"Yes."

"What about him?"

"I found him in Leno's indoor swimming pool."

I gave No Hair a minute to process the news.

"Doing what?"

"Floating. For three days, he's been floating. Nothing to eat and nothing to drink but pool water. His pulse is weak and I think he has hypothermia."

"Where is he now?"

"Under every blanket I own. An ambulance is on the way."

"I'll see you in two."

An hour later, I'd had another hot shower after my impromptu dip in the pool, and His Passed Out Fakeness had been uncuffed from the twin beds and was on his way to central booking. I hoped they'd put him in a holding cell with Cleavon and Candy Smucker. The arresting officer couldn't read him his rights, because he couldn't rouse him. We tried a little bit of everything--ice water, whiffs of straight ammonia, and No Hair patting him about the cheeks, none too gently, probably rearranging his teeth and shuffling his brains. His Fakeness wasn't waking up.

"What'd you do to him, Davis?"

"Why is that always the first place you go, No Hair? What did I do?"

I stole his MacBook. That's what I did.

*   *   *

GameCorp Industries owned and maintained the thirty-eight ATM machines scattered throughout the Bellissimo. With thirty of the machines congregated in the casino, I guess they weren't so scattered. Between the Bellissimo and our fourteen neighbor casinos, GameCorp managed more than one hundred and fifty ATMs in Harrison County, Mississippi alone, and more than three thousand ATMs in casinos nationwide. For each and every casino transaction, be it a ten-dollar withdrawal or a ten-thousand-dollar transfer, GameCorp charged a seven-dollar convenience fee.

Highway robbery.

They charged an additional three dollars on the back end to cover the issuing bank service fee.

I wasn't after the three dollars.

At an average of two hundred transactions per ATM every twenty-four hours, GameCorp was clearing more than five million a day during the week, and up to seven million a day on the weekends. In casino convenience fees.

I stopped to wonder if Bradley's next career move shouldn't be casino ATMs. They made more money than Wheels.

The casino ATM fees in thirty-nine states routed to one dedicated account in Detroit. I chose four hundred random ATMs in thirty states, starting in Nevada and ending in Mississippi—no pattern, there'd be no dots to connect—and rerouted the convenience fees to an anonymous offshore account. From there, I sent the money to MD Anderson. It wasn't like I took a sledgehammer to one of GameCorp's ATMs, which they'd notice right away. What I did was more of a slow leak, seven dollars at a time, one hundred and fifty thousand times, and so scattered across America, it would take a team of forensic accountants six months to find the problem and another six months to find the ATMs with the glitch. I only needed two and a half days.

Or, rather, His Fakeness needed two and a half days.

And I'd have six months to somehow, some way, repay the money.

I set it up, checked it ten times, then hit enter.

The fees began pouring into Greene Gully's patient account immediately.

I shut it down and went to bed, having left most of the uncertainty about the right and wrong of what I was doing at the bottom of Jay Leno's indoor pool.

Still, though, I didn't get much sleep.

Because what I'd done was mostly wrong.

* * *

Bex and Quinn slept soundly all night, so naturally, they were awake at the crack of dawn. Jumping. On my felonious head. "Bite, bite, bite!"

I rallied. My girls were hungry. I needed to talk to Bootsy anyway.

Leverette Urleen was sitting at my kitchen table sipping coffee from my favorite mug like he owned the place. "Urleen," I said, "do you have any other clothes?"

"Good morning to you too, Davis." He crossed his seersuckered legs the other way. "And no. I was called here on a quick consultation. I'm afraid I didn't pack for an extended stay." He straightened his bowtie, a total waste of time. The bowtie, along with the rest of him, was beyond straightening.

"Why don't you go downstairs to Cuffs, the men's shop, and find something else to wear? Then go to your hotel room, shower, and put it on."

"A stellar idea," he said. "One never knows when one might be in the company of the fairer sex, and one must always be prepared. Might I have an account established at this men's shop?"

I clicked Bex and Quinn into their highchairs and poured myself a cup of coffee in Bradley's favorite mug. "An account?"

"A house account. Credit. A reimbursement-for-services-rendered wardrobe stipend I could apply to purchases."

"No, Urleen, you don't. Get off your wallet and buy yourself some clean clothes."

"Would your husband be anywhere near my size?"

"No, Urleen, you're not wearing my husband's clothes."

Bex and Quinn said, "Daddy, daddy, daddy."

"And another thing, Urleen, hit the road. if I need you, I'll call you. Don't come back here."

Bex and Quinn said, "Bye, bye, bye."

"Will your children ever speak in sentences?" he asked.

Vree spoke in sentences. Long run-on sentences. She started one in the kitchen door, wearing pink shortie pajamas with pink slippers. "I don't know how to tell you this, Davis."

Princess. On the loose again.

"I woke up this morning, and first thing, Harley and Princess and I went to the balcony, you know, where the grass is? And it's so pretty out there. It's a really nice morning. I mean, the sun is up, and there's this little breeze, and I watched the beach and watched the beach, and I would have watched the beach all morning but I thought about coffee. And there's no coffee on the balcony. So Harley and Princess and I came back inside—"

Where was she going with this? I served apple juice sippy cups, wheat toast triangles, sliced peaches, and little mountains of dry Lucky Charms, then poured myself a second cup of coffee during her preamble.

"—after I washed my face and brushed my teeth, I thought I'd better check on Bootsy. Because one time—"

"Vree!" I slammed my mug down. "Cut to the chase. What about Bootsy?"

"She's gone, Davis." Vree waved a note.

I grabbed it. *I have a score to settle and a man to see.*

Wednesday would be no better than Tuesday, which was more stressful than Monday, which was worse than Sunday, and it all went back to Saturday, when Meredith didn't come. I dreaded Thursday. And Bootsy Howard was the world's slipperiest witch.

From the kitchen phone, I called July.

"Another long day?"

"Yes," I said. "Can I bring them to you?"

"Of course."

"Ten o'clock."

"I'll see you then," July said.

I'd no more put the phone down when it rang again. It was No Hair.

"Davis, I'd like to see you and Fantasy in my office this morning, and don't bring the girls. You're not going to use them as an Uncle No Hair smokescreen. I need to talk to you. Be here at nine." Then he hung up.

I called July back.

* * *

"Your house is destroyed."

He was right. It was. No Hair's office, on the other hand, was its usual pristine man cave. It smelled like leather and cars. Cold leather, and cold cars, because No Hair kept the air at meat-locker. The only thing that didn't belong was a revolving tie rack full of neckties. In five years, I'd never seen No Hair wear the same tie. The two, three, forty, or zero times I'd seen him that week—halfway through the week and it was such a blur—his ties had been dog themed. The night before, when we'd sent the sheik to the hospital, my unwanted guest to jail, and he'd apparently noticed the chaos that was my home, his tie had been all wagging tails. That day, he was mixing it up. His white tie had a disturbingly large black flea on it.

"Who is the goofball in the seersucker suit?"

"He's a doctor from Pine Apple," Fantasy said.

It was very much like being in the principal's office. No Hair was behind his desk, we were in straight chairs across from him.

"What's he doing here?"

I opened my mouth to make up something, but Fantasy took that one too. "The dead woman. We didn't know what she died of."

"What dead woman?"

"The caregiver," she said.

"Whose caregiver?" No Hair asked.

"The dog's."

"Which dog?"

"The black one. Harley."

No Hair put a hand over his eyes and shook his bald head. When he returned, he told Fantasy to shut up. He'd heard enough from her. He aimed at me. "Start talking."

"Well, No Hair, there's this man. Greene Gully. He owns Jesus Water."

"He owns what?"

"Jesus Water."

"What the hell is Jesus Water, Davis?"

"Blessings in a bottle. Drink the water, be blessed."

No Hair inhaled sharply, and the look on his face said he didn't like my answers any better than he'd liked Fantasy's. "Does this Jesus Water man have anything to do with anything anywhere remotely related to this property? Or is this all you, Davis?"

I scratched my head. "Could you rephrase the question?"

"The Smuckers," Fantasy said.

"What about them? The Jesus Water man has something to do with the Smuckers?" No Hair looked hopeful.

"No," Fantasy said. "I was asking what's going on with the Smuckers."

"Don't do that to me," No Hair said.

"Do what?" she asked.

"Change the subject."

"What was the subject?" I asked.

No Hair slammed a fist on his desk. We jumped.

"We're going to start over," No Hair said. "And I want straight answers."

Our heads rolled compliantly.

"Why were you in the Leno suite?" he asked.

"Tossing to Davis," Fantasy said. "I wasn't in the Leno suite except to lock up and get the wine."

"Is that the problem?" No Hair asked. "Are you two drunk?"

"It's nine o'clock in the morning," I said. "No one's drunk."

"Answer the question," he said.

I couldn't very well say I was there to steal a laptop, I wasn't about to open that bucket of worms, so I went with something safe. "I heard a noise."

"You didn't hear anything in the Leno suite unless you had your ear to the door, Davis. Why would you have your ear to the Leno door?"

I scratched my ear.

No Hair slapped his desk with both hands. "We're getting absolutely nowhere. And I, for one, have work to do." He turned to Fantasy. "Since you asked, the Smuckers were released." Then to me. "You were right. The judge said we didn't have enough to hold them on."

"What about IGT?" I asked. "I thought they were pressing

charges."

"They were. They are. They will. But the drunk tank was past capacity, so in an effort to lower the body count, a judge was called in for middle of the night arraignments. At the time, IGT's lawyers were just landing, they certainly didn't have time to file charges, so the Smuckers are ours again."

"That's terrible news," I said.

"Hang on to your hat, Davis. It gets worse. The man we took from you, the one you had cuffed to the bedposts who you call His Phony?"

"His Fakeness," I said.

"What the hell ever, Davis."

No Hair's face was red. So red.

"He's not in jail either," No Hair said. "The officers took him to the emergency room first, where the man's bloodwork came back with toxic barbiturate levels."

Urleen was the worst doctor ever, ever of all the bad doctors ever.

"Do either one of you think this man drugged himself?" No Hair asked.

Our heads rolled uncertainly.

"No?" No Hair asked. "Do either one of you know who drugged this man?"

"I'm taking the fifth," I said.

"I'll take the sixth," Fantasy said. "Because I don't want to incriminate Davis either."

"Okay," No Hair said. "I get it. You two had such a beef with this guy you pumped him full of barbiturates to the point of almost killing him, then chained him to beds, and yet you either don't remember what he did to piss you off or you don't care to share. How about I share?"

I had a feeling I didn't want to hear what No Hair had to share.

"The drugs wore off in the emergency room," No Hair said. "The man came to. He knocked an orderly over the head with a suction aspirator machine and helped himself to the orderly's clothes and wallet. He walked right past the two patrolmen sleeping in the waiting room, then out the door. The good news is we know his name."

I wanted to hear the name. I hadn't had time to run the print on my phone, and when I'd set up the ATM con on his MacBook, the username I'd bypassed was initials and numbers.

"Rod J. Sebastian."

My heart skipped a beat.

"Does that mean anything to you two? And if it does, would you give me a straight answer? No? Let me connect the dots for you. The man you tried to kill was Rod J. Sebastian, Hiriddhi Al Abbasov's personal secretary, who all but killed Al Abbasov when he pushed him into the pool to spend three days bobbing like a cork with his hands and feet bound and a pool float around his neck barely keeping his head above water. Which means we want him. And we're not the only ones. We ran Mr. Sebastian's prints through the system and found out he's wanted under an alias for child abandonment in Florida, for impersonating the sheik and embezzling donations from a non-profit organization for the blind in Atlanta, and get this," No Hair said, "Animal Control wants him too. The police raided his home and found an illegal dogfighting operation he and two of his cousins are running on a farm just outside city limits."

Any lingering doubt I had about what I'd done on Rod J. Sebastian's laptop flew out the window.

"And not a little operation," No Hair said. "They rescued forty dogs from appalling conditions."

Then out to sea.

"So we want him," No Hair said. "The sheik wants him. The

blind people want him. The mother of the two abandoned children wants him. Animal Control and the feds want him. And you two are the reason we don't have him."

I was having trouble breathing.

"Be warned." No Hair shook his finger at us. "Sebastian's on the loose. And you'd better watch your backs. He might, like me, be more than a little irritated with you." He turned to Fantasy. "I'll see you at noon in the doghouse." Then me. "I'll see you at two for the dog show. And call your husband. He's coughing his head off." No Hair sat back. "That'll be all." He pointed at the door.

We slinked out. We slinked to the elevator. Neither of us had the energy to push the call button, so we slinked down the wall to sit on an upholstered bench in the cold empty vestibule. Fantasy's fog lifted first. "We found Bootsy, then we lost her again. We found the secretary, who we didn't know was a serial-criminal secretary, and his name is Sebastian, just like the fake housekeepers Sebastian, so there's the connection between Al Abbasov and the Smuckers, a serial-criminal-secretary connection we didn't even know we were looking for, but now he's in the wind again, which puts all three Sebastians *and* the witch *and* the dead caregiver in the wind. The Smuckers are out of jail, we can't find their dog's collar, and there's no million dollars."

"About that."

"About what?" she asked. "Which part?"

"The million dollars."

I looked right and left, making sure there were no eavesdroppers. I cupped my hand over her ear and whispered.

She stopped me to whisper in my ear, "He deserves it, Davis. For the dog fighting alone, he deserves it." She stopped me again to whisper, "Seven dollars for a convenience fee is outrageous. GameCorp had this coming too."

When I finished, she said, "Brilliant."

TWENTY

For the final round of the dog competition, the contestant interviews, Bianca had me in a Shetland pony dominatrix getup. The dress looked wet, as in liquefied, and felt like Jell-O. I think it was made of rubber. It was as white as the driven snow, covered just enough of me to be street legal, took twenty minutes to skid into, and that was just the half of it. The other half were the accessories. One was a purse. Or a clutch. I didn't know what to call it, because it was a horse's foot on a gold chain. A whole horse's foot. I didn't know if it was real or not and I didn't want to know. The other accessory went over the dress. The whole wet white dress. It was either a harness or bridle. Whichever, it was silver spiked black leather and laced all the way up the back. Or maybe it laced all the way up the front. Vree was trying to help. "I think this part goes in your mouth."

"In a million years, Vree, I am not walking around with leather straps in my mouth."

"Then they're going to have to hang down. And hanging down, they look, well, they hit you in a bad place. They look like black leather tassel headlights. You know what I mean? They fall right on your...girls."

"Let them fall." I'd be falling with them soon enough. The over-the-knee black leather boots with sliver studs and spurs

Bianca sent had eight-inch needle-thin heels. The accompanying note said, *Updo and smoky eyes, David. Very up and very smoky.*

We studied the final results in the mirror.

"In a way, you look pretty," Vree said.

In every other way, I looked like I'd escaped the mental facility I called home.

When I hobbled into the competition arena carrying a horse's foot and hanging on to Vree for dear life—who wears eight-inch heels?—one of my fellow judges spotted me, startled, then spun around. I could see his shoulders shaking. He turned back around, took a second look, then took a keen interest in the floor. His head started bobbing. At first it was just a chuckle he tried, and failed, to hide. After a few minutes, he was openly laughing to the point of tears. Then through the entire round of dog questions, every ten minutes or so he would lean forward, take another peek at me, then double over again. Near the end, he gave up, laid his head down, and pounded the judges' table with his fist. "Sorry!" he choked out. "I'm so sorry! I can't help it!"

I found his name on the score screen. Menton Williams.

When the last question was posed to the last pooch—"How old are you?"—and he answered with four barks, I slipped my phone out of the horse hoof and checked Greene Gully's MD Anderson account. It had almost three hundred thousand dollars in it, and his patient status had been changed from inactive to pre-op. I read a quick email from my sister. Four Seasons was accommodating the iron-rich diet Greene's doctors had her on. She couldn't do the oysters or lentils, but everything else was fine. She'd check in at MD Anderson at five Friday morning, she'd finish by eight, but wouldn't be released until two. Observation. After, it'd be back to Four Seasons to pick up Bubblegum, then on to the airport for their four o'clock flight to Gulfport-Biloxi International. She'd see me at six Friday.

I couldn't wait until six Friday.

Dog interviews over, the room clearing, I logged into Facebook.

"Where to?" Vree asked.

"Ivories." I had to wrap my arms around her waist to take a baby step. "The piano bar in the casino."

"Do you need me to stay with you?"

"No, Vree. I've got this. Go upstairs and take care of the dogs."

In sunglasses the size of bread plates, my updo on its way down, I hung the horse foot around my neck by the gold chain as I limped into Ivories fist over fist along a brass handrail. Candy Smucker was alone at the bar nursing a big blue drink. She'd freshened up since her mugshot. She was wearing a loose tank top above tight ripped jeans. There was more rip than jean. She came up from her drink and looked at me. "You're in worse shape than I am." She slid off the barstool. "You need a hand?"

I needed a foot. Two of them.

"I love your outfit." She helped me limp along. "Where'd you get your boots?" She helped me onto a barstool. "They're hot."

"You can have them."

"For real?"

"If you can help me take them off, you can have them."

"What size are they?" she asked.

"Six and a half."

"I wear a six on one foot and a seven on the other," she said. "One of my hands is bigger than the other one too."

She displayed.

I made what I hoped was an appropriate noise.

I landed my Clydesdale clutch on the bar.

Candy's mouth dropped open. "Where'd you get that? It's the most beautiful purse I've ever seen in my life." She reached out and stroked the horse hair. "I want one so bad." She picked it up and clacked it on the bar. "Here horsey, horsey!" More clacking. "Where'd you get it?"

"I can't remember."

"Say, you want a drink?" Then, twenty decibels louder, "Hey! Bar boy! Bring me and my friend a drink! Get your ass out here!" She turned to me. "He tried to run me off when I got here. I had to tip him big. Money talks and bullshit walks, you know."

I nodded. I knew.

Ivories didn't officially open until five. The bar was dark, the pianos silent, and the candles on the cocktail tables cold. A male head popped through a cracked door behind the bar. I turned so he wouldn't think he knew me as Candy ordered a round of Flaming Volcanos, which I'd never heard of. Then she sat at my feet and worked down the rows of hook and eye closures on both boots. A woman worth a billion dollars sat on the floor of a bar to help a total stranger whose feet hurt. When she pulled the second boot off, I thanked her. And meant every word of it.

"Thank you too." She stood. "I needed some company."

"Bad day?"

"Woke up in jail." She tossed her new boots. "That always makes for a bad day."

"Sorry."

She waved it off. "It was a nice jail," she said. "I've been in way worser."

"You're Candy, right?"

She slapped the bar. "How'd you know?"

"We're Facebook friends."

"Get out!"

I nodded.

"You from Atlanta?"

"No," I said. "But I'm looking for someone who is."

"His name ain't Cleave, is it?"

I shook my head no, then reached in the horse hoof for my phone. I found a photograph of Brutus and Butch Sebastian. "I'm looking for these men."

She zoomed in and out. She picked my phone up and angled it for better light. "Yeah, I know them."

"I need to find them."

"I wouldn't go looking for these two. They're bad news. What do you want with them?"

"Child support."

Candy nodded gravely. "Which one?"

"I'm not sure."

"Get out! You don't know which one? You go, girl!" She punched me in the arm. My rubber dress took the blow.

"You wouldn't know where they are, would you?"

"Nope."

I studied my white rubber lap as the bartender placed big blue frozen drinks in front of us. When the coast was clear, I looked up and asked Candy how she knew Brutus and Butch Sebastian.

"This one—" she stabbed my phone "—was supposed to be my dog-sitter, and this other one—" stab stab "—was supposed to be my bodyguard. Do you see a bodyguard?" Her arms flailed. "Is there anybody guarding this body? No!"

I waited. She drank.

"Me and Cleave—" she paused to explain "—Cleave's my husband."

I nodded.

"We hired them to come with us sight unseed. Then I told Cleave, 'Cleave, we need to meet them for real,' because anybody with a nose ring can be a bodyguard, but not just anybody can be a dog-sitter. You know what I mean?"

I knew what she meant.

"They got to our place, and our dog throwed a fit. She tore into them the minute she laid her eye on them. She got one of them in the face. The one with the beard."

"That's terrifying." And I meant it. "What'd you do?"

"We got her a hotel room."

"Ah."

"Last night, we got to missing her. We went upstairs to the dog hotel and couldn't find her."

That wasn't the dog hotel, Candy.

"Then Cleave got in a little fight with a slot machine."

I would call what Cleve got into with the Wheel more of a big fight.

"That's when we went to jail."

"Ah."

"It'll be okay," she said. "We got eleventeen hundred lawyers."

You're going to need all eleventeen hundred.

"Have you seen them since?"

"Seen who?" she asked.

I gave my phone a nod.

"Since when?" she asked.

"Since you met them in Atlanta."

"They're here," she said. "Me and Cleave ran into them the other day. I saw them getting into the elevator with a old lady and a black dog. I said, 'Hey, you two! Where you been?' They acted like they didn't even know us, then they were gone. I said, 'Cleave, that was them, right?' Then Cleave said, 'Hell if I know.'" She paused for a sip of Flaming Volcano. "We had tequila for breakfast that day."

"What day was that?"

"The day we had tequila for breakfast."

I was nowhere. The only solid lead I had from Candy placed the fake housekeepers Sebastian with Doris Harrington and Harley in an elevator the day she had tequila for breakfast.

"Those two are the reason Cleave got so worked up last night."

"Really?"

"Them and he got on the whiskey. When Cleave gets on the whiskey, watch out."

Duly noted.

"Here." She reached into her purse and returned with a cardkey. "Take this. Like a trade for the boots. Go get their asses."

"What is it?"

"It's the key to their hotel room. But watch out. They trashed it. It stinks."

"Why do you have their room key?"

"They came with us," she said. "It was our constellation prize to them since our dog drew blood. We don't want anybody suing us, you know?"

Too late.

"We already had their reservations," she said. "So we said, 'Y'all come on.'"

Now I knew why the brothers Sebastian were here, but I still didn't know why the Smuckers were mad at them.

"And them acting like they didn't even know us."

I could think of worse offenses.

"Then last night, a casino woman tracked us down to tell us our room stinks so bad the maids won't go in it. Cleave said, 'What the hell? We haven't even been in our room.' Then she told him we'd charged our room bill up too high. And Cleave said, 'What the hell? You ever heard of cash, lady? I pay cash.' Then she said, 'No, I'm talking about room charges, mister. High charges.' Cleave said, 'What the hell? How high?' She said, 'High, high through the roof.' Then Cleave said, "What the hell? Prove it, lady." She had a paper a mile long with room charges for their room." She stabbed my phone.

Those were worse offenses.

"Cleave went up there to give them a piece of his mind."

"I don't blame him," I said.

"He took his sledgehammer with him."

(Who packs a sledgehammer?)

"Did he find them?"

"Nope. He fell asleep in the elevator. When he woke up he forgot he was looking for them. 'Course he was on the whiskey." She pushed the room key closer. "You give it a try. You got a sledgehammer?"

I shook my head.

"Take a tire iron. Takes longer, works just as good. When you're done with them, tell them Cleave and Candy said we don't appreciate them running up those high charges and stinking up their hotel room." Then she reached back in her purse and whipped out her phone. In one smooth move, she slung an arm around my shoulders, pressed her cheek against mine, and snapped a picture. "What's your name? I'm gonna tag you."

"Bianca Sanders," the bartender, who came out of nowhere, supplied.

"Spell that," Candy said. "I can't spell worth a shit."

*   *   *

I found something the rubber dress was good for.

Blocking death fumes.

I found Doris Harrington's body in Butch and Brutus Sebastian's Bellissimo guest room. I didn't find the brothers Sebastian or Princess's collar.

TWENTY-ONE

Plethora delivered dinner at six. I ordered comfort food. Bex and Quinn were the only takers. At seven, it was "bath, bath, bath," and at eight, I tucked the girls in, then sat on the rug between their little beds and read Corduroy, a story about a bear who'd lost his button. They only said, "again, again, again" three times before sleep found my tired babies. I kissed noses, turned down lights, turned up monitors, then went straight to the coffee pot, where I made a strong pot of coffee. I pulled three mugs from the shelf and waited. Just before the finished beep, I filled two of the mugs and walked them to my security detail at the elevator.

"Anything?" I passed out coffee.

"Nothing," one said.

"Thank you," the other said.

Rod J. Sebastian, last seen the night before leaving the emergency room in an orderly's uniform, hadn't surfaced yet. Not on the twenty-ninth floor, anyway. If and when he did, he wouldn't get far. Back to the kitchen, I poured myself a cup of coffee. It was going to be another long night. The night before, I'd crossed to the dark side, joining the rank and file of cyberthieves. That night, I'd be digging through endless hours of Bellissimo surveillance to establish a timeline, and look for people, answers, and dog collars. While my coffee cooled enough to drink, I did something I'd been trying to do for hours: I called my husband.

"Hey, you," I said.

He coughed.

"Bradley, you sound terrible."

"I feel better than I sound. Guess what night it is?"

I was pretty sure it was Wednesday.

"Casino night." He coughed. "It's like being home, except everyone here knows what they're doing. Can I call you back?" I said goodbye, he coughed it.

Next, I checked Greene Gully's MD Anderson patient account and found a balance of more than eight hundred thousand dollars.

After that, I texted Urleen the Idiot. *Bradley has a new symptom. He's coughing.*

Urleen texted back. *Probably respiratory failure.*

Why did I even bother? *Does the medical examiner know the caregiver's cause of death yet?*

Urleen shot back, *No, but she has a date. With yours truly.*

I blew a raspberry. *I don't care, Urleen. What is she saying the woman on the table died of?*

I told you hours ago. A broken heart.

Not a legitimate cause of death. *What does the real doctor say, Urleen?*

I will forgive you the rude implication, Davis, if for no other reason, I'm a gentleman. The lovely Dr. Gallman-Washburn hasn't made a final determination yet. I'm in as big a hurry as you are. If you could see this woman in scrubs, you too would be anxious to see her out of scrubs.

I traded the phone for the computer.

Pulling surveillance up on all three monitors, I loaded Bootsy Howard's mug on one, Butch and Brutus Sebastian's driver's license pictures on the next, and Rod J. Sebastian's photo on the third screen. It was a good thing Doris Harrington's body had been recovered, because I didn't have a fourth screen.

Bootsy Howard pulled into the Bellissimo parking garage at four Saturday morning, beating Meredith and Bubbles here altogether, and Vree by four hours. I picked her up again when she marched in the Bellissimo through the west entrance, where she wandered to the VIP elevator and ran into Bradley, Bex, and Quinn. I watched until she gave the girls carnival suckers, then jumped all the way to Tuesday afternoon, as Vree pushed the wheelchair full of sleeping Bootsy through my front door after she was released from the hospital. I stayed with the camera on my door, using the video speed changer to fast forward to her exit, sometime the next morning. Sometime turned out to be 4:14. Everyone here was asleep when Bootsy sneaked out, dressed in full witch regalia. She looked right and left, particularly left, in the direction of Jay Leno's—something caught her eye?—then stepped out of the camera's range. Rather than taking the time for a new search from a different angle, I had surveillance look for any additional footage of Bootsy and found only one more shot of her entering the parking garage at 5:50 Wednesday morning. From my front door to the west entrance leading to the parking lot at that time of morning was a ten-minute crawl. I had no idea what she'd been doing all that time. I froze the screen. I couldn't imagine she had the energy, after what she'd been through, to drive to Houston, but the only reason she'd have gone to the parking garage would have been to get in her car and go somewhere. My best guess was to Greene's bedside.

Moving to my second monitor, I cued VIP reception, and sped through Sunday morning check-ins and check-outs until I found Cleave, Candy, and Princess Smucker, changing the Bellissimo forever when they blasted through the VIP double doors. The main act was the Smuckers, all three, and the poor girl behind the desk trying to check them in, Lauren, who'd written No Hair the email about Princess. But it was the sideshow I was after, Butch and

Brutus Sebastian, who'd arrived with the Smuckers. While Cleave and Candy argued, vehemently, with Lauren, the brothers Sebastian quietly and stealthily slipped around the corner. I had to change the camera feed to catch the brothers in quick conversation with their cousin Rod J. Sebastian, who'd obviously been awaiting their arrival. I wished I could read lips. Rod J. Sebastian passed them a blue keycard, turned on his heel and left. I don't know how Rod J. acquired the blue keycard, unless he swiped it from a housekeeping supervisor's cart, but it gave the brothers access to all areas janitorial. Minutes later, they accepted a guest-room keycard portfolio from the Smuckers. For the next fifteen minutes, I followed them at warp speed until they knocked on my front door hours later with a riding-lawn-mower sized floor cleaner, then slowed the feed to a crawl to watch them leave. Like I'd see a Harry Winston collar dangling from one of their pockets. No such luck. It was just after noon Sunday, when they should have been doing what I'd paid them two hundred dollars each to do, which was drive a Bellissimo truck to Fantasy's bonus room and retrieve Bootsy, but instead, they took a left. To Jay Leno's. Their cousin Rod answered the door, where I watched a hushed exchange ensue, most likely including "daughters" and "Ivory Snow" and "there's a dog in there that looks like a weasel and smells like death warmed over," but no sight of, or passing of, the diamond collar. Eventually, after checking over his shoulder, cousin Rod pulled them in, and none too gently. Not having footage of the suite's interior, I had to wait until they exited four minutes later, with Doris Harrington and Harley in tow. She was being manhandled by the bearded Sebastian, and Harley dragged on a leash by the nose-ringed Sebastian. It was terrifying to watch; they'd been in my home just minutes earlier. I lost their party in the elevator, then picked them up eighteen minutes later, turning left onto Beach Boulevard in the Bellissimo truck, on their way to Fantasy's. A chill ran through me as I realized I was watching the very end of Doris Harrington's life. Back at the Bellissimo, I had to assume, having cleared the Leno suite of his minor obstacles, Doris and Harley, Rod J. Sebastian incapacitated his major obstacle, Hiriddhi Al Abbasov, in the indoor pool. I didn't find Butch and Brutus Sebastian's images on Bellissimo surveillance again until hours later, when they made use of the very laundry cart Vree and I left on the loading dock when we'd rolled knocked-out Bootsy Howard to Fantasy's Volvo. The brothers Sebastian used the same laundry cart to transport Doris Harrington's lifeless body to their hotel room, which was registered to the Smuckers, leaving the body there for Cleave and Candy to explain, which, given the controversy already swirling the Smuckers, would have been difficult at best. I fast forwarded to the last recorded surveillance sighting of Butch and Brutus, which was dark and early Wednesday morning leaving via the west entrance. I froze the feed.

Saving the best for last, I pulled up cousin Rod's activities to track him carefully and specifically. There would be no fast-forwarding. I wanted to see his every step, first to last. I poured a second cup of coffee at ten o'clock, then settled in to watch, from his wing-tipped shoe first touching Bellissimo ground when he arrived by limo Saturday morning, through check in, picking him up exiting the twenty-ninth floor elevator at the back of the sheik entourage. I continued to watch his meanderings throughout the grounds and casino on Saturday afternoon, including the passing of an iPad to a little boy in the lobby impatiently waiting for his parents to check out. Fantasy's iPad. It was never in her car. We'd tracked a kid in the backseat playing zombie games for days, thinking we were tracking Bootsy Howard. I fell asleep at my desk somewhere between Rod J.'s Saturday night and my wee hours of Thursday morning. My phone woke me at four. My third cup of coffee was full and cold, and all three computer monitors rolled screen savers. The text message was from Meredith. *Davis, I'm on my way to the hospital. They called a code on Greene. He isn't going to make it until tomorrow for the scheduled procedure. It's now. Bootsy is here. She rode a Trailways bus. Pray.*

Lord, help Greene Gully. And help my sister while she helps him.

I woke up the third screen in front of me, where the surveillance had gone on while I slept. The last sighting of Rod J. Sebastian at the Bellissimo was dark and early Wednesday morning. From behind a marble fountain, and with great interest, he inconspicuously watched the west entrance from behind the cover of eight feet of babbling water. I looked at the time, compared it to the last times and locations of Bootsy Howard and the brothers Sebastian on the first two screens, then changed screen shots to see what Rod J. was so interested in.

He was interested in Bootsy Howard holding Butch and Brutus Sebastian at pink gunpoint.

I found the brothers.

I knew where they were. And for the time being, they could just stay there.

I dialed transportation. "This is Mrs. Cole. I need a jet to Houston. Six passengers, including my daughters and two dogs. We're leaving the Bellissimo in fifteen minutes. Be ready."

I texted Fantasy. *Cover for me. I'm going to Houston.*

I ran down the guest-wing hall. "Vree, wake up." I shook her. "Get the dogs ready. We've got to go."

"Where?"

"Houston."

* * *

We touched down at Houston Executive at 6:22 Thursday morning, the sun just rising, and piled the girls and the dogs into a waiting limo that drove us to MD Anderson via an eighteen-minute stop at Four Seasons on Lamar Street, where Vree and Bubbles were reunited. At 7:40, we blew through the fire exit on the ground floor of MD Anderson's Duncan Building, then sneaked babies and dogs past three nurses' stations to the Gully family's private waiting room, where Preacher Gully, his wife Gina, and Bootsy Howard stared at the collection of women, children, and dogs as if a spaceship had landed in the room. Bootsy said, "I'm not sure they allow dogs, Vreeland." Gina said, "Lord Jesus, is that a dog? What's wrong with his eyes?" Pastor Gully said, "God will bless you for your lifelong days, Davis."

My phone, silent all morning, dinged. It was a message, with an attachment, from Bianca. *DAVID. WHAT IS THIS? WHAT WHAT WHAT IS THIS?*

I clicked the attachment. *It's a photograph of you and a guest, Bianca. Her name is Candy Smucker.*

HOW MANY PEOPLE HAVE SEEN THIS, DAVID?

I'm not sure. How did you see it?

MY PUBLICIST WOKE ME UP WITH THIS ATROCITY, DAVID. HE SAYS IT IS AVAILABLE FOR PUBLIC VIEWING AT FACEWHO. WHY DO I LOOK CRAZED? AS IF I'M DAFT? WHY AM I STARING AT THE CAMERA AS IF I'VE SEEN AN APPIRITION? WHY IS MY MOUTH GAPED OPEN? WHAT IS WRONG WITH MY HAIR? WAS I ATTACKED BY A MULTITUDE OF DOGS AT THE SHOW? WHY AM I WEARING MY $12,000 MAX GALLIANO DRESS BACKWARDS? WHY ARE MY $7,000 JUBILIE LOORE BOOTS UPTURNED IN A CHAIR BEHIND ME? WHERE ARE MY DRESS, MY BOOTS, AND MY $10,000 MATTOX BRAY EQUINE CLUTCH? HOW COULD YOU, DAVID? HOW COULD YOU?

Bianca, a man named Menton Williams took the picture. I

repeatedly asked him not to photograph me (you) and specifically asked him not to distribute it publicly. He's one of the dog-show judges. You should give him a call.

GIVE HIM A CALL? I'M HAVING HIM AND THE MONSTER BEHIND FACEWHAT ARRESTED.

She paid ten thousand dollars for a horse-foot purse?

TWENTY-TWO

The family waiting rooms for surgery patients at MD Anderson were large, private, and accommodating. The main room had several seating areas, two televisions, a desk with a computer, a small stocked kitchen, and an internal phone for communicating with the family's assigned patient liaison. Off the large room, there was a full bath, a prayer room, and a bedroom with three small beds, two large windows, and one sliding-glass door that led to a small private courtyard. The bedroom was now the playroom. Playing in it were Bex, Quinn, Princess, and Harley. I was in the room too. I wasn't playing.

Vree, holding Bubblegum, knocked on the bedroom door at nine. "Coast is clear. The nurse has come and gone."

"Where'd you hide Bubbles?"

"Under a blanket."

I left the door open, chose a seat where I could keep an eye on Bex and Quinn, and joined the adults. "What are they saying?"

"Well." Vree took a deep breath.

Preacher Gully didn't let her use it. "His condition is grave, Sister Davis. His vital signs are unstable, he's unconscious, and the indicators are unfavorable."

Gina was shredding tissues.

"What about Meredith?" I asked.

"They said we could talk to her in thirty minutes," Vree said.

I shot to the edge of my seat. "Talk to her? Can we see her?"

"Skype," Vree said.

"On the computer," Gully said.

I was glad he cleared that up.

Vree held Bubbles in the air. They were nose to nose. Bubblegum's tail was wagging a mile a minute. "Did you hear that, Bubbly Girl? We get to talk to Aunt Meredith!"

I paced the family room, checked on my girls and the dogs, went outside with them for a few minutes, started a fresh pot of coffee, and paced more. Nine thirty finally arrived. The nurse's head popped in. "Connect to Skype on the home screen," she said. "We'll have Miss Way on in a few minutes."

I sat at the desk, connected to Skype, and stared at the gray screen until I saw my sister.

*　*　*

At noon, Greene Gully's condition was upgraded to critical. Meredith was in recovery. She called, mouth full. "I'm done."

I shooed Princess off one of the small beds so I could sit down. She glared at me with her yellow eye, bared her crooked teeth, then backed off. "What are you eating?"

"A cheeseburger," Meredith said. "Have you ordered anything to eat? The food here is incredible."

For a million dollars, it ought to be.

"Between Four Seasons and what they've fed me here, I swear, Davis, I'm going to need to go on a diet."

"When are they going to let you out?"

"I have to stay until my bloodwork is normal," she said. "The nurse said maybe one more cheeseburger. But Davis, I'm not leaving until Greene's out of the woods."

"Meredith, you don't have any more blood to give him."

"You're right about that. But I have to see this through, and they're telling me it won't take long. They'll know soon if the procedure worked, and for the time being, he's not going downhill. Let's put it this way." She took a huge bite of burger. In my ear. "So far, he's not rejecting my plasma."

"How can you eat and talk about Greene's blood at the same time?"

Meredith said she'd call again after her next round of bloodwork.

The morning dragged on. And on. And on.

At noon, I peeked out the bedroom door, where Bex, Quinn, and both dogs had fallen asleep, to ask how things were going, but stopped short to listen to the doctor, who was just coming in with an update. He pulled up a chair, sat close to Gully and Bootsy, totally ignored Bubbles stretched out in front of Vree, and spoke in tones too hushed for me to hear. After several long minutes, a negotiation ensued. "Sister Bootsy, you should go," Gina said.

"No. I'll stay here with Vreeland. You go with Pastor, Gina. I'll go next time."

Greene Gully was being allowed visitors.

That had to be good.

I waited until the doctor escorted the Gullys out, and was about to step out of the bedroom when Bootsy said, "Have a seat, Vreeland. We need to talk." I slid down the doorframe and sat on the floor, ear to the cracked door.

"You have to stop with the witch business."

Nothing from Vree.

"Do you understand I'm not a witch?"

Still nothing from Vree.

Bootsy went back in time. She talked about when her sister died, and she went from being an early thirtysomething with her life on track to a full-time single parent of four rowdy boys in the blink of an eye. Not only did she miss her sister desperately, she knew nothing about parenting. She was overwhelmed, and looking back, she wished she hadn't told the boys she'd turn them into frogs if they didn't pick up after themselves, or that she'd shrink them to the size of crowder peas if they didn't clean their plates, or that she'd see to it that they woke up with warts all over their faces if they didn't do their homework. Before too long, her flowers bloomed again, because Gooch and his brothers spread the word—don't set foot in Bootsy's yard unless you like werewolves. The ding dong ditching stopped, because Gooch and his brothers told their friends Bootsy had bats guarding the door. Her troubles with the school stopped, because the boys told the teachers if they said one word to their Aunt Bootsy, she'd cast a spell on them and their hair would fall out. People began staying out of her way, which, at the time, she liked. Then she woke up one day and everyone was out of her way, with the whole town calling her a witch.

I heard a distant hospital bell ding.

"Why, Vreeland, would you drug me and lock me in that room? I realize what we should have done was sit Meredith and Davis down. They're good girls, they were raised right, and looking back, I think they would have helped without being forced to. And I'll do my best to make it right with them. I made that decision when I woke up locked in a strange place in a strange city surrounded by baseball bats and violent television games again. I thought I'd died and gone to hell."

At that point, Vree could have blamed me and Fantasy.

She didn't.

"It was terrifying, Vreeland. A light bulb exploded in the stairwell outside of the room. I heard it pop, I smelled the smoke, and I thought I'd burn to death locked in that room with no phone, no way out, no help. Then, Vreeland, when I thought you'd come back to get me, the door opened and it wasn't you. It was two horrible men. Vile men, Vreeland. They threw a petrified woman and a dog in with me, with every intention of leaving the three of us there, but they scared her to death before they could. They literally scared the life out of her, right before my eyes. They scared her to death, ran off in the black girl's car, but not before knocking me over the head and throwing me in the bed of a truck to leave me for dead because I'd borne witness. A truck bed, Vreeland. A truck bed. Three days I spent in a truck bed. Be sure your sins will find you out. Mine found me out. I led the Way girls into troubled waters, and the Lord brought down hell on me. Pure hell."

I heard Vree sniff. She must have been crying.

Then I heard nothing.

"Vreeland, say something."

I'd never heard those words before.

No one had ever spoken those words before.

Just when I thought Vree had lost her voice forever, she said, "If you're not a witch, Bootsy, then who put the baby spell on me?"

"What, Vreeland? What are you talking about? What baby spell?"

"Why can't I have a baby?"

Oh, Vree...

* * *

We left through the front door of the Duncan Building at five that afternoon, kids, dogs, the whole kit and caboodle, like a deranged parade, because Meredith had to leave by wheelchair. Insurance regulations. I put Princess at the front of the line and told her to guard us. She marched through like she owned the place, giving everyone we passed her eye, and no one said a word.

"Good dog," I told her.

Greene Gully was in critical but stable condition. The Gullys and Bootsy would stay until his release, which would be after several days in ICU, then several more in general population.

"Sister Davis," Gully started.

I stopped him. "No, Gully. Don't." I didn't want to be thanked for stealing a million dollars. I did want to get home and shut it down. Which reminded me of another thing I needed to do when I got home. I found Bootsy in the mix of people, babies, and dogs. "Where's your car parked?"

Her face turned a shade of purple. "In the casino garage."

"I know that, Bootsy. Where in the garage?"

"At the top."

"The eighth level?" It was Thursday. At least I thought it was Thursday. The eighth level of the parking garage would be all but empty. Friday, it would fill. Saturday, it would be stuffed. Thursday, not so much. "How did you subdue them?"

"I used my magic wand."

She winked.

"Do you have your car keys?"

"They're under the floor mat on the driver's side."

I held my hand out.

From deep in one of her burlap pockets, she produced Fantasy's magic pink gun.

"What was that about?" Meredith was bouncing Quinn on one hip and Bex on the other.

"Tying up loose ends," I said.

From the tarmac, waiting for takeoff, I texted Fantasy. *The brothers are locked in the trunk of Bootsy's car in the parking garage on eight.*

From her: *The fake housekeepers?*

Me: *Yes.*

Her: *Yow. How long have they been there?*

Me: *Since five or so Wednesday morning.*

Her: *Double you.*

Me: *Right.*

Her: *Where's the other one? The cousin?*

Me: *That, we don't know.*

Her: *Two down is better than none down.*

Me: *The keys are under the driver mat.*

Her: *I'd better take a taser or two with me. Or my pink gun.*

Me: *Take a fully loaded gun, No Hair, and the police. I have your pink gun.*

Her: *You took my pink gun to Houston?*

Me: *No, Bootsy borrowed it. She gave it back to me.*

Her: *That Bootsy's a strange bird.*

Me: *Yes and no.*

Her: *I have one word for you—bloomers.*

There was that.

Her: *Hey, hurry back. The Smuckers bought controlling interest in IGT and they're throwing a party in the casino tonight.*

Me: *I want no part of that.*

Her: *All IGT machines will be free.*

Me: *Free? As in they're giving away IGT slot machines?*

Her: *Free to play. The Smuckers are unlocking them. The cash will be flying.*

Who didn't like flying cash?

We took off. Bex and Quinn were buckled on both sides of Meredith.

They said, "Merri, Merri, Merri."

She said, "I love you, I love you, I love you."

TWENTY-THREE

"Davis," my husband said. "Your phone has gone straight to voicemail for more than an hour."

He called as we were pulling into the Bellissimo. He sounded like he was underwater. What in the world was wrong with Bradley? Whatever it was, should I make it worse by telling him my phone had been in airplane mode? Then tell him where I'd been? Then tell him about Meredith, Greene Gully, Princess, Harley, Bootsy, the Sebastians, and Hiriddhi Al Abbasov?

Then probably wasn't the best time.

"Davis, I need your help."

"Bradley, you need to come home."

"I am," he said. "Tomorrow morning. I woke up this morning feeling better, then spent the day in Nashville. I toured Brentwood, Harpeth Hall, and the Vanderbilt campus. Every step I took I felt worse. I'll be home tomorrow morning."

"Why don't you come home now?" I asked. "Right now? Why are you waiting until tomorrow morning?"

"Obviously, Davis, I caught a bug. I want to go to the doctor before I'm around the girls, because we don't need two sick little girls. I couldn't get an appointment until tomorrow morning. I'm flying out at seven, and I'll see the doctor at eight thirty."

Bradley hadn't been sick in forever, and I couldn't remember the last time he'd been to the doctor other than routine checkups at Bellissimo Employee Health Fairs. "Where's your appointment?" I asked. "I'll meet you. I want to go with you."

"I had my office set it up. A doctor I've never met. Levon Urlens, maybe? Leonard Orleans? Everett Urlelo? I don't remember."

Leverette Urleen.

That wasn't going to happen.

In a million years, that wasn't going to happen.

"Where did your office find this doctor, Bradley?"

"He applied for the Bellissimo staff physician job. What better way to interview him?"

I could think of several better ways.

"Let's worry about tomorrow tomorrow, Bradley, and tonight tonight. What do you need help with?"

"The casino guests, the Smuckers. I know you've had a busy week with the girls, the dog show, and Vree, but you couldn't have been so busy you didn't hear about the Smuckers."

"I've heard." Boy, had I heard.

"Davis, they've bought controlling interest in IGT to stave off a lawsuit."

I'd heard that too.

"I'd like for you to track them down," Bradley said. "Explain to them that opening our IGT machines will cost them millions."

"Bradley, I don't think they care. They cleared more than a billion when they won the lottery."

"It doesn't matter if they cleared ten billion, I have a responsibility to make sure they know what they're doing."

The Smuckers most definitely did not know what they were doing when it came to money.

"I'll talk to them, but I don't think it will do any good. You know those people who won't stop until they lose? The people who don't think they deserve their money and are determined to get rid of it? The winner's guilt people?"

"I do," he said.

"Well, meet the Smuckers."

"Will you try to talk some sense into them anyway?"

"I will."

"I don't know how you'll find them," he said. "I'm sure word is out and the casino is packed."

I knew how to find them.

"I'll see you in the morning, Davis."

"I love you, Bradley."

We talked through the lobby, up the VIP elevator, and through my door, where No Hair was waiting. No Hair and three men in power suits carrying briefcases. "Welcome home, Davis." His face registered no emotion. Which was far past rage for No Hair. "How was Houston?"

The jig was up.

The secrets I'd been keeping were about to be revealed. My most fervent wish was that I not be arrested for embezzling GameCorp convenience fees in front of my daughters.

* * *

No Hair led me and the three suits into Bradley's home office, then slammed the door. He took the desk seat. He put me in the corner.

(No, he didn't.)

He introduced me to Robert Miller and Richard Martin of Garland Law Group, Atlanta, Georgia, and Neil Spenser, the firm's private investigator. The men were there on behalf of Hiriddhi Al Abbasov. Not GameCorp. I tried to contain my relief. I doubt if I did, because I was dish-rag limp with it. It took me forever to find my voice. "How is His Excellency?"

One of the attorneys said, "He's young, he's strong, he'll be okay."

The other said, "He wants his dog."

The private investigator said, "He wants to speak to Rod J. Sebastian. Where is he?"

"Just one of many subjects we'd like to discuss with you, Davis," No Hair said. "Start at the beginning."

I couldn't do that. The beginning was Saturday morning, when Meredith didn't show. I couldn't talk about that, because talking about Meredith would mean talking about Greene Gully. And talking about Greene Gully would mean talking about GameCorp. Talking about GameCorp would mean handcuffs. On my hands.

The four men waited. Expectantly.

"Let's hear it, Davis," No Hair said.

What if I ripped a page from the Book of Vree? What if I started talking and didn't stop? What if I threw so much so fast at the men in front of me, they couldn't get a word in edgewise, much less ask leading, or compromising, or incriminating questions? If I controlled the entire conversation, I could avoid the subjects I didn't want to discuss. With that in mind, I took a deep breath.

"Well."

I reminded myself to keep my hands going the whole time.

Lots of inflection.

Lots of heart.

Tangents. Side roads. No detail too small.

Channeling my Vree, I gave them everything I had.

Soundbites from my lengthy confession, in no particular order, included, "And Candy Smucker isn't a monster. She's not a bad person. In fact, she's a very good person. I believe the borderline obsessive Facebook business is about wanting to connect. She'd help anyone with anything. Her only problem is she's been thrown into a life she couldn't possibly have prepared for. And where society accepted her for exactly who and what she was before, it doesn't now, which isn't fair. Cleave and Candy lived in a world where problems were solved by bar fights. Everything escalated for them, including the size of the bars, and thus, the size of the fights. The only thing they're guilty of is not adjusting to society's demands and expectations fast enough. And packing sledgehammers. Packing a sledgehammer was a bad idea, I'll give you that."

And, "I did *not* put the fake housekeepers in the trunk of that car. I absolutely did not. I didn't use a tranquilizer gun on them, I didn't zip tie their hands, I didn't duct tape their mouths, and I didn't see it happen so I can't say who did. And while I'm sorry that man's nose is infected, it's his own fault. In my opinion, when you sign a waiver agreeing to having your nose pierced, you're asking for an infection. The nose pierce people should pass out antibiotics at the nose pierce store. We need better surveillance in the parking garage."

And, "The hardest thing about Harley has been how much space he takes up. If it weren't for how big he is and how much he eats, I wouldn't have known he was here. Not that I don't have a big home, I do. Really big in terms of vacuuming, but with two dogs in it, and one of those dogs being Princess, it got small fast. Please, don't get me started on Princess. That dog lives on a steady diet of manicotti. I'll never eat manicotti again. I don't even want to hear the word manicotti again, much less eat it. And I don't know what to do about the garlic smell. I feel like it's in my fabrics, you know? Like it's permeated my window treatments, fabrics, and upholstery. I can't see replacing everything. I'm thinking I'll have to wait it out. I have no idea how long it takes to wait out garlic."

And, "I've never believed in witches. I've heard it all my life, you can't grow up in Pine Apple and not hear, 'Bootsy Howard is a witch! She will make your innards twitch!' I ignored it. Not completely, but I always thought she was just mean, as opposed to otherworldly. As it turns out, she's neither. She wants what everyone else wants. Someone to love who loves her back. That's it. It is spooky, how much happens when Bootsy's around, I'll give you that, but even Fantasy's lips weren't Bootsy. Fantasy accidentally used her husband's prescription toothpaste, and Fantasy's allergic to everything under the sun, although it turns out she's not allergic to dogs, and have you even heard of prescription toothpaste?"

And, "I had to be cut out of Bianca's dress. Vree cut it off me, not that I'm blaming Vree. I asked her to cut it off me. Vree is my sister Meredith's best friend. And the poor thing has been trying to get pregnant since she was twenty-seven years old. I couldn't have made it through this week without Vree. For one thing, I'd still be wearing the rubber dress. At the time, I had no idea Bianca paid twelve thousand dollars for it. I'd have never let Vree at it with scissors had I known. If she hadn't, though, I'd be waiting for it to melt off. I barely got it on; I would have never gotten it off. It took fifteen minutes to even find scissors, because my house is completely baby proofed. You know how you hide things from the children, then it's the adults who can't find them?"

And, "I should have known he was an imposter. I can't believe I didn't know. In my defense, there are no pictures of His Excellency on the internet, so it's not like I knew what he was supposed to look like. I'll tell you how Rod J. fooled me: Harley. Harley was so glad to see him. I've never had a dog. My grandmother was bitten by a dog when she was a little girl, and I didn't grow up in a dog family. I've never really been around dogs. I have a cat, Anderson Cooper, but she moved in with my parents. She sleeps on my father's head. Cats, I know. Dogs? Not so much. Not that I have a thing against dogs, I don't. I've always been under the impression that dogs adored their owners. Well, Harley adored his imposter owner. What I didn't know then that I know now is

Harley adores *everyone*. Harley wouldn't know the difference in a serial killer and a flower-delivery girl. He'd greet them both like they were his very best friend. I could bring him in here right now, and having never met any of you, he'd still try to lick you to death. He doesn't have an aggressive bone in his body. If he did, he'd have ripped Rod J. the secretary to pieces. My best guess is we'll never see Rod J. again. He's long gone. I know if it were me, I would be too. I'd hightail it out of town before my boss, who I left bobbing in a swimming pool for three days, caught up with me. I'd have as much space between myself and the waterlogged sheik as geographically possible."

And, "I've thought all along it was a head cold. In five years, my husband hasn't been sick a single day. Not one. Not the flu, or strep, not anything. I mean, honestly, he's as healthy as a horse. The sneezing alone was a shock. A big part of me feels guilty for not rushing to his bedside with chicken soup from Chops, which is just another example of how bad this week has been. Any other time, I'd have been spoon feeding him the soup and dabbing his chin with a napkin. All I've done all week is say, 'Oh, everything's okay, Bradley. Stay where you are, Bradley. Get better, Bradley. Don't drink hot Jack Daniels, Bradley.' When I slowed down enough to even think about my husband, it was along the lines of I hoped I could make it through this week married, not I hoped he lived through the week. I feel so guilty, but kept telling myself it was just a cold. The common cold! No big deal! He'll be fine!"

And, "If Urleen tells you your left arm is broken, rest assured it's your right ankle that's sprained. He is Chief of Staff at Idiot Hospital. President of the Crazy Doctor Club. Head Quack of Quackville General. Calling Dr. Ridiculous! Calling Dr. Ridiculous! I didn't believe him for one minute when he said Doris Harrington died of a broken heart, then the ME ruled the cause of death heart failure. The poor woman, who had nothing to do with anything, actually *did* die of a broken heart. You know what I think? I think the brothers double crossed the cousin. They have that collar. They marched into my house with their lawn mower and took Princess's collar, then hid it somewhere. I believe they lied to their cousin Rod J. and told him they couldn't find it. Not wanting his criminal vacation to be a total bust, he said, 'Plan B, we dognap Harley. Take the old woman with you. I'll dispose of Sheiky and offer a million-dollar reward with his money, you two show up with the old woman and the dog, then we'll split the reward.' And that poor woman died of a broken heart. Not that I'm giving Urleen any credit. I'm not. Now, his nurse, Jenna Ray—"

"STOP."

No Hair's boom echoed off the walls.

I scanned the faces of my numb audience. One attorney's head jerked in a nervous tic way, and the other's head was tilted with an open palm to his ear, pressing it, like he had water trapped in there. The private investigator was mumbling under his breath. It sounded like, "Tata tata tata."

Thirty empty seconds passed.

No Hair said, "Would you like a glass of water?"

I nodded.

"Would you mind if one of these gentlemen spoke?"

I shook my head.

They declined. Six hands waved off any additional communication. Those men wanted out. They stood. They picked up their briefcases. They took two steps in my direction and sat the briefcases down in front of me.

"What's this?"

"Your reward, Mrs. Cole," one of the suits said.

"I don't want it." I opened my mouth to explain I didn't want reward money for finding Harley, because I wasn't even looking for him. And I certainly didn't want reward money for finding Doris

Harrington, because for sure, I didn't find her in time. May she rest in peace.

The suit didn't give me the chance. "The reward is for saving His Excellency's life. To not accept it would be a great insult."

Well.

In that case.

I could sure use a million dollars.

I walked them to the elevator with Harley in tow. The guards stepped aside.

I said, "Harley. Blow me a kiss."

Harley blew me a kiss.

"Good dog."

*   *   *

"Vree! Get in here! I'm going to show you what a million dollars looks like!"

Bex and Quinn led the pack. "Penny, penny, penny!"

So many pennies.

Meredith stood over the money and asked, "Do I want to know?"

Fantasy arrived while I'd been behind closed doors going on. And on. And on. She said, "No, Meredith. You don't want to know."

"Take a good hard look at it, Vree," I said.

"Why?"

"Because I'm getting ready to stuff it in an ATM."

TWENTY-FOUR

It was nine o'clock Thursday night. Bex and Quinn had been in bed for an hour, Bubblegum was stretched out on my sofa like it was her sofa watching Princess in her upside-down playpen, who was busy with Madeleine Albright. Fantasy, Vree, and Meredith were around the kitchen table, and my sister was telling Vree that she had no interest in the Smucker IGT party in the casino. I was at my desk, doing cyber chores and eavesdropping.

"You don't want to see them?" Vree asked. "I mean, Meredith, when will you ever have the chance to be in the same room with billionaires again? I guess, though, you're in the same room with a millionaire now—"

"Not for long, Vree," I yelled through my office door. "And Meredith had her blood sucked out this morning. If she doesn't want to go, she doesn't want to go. Let her rest."

"You go, Vree. I'll stay," Meredith said. "Someone needs to stay with Bexley and Quinn anyway, not to mention these dogs. Pass me a bottle of wine and the remote control. You kids have fun."

I shut down the computer and turned off the office light, having stopped the flow of GameCorp's convenience fees to Greene Gully's MD Anderson patient account at one million and eleven dollars, then deleted the deposit account, so if auditors ever showed up at the hospital there'd be no money trail to follow. I sat down beside my sister at the kitchen table. "We're not going to have fun tonight anyway, Meredith. You're not missing a thing."

"Can't we take care of the ATM business later?" Fantasy asked. "I get that you want to pay the money back, so you won't feel like a big fat thief, but does it have to be tonight? Let's do it tomorrow. Or next year. I'm on call until midnight. Twiddling my thumbs. I'd like to twiddle them at the Smucker Show."

"Where am I going to hide a million dollars for a year, Fantasy? Tomorrow won't work because Bradley will be home tomorrow morning. I have to do the ATM thing tonight. If for no other reason, I'd like to get a good night's sleep without this hanging over my head."

"Okay," Fantasy said. "We'll throw the money in an ATM, then go see the Smucker Show."

"We can't just throw the money in," I said.

"Why not?"

"I hacked four hundred ATMs."

"Bragger," my sister said.

"Okay," Fantasy said. "So?"

"We need to put the million dollars into a hacked ATM. We can't just toss it in the first ATM we see."

"Why not?" Vree asked.

Fantasy said, "Because Davis says so, Vree." Then to me, "Why not?"

"So Rod J. Sebastian pays for what he's done," I said. "We don't really have anything on him. Even if we knew where he was, which we don't, the only thing he did to us was impersonate an oil sheik. Doris Harrington died of natural causes. He won't be charged, even though she died during the commission of a crime he masterminded, because the medical examiner's report showed she had a long history of heart disease. Even a bad lawyer could get it dismissed. He won't pay for what he did to Bootsy either, because he wasn't the one who hit her over the head and left her in a truck bed for three days. He'll throw his cousins under the truck and walk away from those charges too, because the cousins actually were the ones who hit Bootsy over the head and left her in a truck bed for three days. And while he's at it, chances are he'll blame embezzling from the blind people and the dog fighting on the cousins too, then pay his back child support and disappear. Linking Rod J. Sebastian to the ambushed convenience fees is the only path to justice. GameCorp will ask why there's an extra million dollars sitting in one of their ATMs. They'll run diagnostics on the machine, and if they don't find the glitch, he'll never be caught. If we put the money into an ATM I hacked, GameCorp will run the same diagnostics, find the glitch, and it will lead straight to Rod J. Sebastian. GameCorp has the resources to track him down. And when they do, they'll throw the book at him for breaching their system."

Confusion played all over Vree's face. She started and stopped several times.

"What, Vree?" I asked. "What?"

"Wouldn't that be him paying for what you did, Davis? I mean, aren't you the one who breached their system?"

An immediate hush fell over the kitchen.

From the living room, we heard Madeline Albright say, "I think 'guilt' is every woman's middle name."

* * *

"No, Fantasy." She grabbed my arm as I rose from the table. I shook her off. "I need a minute." I wandered out the kitchen door to the terrace, where my guilty conscience and I were met by a starless night and a cool ocean breeze.

Meredith spoke softly, but I still heard her through the open door. "Vree, Davis bent the rules. She does that when she has to. If she hadn't, Greene would be dead. And she's trying to make it right. Clearly, this man Rod broke the rules. She's trying to make that right too."

True, I said to my criminal self.

"Everything Davis did was to help someone else, Vree," Fantasy said. "Everything he did was to help himself."

True again.

Which didn't make what Vree said untrue. No two ways about it, I'd stolen a million dollars from GameCorp and was willing to let Rod J. go down for my crime so he wouldn't get away with his own.

"But I didn't mean anything by it." Vree sounded pitiful. "I was just trying to understand."

And there it was. GameCorp would catch Rod J., and justice would be served, but since he wasn't the one who breached their system, they'd never understand.

"I was confused!" Vree said. "I get confused!"

They'd be confused. In a million years, Rod J. wouldn't be able to explain what happened.

"Davis!" It was Vree. "Please come back!"

Only I could explain it.

"Davis!" It was Vree again. "I'm sorry!"

If I could hack GameCorp's ATMs and make off with a small percentage of their convenience fees for two days, imagine what a real cyberpunk could do.

"Davis?" My sister sneaked up behind me and tugged my ponytail.

GameCorp's security was all about the cash. They hadn't bothered to secure the fees.

"Shake it off," Meredith said. "She really didn't mean anything by it."

Honestly, who was to say ATMs worldwide weren't just as vulnerable?

"Vree's forever saying things better left unsaid. You know that, Davis."

I'd need to leave Rod J.'s laptop with the money. It would be a roadmap for GameCorp's security-management programmers, who could eliminate the threat faster than I'd uncovered it. Then they could develop the program for other ATM owners, sell it, and be richer than they already were.

Maybe then, I could sleep.

* * *

I spent the next ten minutes on the home screen of Rod J.'s laptop.

I typed, "Dear GameCorp," first. Then I spelled out, in bits and bytes, where their system was weak and exactly how it'd been compromised. I suggested they build firewalls along the convenience-fee route, then went on to suggest they develop and patent the program. The last words I typed were, "Seven dollars for a casino convenience fee is ridiculous. Please consider lowering it."

My work done, I reclaimed my seat at the kitchen table with newly acquired determination to make things right for everyone— Rod J., GameCorp, and myself. To Vree, puffy-eyed and red-nosed, I said, "It's okay, Vree. You weren't wrong."

"I would never hurt your feelings, Davis. Ever. I mean—"

"You were right, Vree. I stole the money."

"And you're going to replace it." Fantasy slapped the table. "Let's go."

"You don't understand," I told her. "We can't just go. The hacked ATMs are all over America, and we can't get all over America and back tonight. Half of the glitched ATMs are in Vegas."

"Where are the other half? Surely there are a few closer than Vegas. Where's the closest one?" Meredith asked.

"There are two here," I said.

"Here, where?" she asked.

"Here Biloxi. One is downstairs."

"That's a no-brainer, Davis," Fantasy said. "Let's sneak into Human Resources, get engineering uniforms, bust into the ATM like we're repairing it, dump the money and be done with it."

"We can't," I said. "We can't bust into an ATM. We need a key. That's problem one."

"Keys, piece of cake," Fantasy said. "You distract, I'll nab."

"Distract who?" Vree sniffed. "Nab what?"

"We'll distract a High Limits slot attendant," Fantasy said. "You can always hear them coming, because their keys jingle. One of the keys they carry is a GameCorp universal ATM key, which is what we'll nab, because the only way into an ATM is a key, dynamite, or a nuclear bomb. It'd be best if we went the key route. Between me and Davis, one will distract and the other will nab." She turned to me. "If there was ever a night to nab a key off a slot attendant, tonight's the night. You know they're running their legs off paying out IGT jackpots. We can have a key in five minutes, tops. We get the key, go to an ATM, dump the money, and then go to the Smucker Show."

"How is all that money going to fit into an ATM?" Vree asked.

"Casino ATMs are big, Vree, in big cabinets so you can't miss them," I said. "Inside, they're ninety-percent nothing. One little data line, one little printer, one little cash tray. There's plenty of room."

"The money will fit," Fantasy said. "They're serviced every six hours, and we'll fit it in there so it falls all over the technician's feet when he opens the cabinet. The search for Rod J. will start two minutes later." She turned to me. "Where's the glitched ATM we're going to fit it in?"

"That's our second problem," I said. "Location, location,

location."

Meredith yawned.

"What are our choices?" Fantasy asked.

"One is the cage."

Fantasy shook her head at the ceiling.

"What?" Vree asked. "Like a bird cage? Like a hamster cage? Like a cat cage?"

"The cash cage," Fantasy said. "It's the banking center of the casino and the ATM is dead bullseye in the middle of it. There are cameras covering every square inch. Cameras, and wall-to-wall people."

"Ah," Vree said. "One time I was at the bank depositing Gooch's insurance check from when Gator Moore rear ended him, and—"

Meredith interrupted. "I don't understand. You're not taking money, you're giving money. So what if someone sees you? And what is up with that dog and Madeleine Albright?"

"The cage ATM won't work. Where's the other one?" Fantasy asked.

I took a deep breath. "In the men's room."

"No," Fantasy said.

"Yes. It's the ATM at the cage or the ATM in the men's room, Fantasy. Those are our choices."

"*Why*?" she asked.

"I was picking from a list of general locations in our zip code. I chose casino and lobby," I said. "I didn't know the casino ATM was the cage or the lobby ATM was the men's room until five minutes ago."

"Why would someone put an ATM in a men's room?" Vree asked. "Do all men's rooms have ATMs? Gooch has never come out of a men's room with money. That I know of. I mean—"

"Which lobby men's room?" Fantasy asked. "Like the lobby

men's room behind valet or the lobby men's room behind Beans?"

"What's Beans?" Vree asked.

"The coffee shop." Fantasy and I said it on the same beat.

"What difference does it make?" Vree asked.

Meredith yawned again.

"Same as the cage, Vree," Fantasy said. "Traffic. It's crowded tonight. The valet men's room will have a revolving door. In and out. Too much traffic. The men's room in the coffee shop won't. Which one, Davis? There are five lobby men's rooms."

"No," I said. "Just one."

"Five," she said. "Counting the one behind Rocks. Five."

"What's Rocks?" Vree asked.

"The jewelry store in the lobby." I turned to Fantasy. "I never said the ATM was in a men's room in *our* lobby."

"Oh, no," she said. "Whose lobby?"

My head thunked down on the table. "The Resort."

"Which resort?" Meredith asked.

"The Last Resort." Fantasy's head hit the table too.

"Wouldn't that be even better?" Meredith asked. "Your chances of being recognized at another casino are considerably less. Right?"

"Well," Fantasy said to the table.

"Well," I said to the table.

"You two sit up," Meredith said. "What's wrong with the Resort?"

"Everything," Fantasy said. "It's a dump, the likes of which you can't imagine. I roll up my windows when I drive within a mile of it. I don't want to set foot in it, much less get within five miles of a men's room there."

"It can't be that bad," Vree said.

"Vree," I said, "their slot machines take government-assistance checks and their buffet takes food stamps."

"That buffet filled three hospitals last Thanksgiving," Fantasy said.

Meredith shivered. "Don't say hospital."

I asked Vree if she remembered Shoney's.

"Shoney?" She gave me a blank look. "Did we go to high school with her?"

"It's an old restaurant," Meredith said. "There was one in Greenville by the mall. They had a fat boy holding a cheeseburger in the parking lot."

"Hot fudge cake," Vree said.

"That's the one," I said. "They used to have hotels. About a million years ago. After Hurricane Katrina ripped through Biloxi, one of the only things left standing was the old Shoney's Inn. It's been sitting empty for decades, before and after the storm, until two mobster shrimpers got a small-business loan and opened the Last Resort Casino six months ago. The fifty-year-old dilapidated restaurant is now a casino. The fifty-year-old decrepit hotel rooms are now, well, fifty-year-old decrepit hotel rooms. It's nasty."

"Are the owners mobsters or are they shrimpers?" Meredith asked.

"Both," Fantasy and I said.

"Who in the world goes there?" Vree asked.

"Three kinds of people," I said. "People down on their luck, people who have nowhere else to go, and money launderers. Which brings us to our third problem."

"This had better be our last problem," Fantasy said.

"It is."

"What, Davis?" Vree asked. "What's our last problem?"

"We have to clean this money."

"What's dirty about it?" Vree asked.

"Davis is right," Fantasy said. "The sheik's money in the ATM won't work. It will lead straight back to him. If we dump it in a hacked ATM, the sheik will go down with the secretary."

"We have to clean it before we dump it."

"How do you clean money?" Vree's head was spinning. "Febreze? Lysol? Clorox Clean Up?"

Fantasy finally stood. "The Last Resort it is. We can launder the money and dump it at the same...dump."

"How can I help?" Vree stood.

"You don't have to, Vree," I said. "You've helped enough."

"But I want to. I really do."

"Vree," I said, "it's risky. Sometimes we get into...sticky situations. What Fantasy and I do isn't always easy."

"Or by the book," Fantasy said.

"Please."

"Okay, Vree. You can be our money launderer and our getaway driver." I looked at my watch. "Let's hit it."

*　　*　　*

It was our first plumbing gig.

Our secret spy days had seen me and Fantasy in many disguises. We'd infiltrated restaurants disguised as waitresses, most recently because a thousand dollars a day of Kobe beef was sneaking out the back door of Chops, the steak house. It was the sous chef doing the sneaking. We'd worn horticulture aprons and drowned fake plants with water canisters for hours on end, waiting on the right, or wrong, person to walk by. We'd worn front desk, concierge, housekeeping, valet, and pool bikini uniforms. We'd dressed up as old ladies and played penny slots; we'd dressed up as new socialites and played five-hundred-dollar slots. But we'd never been plumbers. I kissed my sleeping babies one more time, hugged my sister tight, then we hit the Bellissimo janitorial supply room. Hard.

We dressed in gray Dungaree pants and matching short-sleeved shirts, the only uniforms we could find without the Bellissimo logo. Mine didn't begin to fit and smelled like motor oil. Fantasy's fit fine and smelled like sawdust. We had Vree dressed as a mob boss wife—short black dress, stiletto black heels, push-up bra, big hair, blood red lipstick—and she smelled like birthday cake.

Fantasy and I stuffed our hair into Biloxi Shuckers baseball caps and hid our faces behind welding goggles. I didn't want to say anything, but Fantasy didn't look like a plumber at all.

"Davis," she said, "you don't look a bit like a plumber."

"I think you do," Vree said.

I thanked her.

"What is this?" Fantasy's fingers were wrapped around a black handlebar above a giant circular sandpaper machine.

"It doesn't look very plumbing related," I said. "Skip it."

"What's a flood remediation machine?" Vree was bent over a black box-shaped contraption with a funnel on one end and a fifty-foot hose on the other.

"I have no idea," I said. "But it sounds like it sucks up water. We don't need it."

"What do we need, Davis?" Fantasy asked.

"Plumber hammers? Plumber nails? Pipes? Sinks? Bathtubs? I don't know.'"

"Drano," Fantasy said. "We need Drano."

There was no Drano.

Fantasy shook a plunger at me.

"No thank you," I said.

She shook it at me again.

I took the plunger.

And to think how much fun everyone was having in the casino.

We transferred the ten shrink-wrapped stacks of money, plus everything Bradley and I had in our home safe, four thousand dollars, and everything I had in my secret cash cookie jar, six hundred and seventy dollars, into the larger of Vree's hot pink rolling suitcases. We stuffed the plumbing hammers and Rod J. Sebastian's laptop in a canvas bag we found in the janitorial supply room. I rolled the suitcase while Fantasy dragged our plumber hammer bag to the loading dock. Vree drove her car around and was waiting on us. She popped open the back hatch and we loaded up.

"Do you have plenty of ammo, Davis, or are you planning on hitting someone with the computer?"

"Yes, I have plenty of ammo," I said. "But I don't plan on shooting anyone. And I need the computer. GameCorp needs what's on it, and I'll need to shut down the Resort's surveillance. I surrendered my laptop to a yellow-eyed dog, thank you."

"Do you honestly think the Resort has surveillance?"

"You never know."

We slammed the hatch and climbed into the backseat.

It was a quiet ride to The Last Resort.

"Take a right, Vree," I said. "We're here. See the fat boy with the cheeseburger?"

Vree peered out the windshield. "You're kidding, right?"

Half of fat boy's head was gone. All of the cheeseburger was gone. A faded vinyl banner over the fat boy's red-checkered overalls barely said, THE LAST RESORT CASINO.

We counted four people sleeping around the front door. One lobbed over a metal canister ashtray, two on a sagging wooden bench, and one stretched out on the ground.

"Keep going straight, Vree. The parking garage is past the building."

She said, "This is the ugliest place I've ever seen. I mean—"

"Here we are," Fantasy said. "This is the parking garage. Pull in."

"There's a tree growing out of it." She inched forward. "There are lots of trees growing out of it."

There were no lights in the two-story parking garage. Lots of scraggy vegetation, no lights. I'd never seen anything spookier in my life. My whole life.

We passed a wrecked Jeep Liberty and a twenty-year-old Lincoln Town Car missing a door. We drove by an old Ford Bronco with everything past the cab chopped off down to the wheel base, and an unrecognizable beat-up car Fantasy said was a Gremlin. "That thing must be forty years old." The used and abused car lot continued to the second level, where we found a diamond in the rough. A shiny white Volvo XC90 hiding between a rusty truck and what might have been the very first Ford Taurus off the production line. "Would you look at that?" Fantasy said. "There's my car."

Vree braked. "How did your car get here, Fantasy?"

I closed my eyes and let my weary head fall back. It was going to be another long sleepless night. "I'd say Rod J. Sebastian drove it here."

TWENTY-FIVE

Vree backed into a parking place opposite Fantasy's car and killed the lights. Then it was pitch black. Black black. We locked the doors.

"Does anyone have a lighter?" Vree asked.

"I'll turn on my phone flashlight," I said.

"And what?" Fantasy asked. "Draw attention to us?"

"We have to sit here until we figure out what to do, Fantasy."

"Why don't we go sit somewhere else until we figure out what to do? This parking lot is freaking me out."

Vree, in the front seat, started praying. "Now I lay me down to sleep—"

"Vree, pray with your eyes open," I said. "You're our lookout."

Her eyes popped open. "I pray the Lord my soul to keep."

"How are you so sure Rod J. is here, Davis?"

"Who had your car last?"

"The brothers."

"And where are the brothers?"

"In jail."

"At some point, Fantasy, they passed off your car to Rod J."

"If I should die before I wake—"

"Here's another example of a dumber than dumb criminal," Fantasy said. "He could be in Aruba by now. If I left an oil sheik to drown, I'd run like the wind."

"We should have dropped everything and chased him down when he fell off the grid Tuesday," I whispered. "Or Monday. Or Wednesday. Whatever night he disappeared from the emergency room."

"Well, we didn't," Fantasy said. "We were busy."

"—I pray the Lord my soul to take."

"Davis, why is he still here?"

"The dog collar, Fantasy. He wants the collar."

"Amen."

"The brothers hid it somewhere," I said. "They stole it from my house and hid it. The cousin either doesn't know where, or he knows where and he's laying low until he can get it."

"It wasn't in the brothers' Bellissimo room," Fantasy said. "The crime scene people ripped that room apart."

"And he didn't leave it in the Leno suite," I said. "They went over every square inch there too."

"Now we have three things to do here," she said. "Launder the money, get it in the ATM, and take down Rod J."

"God is great. God is good. Let us thank him for our food."

"We can't get in the ATM, Fantasy."

"Why not?"

"We forgot to nab an ATM key."

"Amen."

* * *

Once we were out of the terrifying parking lot, our burdens lifted a little. Which could have been the praying. We parked behind a dumpster near the side entrance to the casino. The paint above the door was long gone, but I could see where it used to say Curb Service for Take Home Dining. There were no cameras. One flickering yellow street light half a block away, no cameras. Clicking away on Rod J.'s laptop, thankfully, I found cameras inside. When I finally hacked my way into the Resort's archaic surveillance feed, I said, "Okay, Vree. You're on."

"Gooch is going to kill me if I get killed in here."

"You're not going to get killed in there. Fantasy will be right behind you with a gun and I'll be watching you on the computer the whole time. The casino banking center is the old salad bar, right inside this door. You're going to be fine."

I believed about half of those words. The salad-bar part, I believed.

"Just roll your suitcase up to the salad bar and tell the cashier you need to trade your money," I said. "She's going to ask why you want to trade the money, and you're going to say—" I hadn't gotten that far.

"Tell her your ex-husband gave you the money and it has bad juju," Fantasy said.

"Good one," I said. "Tell her that, Vree."

"Why would someone's ex-husband give them a million dollars? I mean—"

Fantasy said, "Now is not the time for details."

"What do I do if she doesn't believe me?" Vree asked.

"You tip her the four thousand dollars," I said. "That'll make a believer out of her."

"Then what?" Vree asked.

"Bring the suitcase with the new money back to the car."

Twenty excruciating minutes later, we had Resort cash.

Popping the hatch again, I played the part of the parking lot armed guard while Fantasy, working out of the back of Vree's car, transferred the money from the pink suitcase to the plumber bag. She passed the loose change, which was all the cash I had in the world, the money from my cookie jar, to me. We piled back in the car and locked the doors.

"Guess where their vault is, Davis?" Fantasy asked.

I saw it on surveillance before I disconnected it—the walk-in refrigerator. The old Shoney's walk-in refrigerator was the Last Resort's vault. How were the doors still open?

"What now?" Vree asked.

"We're going in," Fantasy said.

"And leaving me alone?"

"You're our getaway driver, Vree. The getaway driver stays with the car. Don't you watch *Blue Bloods*?"

She broke into song. "*This little light of mine.*"

I wondered what people who lived in Nashville were doing.

"Are you ready?" I asked Fantasy.

"I'm ready."

"*I'm going to let it shine.*"

Fantasy was just about to open the car door when she stopped. "What about the ATM key?"

"*This little light of mine.*"

The entire time I watched Vree at the salad bar, wondering why in the world Resort cashiers were so willing to exchange what could very well be counterfeit cash—they didn't know Vree—for what could very well be more counterfeit cash—I doubted the Resort followed federal banking laws—I hadn't once remembered we'd forgotten to nab an ATM key.

"Davis, do we want to go back to the Bellissimo for a key or keep going?"

I bet Nashville mothers were home with their Nashville babies. Doing Nashville mother things. Or maybe—a novel idea—Nashville sleeping.

I said, "We keep going. Plan B."

"*I'm going to let it shine.*"

"What's Plan B, Davis?"

"Give me a minute."

"*Let it shine, let it shine, let it shine.*"

*   *   *

We drove to the front entrance and backed into a handicap space where Vree would be safer alone. There was an operable street light and we could see Beach Boulevard in the distance, a comforting glimpse of the real world. Now that we'd gone to Plan B, the problem was how we were dressed. The good news was we fit right in. No one would blink an eye. The bad news was, without an ATM key, our plumbing gig was up, and we didn't have a change of clothes. A million dollars, yes. Change of clothes? No. Vree was the only one who'd grabbed her purse on the way out—we'd grabbed firearms—and the only thing in it close to makeup was a tube of MAC Lipglass in Peach Blossom Pink.

"Not my color." Fantasy dotted the gloss on her cheeks, smeared it in, then slathered it on her lips. She passed it to me and I did the same. We tossed our bras and unbuttoned our plumber shirts as far as we could get away with. "Pop your collar, Davis." I popped my collar. "Knot your shirt." I tied the tail of my plumber shirt into a front knot. "Fluff your hair."

Vree watched us in the rearview mirror. "In a way, you guys look really cute."

Fantasy slung the money bag over her shoulder like it was a sack of potatoes, then we moseyed to the front desk of the Last Resort Casino like it was just another night at the casino. There was a girl behind what used to be Shoney's hostess stand.

"Excuse me." Fantasy knocked on the hostess stand. The girl looked up from her phone. "We have a date. We need his room number and we need a key."

I pushed Rod J.'s picture at her.

"Have you seen him?" Fantasy asked.

She nodded.

"He's here?" Fantasy asked.

She nodded again.

"We need his room number and key."

The girl shook her head. "I can't do that. I'll get fired."

I pulled my cookie jar money out of my Dungaree pocket. Six hundred and seventy dollars. I slid it across the hostess stand. "How about now?"

"Fifteen." She landed a box of loose keys on the hostess stand and dug around until she found a rusty key on a diamond-shaped plastic fob for guest room fifteen.

Fantasy took the key, then leaned in. "If you see our date, don't tell him we're here. It's a surprise. If you tell him, I'll hunt you down. Do you hear me?"

The wide-eyed girl nodded.

"Don't make me hunt you down."

She shook her head.

*   *   *

The room was easy enough to find.

Looking both ways, we pulled on latex gloves. I put an ear as close to the door as I could without actually putting my ear to the door. Fantasy raised an eyebrow. I shook my head in a quick no. If Rod J. was in the room, I couldn't hear him. Weapons at the ready, plumber hammer bag full of money between us, we went in dark and quiet. The bedroom was (filthy) clear. She took the closet; I took the bathroom. Rod J. wasn't in his room. He'd been there. By the looks of the half-eaten Chinese takeout containers, he'd been there for days. The ashtrays were overflowing, empty beer bottles littered every flat surface, the bed was a tangled mess, and on the nightstand, Doyle Brunson's *Super System, A Course in Power Poker*. Rod J. was probably in the Resort's poker room.

Fantasy dumped the million on the bed, then dropped the plumber bag in the shower stall. She emptied out a mini shampoo on the bag, then turned on the shower, full blast, to send any traces of us down the Resort drain, while I wiped Rod J.'s laptop clean of my fingerprints, then placed it on top of the money. After, I picked up the house phone on the desk. No dial tone.

"Try zero," Fantasy said.

"Last Resort. May I help you?"

It was the check-in girl.

"I need an outside line."

"Here you go."

I listened to the outside line.

"What?" Fantasy said. "Call them already."

"Fantasy, I don't have GameCorp's phone number."

"Get the computer." She pointed. "Look it up."

"I shut down the wi-fi when I shut down surveillance. I can't look it up."

We flipped. I lost.

The next seven minutes were the worst seven minutes of my life. Fantasy stayed in room fifteen while I went to the very occupied men's room in the lobby to find GameCorp's toll-free service number on the ATM.

She let me back in. "Well?"

"I don't want to talk about it, Fantasy. I don't ever want to talk about it. We will never ever ever speak of it. Ever."

From room fifteen, I called GameCorp. A service rep answered. "Listen carefully. I'm only going to say this once." I sucked in stale Chinese hotel air. "A million dollars was stolen from your company by siphoning convenience fees from four hundred of your ATMs. You need to see a man named Rod J. Sebastian about it. He's in the poker room of the Last Resort Casino in Biloxi, Mississippi. The money is in on the bed in room fifteen along with the computer used to set it up. It's all there." I hung up, then dialed No Hair from my cell phone.

"This had better be good, Davis."

"It is. We have the man who tried to drown my neighbor. The secretary. The deadbeat dad. The animal abuser. Rod J. Sebastian."

"Where are you?"

I told him.

"You can't be serious, Davis. Hold on."

I held for the two seconds it took him to call it in.

"Hey," he said. "One, get out of there. And two, don't get the salad bar."

"What?"

"Don't go near the salad bar. Those are feds. They're giving it another week or so with a money-laundering net. Steer clear of the salad bar."

We watched from the cracked fire-exit door at the end of the hall until we saw Biloxi's finest boys in blue turn the corner. We ran.

Boy, did we run.

We piled into Vree's car. "Drive, Vree."

TWENTY-SIX

If Meredith hadn't woken me Friday morning to say goodbye I might have slept through Bradley coming home. My eyes flew to the video monitor on the nightstand. Bex and Quinn were still asleep. Meredith climbed into bed with me and passed me a cup of coffee.

"Why are you leaving so early, Mer?"

"I'm ready to go home," she said. "See my girl. See Mother and Daddy. Sleep in my own bed. Let you have your life back."

"How are you feeling?"

"Great."

"How's Greene this morning?"

"He's good." She reached for my hand. "Thanks to you."

"No, Mer. Thanks to you."

"We both helped Greene, Davis."

Vree knocked on the open door. "Is three a crowd? I know if I had a sister and I was saying bye, I might not want someone to barge in on my sister party. I mean—"

I waved her in. She sat on the edge of the bed.

"Davis, I packed Princess's things. Bubbles is saying bye to her."

Bradley, Meredith, Vree, Bubbles, and Princess were all coming or going home today. Life as I knew it, like Meredith said, may very well resume. I had Bianca to deal with, having not given the dog-show awards ceremony the night before even a passing thought, but I always had Bianca to deal with. If it weren't me humiliating her by shirking my dog-show duties, it would be something else. I had No Hair to deal with. He sent a two-a.m. message I slept through asking if I had any idea why GameCorp was crawling all over Last Resort fighting with the local authorities, Hiriddhi Al Abbasov's attorneys, the Atlanta Council for the Blind, Animal Control, and Child Services as to who deserved first swing at Rod J. Sebastian. I had the feds to deal with. I'd need to intervene on Vree's behalf before they knocked on her Pine Apple door and accused her of laundering money. I had Candy Smucker to deal with, who, according to Facebook, made it to her hotel room six hours earlier and sixteen million dollars lighter in the wallet. I didn't have her dog's diamond collar, and she deserved to hear it from me. All of which paled at the thought of my husband coming home to tell me we were leaving Biloxi, the Bellissimo, everyone and everything we knew and loved, and moving to Nashville.

I checked the time. He was on his way.

* * *

I walked Meredith, Vree, and Bubblegum to the door.

Part of me wanted to ask them to stay. Part of me wanted to go with them. Most of me wanted to roll back the clock and start our girls' week over. With noted exceptions.

Meredith and I had communicated without words our entire lives, and we never said goodbye. Our smiles were sadder that morning, maybe wearier, or maybe just wiser. We held onto each other longer than we usually did.

And then there was Vree.

"Davis." She looked above me, below me, behind me, and through me. Everywhere but at me. She fidgeted, she tapped a foot, and she cleared her throat. She closed her eyes and took a deep breath. She finally spoke. "I've never had more fun in my life."

I waited.

That was it.

And then they were gone.

Had it not been for my babies, who woke when Aunt Merri kissed them bye, and Madeleine Albright, going on and on in the Pop N' Play, my house would have felt end-of-the-world empty.

I asked Bex and Quinn, "Who wants to go with Mommy to take Princess home?"

"Me, me, me!"

I loaded the double stroller with Bex, Quinn, Princess, her red satin duffel bag, and Bianca's nasty horse purse. Inside the horse's foot, a long note from me. The elevator was too small for the garlic, and the short ride to twenty-seven was too long.

I knocked gently. I knocked with enthusiasm. I knocked long and loud; I knocked slow and steady. I had the Bellissimo operator ring the room phone. Repeatedly. No answer. The last trick I had up my sleeve worked; I sent Candy a Facebook message. *This is your Flaming Volcano friend. The boots? I'm at your door. I have something for you.*

Three minutes later, the door flew open. Candy, wearing a Bellissimo bedsheet, screamed, "Miss Priss!" Princess catapulted from the stroller and into her arms. Candy and Princess, much like how my sister and I said goodbye, shared a sweet silent hello. If I'd learned anything that week, it was this—people were crazy about their dogs, even if the dogs were crazy, and dogs were crazy about their owners, even if the owners were crazy.

Candy, bedsheet slipping, looked at me over Princess's head. "Hey, girl!"

"Hi, Candy."

Bex and Quinn said, "Hi, hi, hi."

Candy said, "Aren't you two cute? If I had my phone on me, you better believe I'd post you." Then to me, "I like your red."

My hair. I'd forgotten Candy met Bianca blonde me.

"I'd ask you in, but Cleave's butt naked."

I passed her the horse foot.

"For real?"

"It's yours." To Princess, I said, "Good girl."

* * *

We rode the elevator home, and for the first time in days, the security guards weren't waiting. Which could only mean one thing. I said, "Girls! Daddy's home!"

"Daddy, Daddy, Daddy!"

Except he wasn't.

Before I could push the stroller out of the elevator, he called to tell me he was in his office, the doctor was just leaving, where were we?

The girls and I flew past Bradley's assistant, barely saying hello. Bex and Quinn jumped out of their stroller and into their father's waiting arms. I wedged myself in the mix.

"Davis? What's wrong?"

"I'm just so glad to see you," I said to his chest.

"Daddy, Daddy, Daddy!"

"Guess what's wrong with me?"

There was no telling.

"I have urban allergies," he said. "I'm allergic to Nashville. Have you ever heard of being allergic to a city? The doctor, Urleen is his name, and I hired him by the way, said I had a negative reaction to the environmental conditions in Nashville. Urban allergies. Can you believe it?"

No.

"He's an out-of-the-box thinker, Davis."

He was out all right. To lunch.

"It's true," Bradley said. "It has to be. I felt horrible all week, boarded the plane this morning miserable, and stepped off an hour later in perfect health. I could breathe, I could see, and I didn't have a headache. I'm fine!"

We wouldn't be moving to Nashville.

"Let's go home," he said. "I have a surprise."

I was done with surprises.

His phone rang before we could get there. I glanced. No Hair. No telling what he was going to tell Bradley before I had the chance to. Bradley listened for a minute, then said, "Good."

"Good, what?"

Bradley said, "The Smuckers have left the building."

That fast?

"The woman, wearing a bedsheet, said they were going home and never coming back."

Then the Cole family went home. With his hand on the doorknob, Bradley said, "Who's ready for their surprise?"

"Me, me, me!"

(Not me, not me, not me.)

A white wicker basket sat in the middle of the foyer floor. A furry head popped up from it. It was a puppy. A round little puppy with bright dark eyes, gold curls, and a furiously wagging tail.

Guess what the girls did? They did not say, "Dog, dog, dog!" and rush to it. They shared a silent glance, then made a run for their playroom. Right past the puppy. Bradley and I looked at each other curiously. Before we could follow them, we heard four little feet returning. With Princess's collar. It had been in their toybox the whole time. We named our Goldendoodle girl Candy. (Candy, Candy.)

Gretchen Archer

Gretchen Archer is a Tennessee housewife who began writing when her daughters, seeking higher educations, ran off and left her. She lives on Lookout Mountain with her husband, son, and a Yorkie named Bently. *Double Whammy*, her first Davis Way Crime Caper, was a Daphne du Maurier Award finalist and hit the USA TODAY Bestsellers List. *Double Dog Dare* is the seventh Davis Way crime caper. You can visit her at www.gretchenarcher.com.

**The Davis Way Crime Caper Series
by Gretchen Archer**

Novels

Bellissimo Casino Crime Caper Short Stories

Henery Press Mystery Books

And finally, before you go...
Here are a few other mysteries
you might enjoy:

THE DEEP END

Julie Mulhern

The Country Club Murders (#1)

Swimming into the lifeless body of her husband's mistress tends to ruin a woman's day, but becoming a murder suspect can ruin her whole life.

It's 1974 and Ellison Russell's life revolves around her daughter and her art. She's long since stopped caring about her cheating husband, until she becomes a suspect in Madeline Harper's death. The murder forces Ellison to confront her husband's proclivities and his crimes—kinky sex, petty cruelties and blackmail.

As the body count approaches par on the seventh hole, Ellison knows she has to catch a killer. But with an interfering mother, an adoring father, a teenage daughter, and a cadre of well-meaning friends, can Ellison find the killer before he finds her?

Available at booksellers nationwide and online

Visit www.henerypress.com for details

NUN TOO SOON

Alice Loweecey

A Giulia Driscoll Mystery (#1)

Giulia Falcone-Driscoll has just taken on her first impossible client: The Silk Tie Killer. He's hired Driscoll Investigations to prove his innocence with only thirteen days to accomplish it. Everyone in town is sure Roger Fitch strangled his girlfriend with one of his silk neckties. On top of all that, her assistant's first baby is due any second, her scary smart admin still doesn't relate well to humans, and her police detective husband insists her client is guilty.

Giulia's ownership of Driscoll Investigations hasn't changed her passion for justice from her convent years. But the more dirt she digs up, the more she's worried her efforts will help a murderer escape. As the client accuses DI of dragging its heels on purpose, Giulia thinks The Silk Tie Killer might be choosing one of his ties for her own neck.

Available at booksellers nationwide and online

Visit www.henerypress.com for details

BONES TO PICK

Linda Lovely

A Brie Hooker Mystery (#1)

Living on a farm with four hundred goats and a cantankerous carnivore isn't among vegan chef Brie Hooker's list of lifetime ambitions. But she can't walk away from her Aunt Eva, who needs help operating her dairy.

Once she calls her aunt's goat farm home, grisly discoveries offer ample inducements for Brie to employ her entire vocabulary of cheese-and-meat curses. The troubles begin when the farm's pot-bellied pig unearths the skull of Eva's missing husband. The sheriff, kin to the deceased, sets out to pin the murder on Eva. He doesn't reckon on Brie's resolve to prove her aunt's innocence. Death threats, ruinous pedicures, psychic shenanigans, and biker bar fisticuffs won't stop Brie from unmasking the killer, even when romantic befuddlement throws her a curve.

Available at booksellers nationwide and online

Visit www.henerypress.com for details

FINDING SKY

Susan O'Brien

A Nicki Valentine Mystery

Suburban widow and P.I. in training Nicki Valentine can barely keep track of her two kids, never mind anyone else. But when her best friend's adoption plan is jeopardized by the young birth mother's disappearance, Nicki is persuaded to help. Nearly everyone else believes the teenager ran away, but Nicki trusts her BFF's judgment, and the feeling is mutual.

The case leads where few moms go (teen parties, gang shootings) and places they can't avoid (preschool parties, OB-GYNs' offices). Nicki has everything to lose and much to gain—like the attention of her unnervingly hot P.I. instructor. Thankfully, Nicki is armed with her pesky conscience, occasional babysitters, a fully stocked minivan, and nature's best defense system: women's intuition.

Available at booksellers nationwide and online

Visit www.henerypress.com for details

Made in the USA
Monee, IL
03 March 2020

22651447R00154